ELA

DOMENICA DI TOMA

Dedication

To my wonderful children, Madeleine and Maxwell. You inspire everything I do. I love you all the universe.

And to my husband, Mike, your kindness, encouragement, patience, and love never go unnoticed. I love you.

"Your memory feels like home to me. So whenever my mind wanders, it always finds its way back to you."

— Ranata Suzuki

Chapter One

Damn it! Why do things like this only happen when you're running late?

Jennifer turns her neck slowly from side to side. There doesn't seem to be any damage to her body. She glances in the rearview mirror at the offending SUV and hopes there isn't any damage to her car, either. She sighs. Time to get this over with.

She scrounges through her glove box for the Ziploc bag that holds a ridiculous number of expired insurance cards, finally unearthing the current one. Jennifer normally wouldn't get out of the car on a dark road at night, but she needs to exchange information with the driver who rear-ended her, and she's already running late to her blind date. Although, the success she's been having with dating lately makes a car accident seem like a win. It turns out that being a forty-four-year-old, well-educated, financially independent, successful single woman who is looking for an equal means you might as well be an Arthurian knight seeking the Holy Grail.

As she approaches the driver, who's standing alongside his SUV waving his insurance card, she can feel her auburn hair beginning to frizz in the damp air. That's DC in June for you.

Now she'll show up for the date looking like she put her finger in an electrical socket.

As Jennifer gets close enough to look this guy in the eyes, she opens her mouth to let a few choice expletives fly. Before she can unleash her anger, she hears someone behind her, then feels a soft cloth pressed into her face. And then nothing.

Jennifer feels herself surface into a murky consciousness, slowly recalling the SUV, the dark road, the cloth. She stretches and blinks, taking in her surroundings. If she were abducted, shouldn't she be in the back of a windowless white van, or some derelict basement chained to the wall? (Okay, maybe she's devoured too many crime novels or episodes of *Criminal Minds*.) What she's seeing just doesn't add up.

She appears to be in total luxury. Like, "beautiful suite at the Ritz-Carlton or the Four Seasons" luxury. Immaculate crown molding tops the walls, painted in a cream color Jennifer is sure she's seen in fancy interior decorating magazines. Looking past the plush bed in which she finds herself, she sees a posh sitting area with white roses in a vase on the coffee table. Above her head is a chandelier which, like the furniture, looks modern and expensive with an understated elegance. Someone has excellent taste.

Jennifer warily gets up from the bed, piled high with sumptuous white pillows, and makes her way to the very solid-looking door. Miraculously, it opens. After a steadying breath, she takes a tentative look out. Nothing but a hallway with a couple of closed doors. She considers venturing out, but decides to stay put and explore the room a bit more. She turns around slowly, stopping when she spots floor-to-ceiling windows covered by stiff blinds.

She snatches up a small electronic tablet on the bedside table. Getting desperate, she tries a few buttons. The lights turn on, then they dim. Music begins to play—soft piano—then stops at the press of another button. Finally, a winner. With the slightest hum of a motor, the blinds open. Peering out into the bright light of day, Jennifer suddenly realizes why her door was unlocked: There's nowhere for her to run to, because it seems she's on some sort of boat. No, she corrects herself, taking in the wide deck lined with clean white lounge chairs, it's more like a yacht. More importantly, it's on open water. She sees the distant horizon without a speck of land obscuring the view.

"Excuse me, doctor. I hope you had a lovely rest and that your accommodations please you."

Jennifer whips around to find an attractive, middle-aged man in a crisp, dark blue suit standing in the doorway. His black hair is speckled with gray, and he has the most mesmerizing blue eyes.

"There are some clean clothes in the closet," he continues breezily. "Why don't you take a nice, hot shower? I will return in thirty minutes to collect you so that your host may formally welcome you."

Jennifer is stunned. "You have got to be kidding me," she sputters. "Who are you? Where am I? What the fuck is all of this about? How long have I been knocked out?" As she shakes the last bits of unconsciousness from her brain, she grows more angry. Jennifer considers physically lashing out at this man, but her prefrontal cortex tells her limbic system to stand down.

The man doesn't blink. "I am Iserate, you are on the yacht *Kayıp Aşk*, and your host will explain all. Please," he says, gesturing towards a door to his right.

The thought of a hot shower and clean clothes does sound appealing, and Jennifer does want some answers. She pauses to think. If whoever has taken her on this nonconsensual luxury cruise wanted to harm or kill her, they would have done so by now. She nods her assent, enters the door the man gestured to, and locks it behind her.

The room is a spacious, beautifully outfitted closet complete with clothes, shoes, and accessories that all appear to be in Jennifer's size. Even more disturbing, it all perfectly reflects her style: breezy linens, elegant but understated resort wear, flowing silhouettes, and sexy cocktail dresses. Many of the pieces are in various shades of green that Jennifer favors to bring out her hazel eyes. Through the next doorway is a marble-lined bathroom, deep grey veins running down the walls and surfaces.

Jennifer is dumbfounded. Who the hell owns this yacht and what the hell do they want with her? Instead of driving herself mad trying to figure it out, she turns on the shower so she can freshen up and go see what this surreal situation is all about.

Feeling human again, clothed in a summer dress that feels bespoke, Jennifer takes a seat by the window of her room and watches the sea (ocean?) roll by. Her auburn hair begins to dry and resume its natural state of unruly curls. A few minutes later, Mr. Blue Eyes comes to fetch her and nods approvingly when he sees she has followed his directions.

As he escorts her into the hall, past mostly closed doors, Jennifer tries to take in what little she can of her surroundings. The passage opens into a main salon that could fit her entire condo inside of it. She tries not to appear stunned by the sheer beauty of yet another meticulously appointed room with floor-to-ceiling views of the water on all sides. Breathtaking. Mr. Blue Eyes clears his throat once again, pointing toward the back of a modern-looking armchair with … are those *diamonds* on the buttons?

Then Jennifer sees him. Rising from the diamond chair, still with his back to her, is a man. He's probably six-foot-two with a thick head of lush black hair and a body that looks like an ancient Greek statue come to life: broad shoulders, narrow waist, and long, powerful legs. Oddly, he's wearing shorts and a T-shirt amid all this finery. Before she can process that juxtaposition, he turns to face her.

Jennifer knows him, but she also doesn't. He is familiar, but it's as though she's recalling something from a dream, just out of reach. The look of joy on his face takes her back. It is a look of elation and intimacy shared when lovers reunite. But she still can't place the face, even as she searches those deep brown eyes.

"You look more beautiful than ever, Ela," he says in a seductive, slightly familiar accent. Jennifer can tell he's trying to hide his smile at the look of shock on her face.

Ela. No one has called Jennifer that in twenty years.

Chapter Two

1999

This sure beats working. Jennifer looks out the train window, eyes wide in awe at the lush countryside. Trains are one of her favorite things about this trip, Jennifer thinks. And since she left Los Angeles, she's seen her fair share of transit. About a year ago, she just picked up her life and headed west from the city, stopping wherever interests her. She's not planning to end this adventure until she hits L.A. again.

Jennifer worked her ass off in college, graduating in three years while working in a corporate communications position for a high-tech firm. Getting a job after graduating was easy: She had three years' experience in her chosen profession, a degree, and—as she's been told ever since she was sixteen and "blossomed"—a rare mix of brains and beauty. The compliment always makes her roll her eyes.

But after three years of the corporate communications grind—not to mention being played for a fool by a male colleague sixteen years her senior—she felt the need for a sea change.

To fund her journey, Jennifer had a small inheritance from her grandma, who always taught her to budget well. She raised Jennifer from the age of six, after her parents' demise. Well, they didn't die, but they were dead to Jennifer. Dad had taken off to who-knows-where, but most likely some country that doesn't have an extradition treaty with the US. And mom was institutionalized after multiple drug-induced breakdowns. Grandma, on the other hand, was wise, kind, strict (in a loving way), and fun. She gave Jennifer the desire to make something of herself.

Last year, her grandma passed away after a full, rich life. She hadn't exactly planned on raising a child in her later years, but she said the joy she got from watching Jennifer grow up made it all worthwhile.

Setting off on this westbound trip was just what Jennifer needed to mend a broken heart and evaluate what to do with the rest of her life. Now, after traveling through New Zealand, Australia, the Philippines, Greece, Italy, Germany, France, and Spain, she finds herself on the road again—this time heading east to help out some friends.

Jennifer's college roommate, Anna, married a German exchange student and moved to Germany two years ago. They opened a California-style Mexican food restaurant in a small hamlet called Freigericht. The business was doing well, but had a long way to go before becoming a thriving enterprise. Jennifer had a quick visit with them two months ago when she was in between trains on her way to France, and planned to return for a longer visit after the restaurant's busy season.

Then, a couple of days ago, Jennifer received a frantic phone call from Anna. Apparently Anna had broken her leg skiing and would be out of commission for up to six weeks. The restaurant couldn't afford for her to be out, but she had no choice. Since Jennifer knows her way around a kitchen, she agreed to come help, and a grateful Anna offered up their guest room for her to stay in.

In college, Jennifer was the friend who would cook for everyone. When someone wanted to impress their date with a home-cooked meal, she would be roped into going over early in the day, cooking the meal, then slipping out before the date arrived. Jennifer never minded the deception: She loved cooking and was always given a portion to take home, so the arrangement benefited everyone.

Now, as evening sets in and the train arrives at the Gelnhausen station, Jennifer dons her backpack to make the seven-minute walk to the bus station. As the bus approaches Freigericht's town center, she can just make out the steeple across the main square in the twilight. As promised, Tobias is waiting at the bus station to walk her to their home above the restaurant. Freigericht has a fairytale quality about it. Jennifer feels like she's stepped into a Brothers Grimm story as they walk through the cobbled streets.

"Truly, we can't tell you how much we appreciate this," Tobias says, glancing sideways at Jennifer. "Anna was beside herself with worry about keeping the restaurant open while she convalesces. This was the only way we could think of keeping things going. We have Hilda, who washes dishes and keeps the kitchen tidy, but she can't cook—believe me, we tested that out and will never do it again. We hate to impose on your vacation—"

"First of all, I'm not on vacation, I'm just living in different places for a while," Jennifer interrupts. "And secondly, what are friends for? I'm actually looking forward to it. I should be thanking you."

They enter through the back of the restaurant, which leads to a staircase to the apartment above. The warm glow of a fire greets them as they enter the cozy living room, along with Anna, sitting in a comfortable chair. Her leg, encased in a neon-pink cast, is propped up on a pillow on top of an ottoman. She smiles broadly and extends her arms for a hug. Jennifer rushes into it and collapses against her before remembering Anna's injury.

"Damn, I have to be more careful," Jennnifer says with a wince. "I didn't hurt you, did I? I have to learn to moderate my enthusiasm!"

Anna laughs and blinks back tears from her big brown eyes. "You'll never learn to moderate that enthusiasm of yours. But it's one of the reasons I love you." She pats her flawless blond bob, a look she has sported since college. Jennifer recognizes the gesture as her way of trying to smooth out a situation she can't control. "It's so good to see you again—and much sooner than we thought."

Jennifer laughs. "We can catch up after I get the lay of the land in the kitchen and make us all some dinner. You both relax and let me spoil you a bit."

She tosses her bag into the guest room and heads back down to the restaurant level. A professional kitchen is such a treat! Before long, Jennifer is bustling around the space, kneading eggs and flour into homemade pasta, and simmering tomatoes for a quick sauce.

Jennifer has always loved cooking. Whenever Grandma didn't feel well, Jennifer would take over the household duties. At a young age, she began her culinary experimenting. The results weren't always a success, but she learned so much and developed the confidence to express herself through the art of cooking, so it was all worth it. Although, as her guinea pigs, Grandma and her friends may have disagreed. Somehow the banana and asparagus cake missed the mark, as did her attempt at Italian-and-Indian fusion.

After dinner, Tobias insists on cleaning up while Anna and Jennifer review what she needs to do tomorrow. And although they all need a good sleep, they stay up late, reminiscing about the past over a lovely bottle of Gewürztraminer. Finally, Tobias helps Anna to bed and Jennifer retreats to the guest room to quickly write in her journal. It's a habit she picked up a couple of years ago when she was trying to make sense of yet another relationship gone bad. Jennifer appreciates that once she makes it through whatever challenge life has tossed at her, she can read her own words and remind herself that yet again, she's come out the other end stronger and more resilient than ever. As she finishes an entry about today and the beginning of a new adventure, Jennifer's eyelids grow heavy with fatigue and she drifts off to sleep.

After a few days getting up to speed, Jennifer starts to enjoy the routine. Her favorite part of the evening is when all the orders are out and the restaurant is filled with locals having drinks and socializing. There's Hans, a seventy-something year-old man who always has a kind word and dad joke to share, and Marietta and her husband Larry, who tell Jennifer all about their time living in California while Marietta was a visiting professor. Jennifer finds herself drawn to her stories and wants to learn as much as she can about becoming a professor, too. The money may not be as good as the tech field, but the intellectual stimulation—not to mention the time off each year—are very appealing to her.

At the end of her second week, Jennifer notices a table of six young men—well, teenagers is more appropriate—who tend to sit for a couple of hours each night over beers and nachos. Five of them speak perfect German and seemed to know everyone, so Jennifer assumes their families are locals. But one of them has inky dark hair and large dark eyes and speaks with an accent. The local boys don't seem to be especially nice to the dark-haired teen, even though he always seems to pay for everything. He's always sitting on the edge of an overstuffed booth, his companions keeping their backs turned to him even when he tries to engage in conversation.

Over glasses of wine after a long shift one night, Jennifer asks Anna about the mismatched friends. Her friend explains that the teen with the accent is a Turkish immigrant named Emre, who is living with some family friends after his parents passed away in a car crash a year ago.

"Those German boys are not very nice," Anna says with a frown. "All they like to do is sit around and get drunk. And have you noticed Emre pays for everything? They are all in gymnasium—you know, high school—together, but Emre also works very hard. He started a couple of small businesses obtaining Turkish products and then selling them to his community. To be honest, he is a much better person than the rest of them."

"Why does he put up with it?" Jennifer asks. She's not sure why she's so curious about this.

"He's a smart young man and has aligned himself with peers whose families are important in town. It's as though at this young age, he is already playing the long game," Anna muses. "I think he'll really make something of himself one day. And I don't want this to sound creepy," she adds, leaning in conspiratorially, "but I bet he's going to be a hottie."

Jennifer has to agree. She decides to go out of her way to make Emre feel seen and appreciated. Her grandma always said that if you saw an injustice being done and did not do something to stop it, then you were just as culpable as the perpetrator. Even though that lesson had put Jennifer in some difficult situations, she still abides by it.

So the next night, after all of the meals are on the tables and Hilda is cleaning up the kitchen, she heads over to the teens' booth. Jennifer had noticed that Emre always had a book with him—this time it's Jack London's *Martin Eden,* in English. One of Jennifer's all-time favorite books. She figures it's an easy way to start a conversation in which he could be the center of attention.

"How are you enjoying the tale of Mr. Eden?" Jennifer asks as she approaches the booth. All the boys stop speaking and stare at her, mouths agape.

It takes all her control not to burst out laughing. You would have thought they had seen a ghost or something. It looks like what Tobias told her was true: The German teens considered Jennifer a great mystery, "some sexy American woman" they were all speculating about. According to Tobias, one or two of them had even bragged that Jennifer had flirted with them. It was quite obvious from their reactions that none of them had ever even said hello to her.

Emre, on the other hand, holds Jennifer's eyes in a respectful yet confident stare, while his friends begin intently studying the wood grain of the tabletop.

He smiles. "A tourist left this book here and Anna gave it to me," he says. His voice is soft. "I am enjoying it very much. I greatly appreciate the effective examination of the social class system. It appears little has changed since 1909."

"Very insightful," Jennifer says, and introduces herself. "I'd love to chat about what you've been reading."

"My name is Emre Sydin. That would be wonderful. I don't really have anyone to discuss my books with as my friends don't read much," He smiles shyly. "I'm sorry that my English is not so good."

Jennifer scoffs. "Are you kidding me? Your English is perfect. Much better than my German!" She sweeps a dismissive glance past his friends, then looks back at Emre. "It's a date. If you like, we can chat once I'm finished in the kitchen tomorrow night. It will be fun."

She saunters away, hoping she didn't lay it on too thick. It felt really good to see the envious looks the boys covertly directed at Emre. She can't cause too much disruption, Jennifer reasons with herself—there's only another three to four weeks before she moves on.

The next night, after making sure the kitchen is ready for Hilda to clean, Jennifer loads up a tray with freshly made nachos and a couple bottles of soda water. At the last minute, she swaps one bottle out for orange soda—she's noticed that it's Emre's drink of choice. She carefully backs through the swinging door and into the dining room, waving Emre over to join her at an empty table. The look of delight on his face makes Jennifer's day.

As he slides in across the booth, Jennifer notices that in place of his usual T-shirt and jeans, he is sporting a light blue button down under a maroon pullover cable-knit sweater and navy-blue chinos. She smiles sweetly at the effort he made. She looks down at her jeans and ratty old Nirvana *Nevermind* T-shirt and shrugs. This isn't a date, she reminds herself. Jennifer hands him the soda and pushes the nachos towards him—a silent invitation to share the meal. It's about time someone treats him.

"This is so great," he says, uncapping the soda. "I thought maybe you would forget, or that maybe you didn't mean it."

"Never. I've been looking forward to this all day!" Jennifer tells him around a mouthful of chips and cheese. "Okay, where are you in the book?"

They spend the next hour eating nachos and enthusiastically discussing *Martin Eden*. Jennifer finds herself impressed by his interpretations of the subtext. He is a brilliant young man. Before she knows it, she's made plans to discuss another London novel with him later in the week.

"Anna told me you came from Istanbul," Jennifer says, polishing off her soda water. "Did any of your family get hurt in the big earthquake that hit in August?"

"I don't have any family left," he says, casting his eyes downward. "That's why I am here in Germany, with a couple of dear friends of my parents'. But it is very sad—that earthquake killed seventeen thousand people and left half a million homeless."

"Oh, I'm so sorry for your country," Jennifer replies. She really didn't mean to end their lovely evening on such a sad topic, but she can feel the day catching up to her. She smiles to break the tension. "It's getting late and I think we both need our sleep. I'll see you Tuesday, Emre, okay?"

"Yes, I look forward to it, Ela." His eyes go wide. "Um, Jennifer I mean." He attempts to hide his embarrassment by looking at his book.

"Ela, what is that?" Jennifer asks.

"It is a name in my language. It means hazel, like the color of your eyes. They are so beautiful," he says then quickly adds, "I am sorry, I did not mean to be so familiar. But your eyes are captivating."

Jennifer smiles, touched by the unaffected sweetness with which he says this. "You can call me that if you'd like," she says before she can stop herself. "I like the name. And I love the grove of hazel trees in the woods at the end of town. I walk there often."

After they say their goodbyes, Jennifer races upstairs to retreat to her journal. Was that weird? The last thing she wants is for Emre to develop a crush on her. He is eight years younger than Jennifer's twenty-four years—at this stage of life, that is a huge age difference. But—and she would only admit this to her pages—if he were older he would be hard to resist. He is kind, a smooth—yet sincere—talker, and wicked smart.

The next day being a Monday, the restaurant is closed. Jennifer decides to wander around town and stop by the local Christmas market. It has all the requisite German festival foods, beer and Glühwein, local crafts, and local bands. She sees a lot of the restaurant's regulars; they all say hello and are friendly enough, but they move on quickly to spend time with their families.

This Christmas is harder than Jennifer thought it would be. Grandma always made a big deal about the holidays. As she shuffles through the happy families, Jennifer realizes she doesn't want to be alone. She turns to head back home and runs right into Emre.

He smiles and Jennifer is surprised when he says exactly what she had just been thinking. "I was just about to head home because I'm feeling out of place," he says, stuffing his hands in his pockets. "My friends are all with their families, and I am not exactly welcome to join them."

"Why is that?" Jennifer asks, blowing on her hands to warm them. "They seem to be fine hanging out with you at the restaurant."

"Well, it is unfortunate," Emre says, shuffling from foot to foot. "Some of the German people don't like us Turks in Deutschland. When the guest worker program started thirty years ago, it wasn't as much of a problem. Turkish workers would migrate here and work hard and bring the money back to Turkey to make a better life for their families. But now, we are reaching close to two million living here and some of the local people do not like it so much."

He has a sad expression as he continues. "I don't understand how a country that went through the atrocities of World War II can choose to vilify others just because they look different, worship differently, and speak with an accent. Do we never learn from history?"

"I don't know the answer to that," Jennifer says honestly. "It appears that as soon as the generation that lived through an earth-shattering event dies off, the next generation forgets. I don't think it's history that repeats itself, it is humans that repeat themselves, sadly."

He gives Jennifer one of his penetrating looks. Suddenly, he smiles, "Come now, Ela, no more sad talk. Let me show you around.

And no arguing with me: Let me buy you some of this tasty food. You, for once, do not have to cook!"

Jennifer laughs and they start back toward the market. "I never thought I would say this, but a day off from cooking sounds heavenly," she admits as they walk. "Don't get me wrong—I love cooking, but I've never had to do it as a job before, it has always just been for pleasure. But it is only for another three weeks and then…"

He interrupts her. "What? Only three more weeks? I didn't know. I mean, do you have to leave then?"

"Anna is healing very well. Her doctor said the cast can come off on week five and then by week six she can resume her regular activities. There is no need for me to stay around once she is back at it. I will just be in the way." Jennifer shrugs. "I'm sure that she and Tobias just want to get back to their normal routine and I need to continue on with my life and my travels. Heading west until I reach home again."

Jennifer smiles at him, hoping to lift the mood. "Where's this yummy food you were talking about?"

They find a table and load it up with bratwurst, kartoffelpuffer, some big pretzels and obatzda to dip them in. As the afternoon sun gets lower in the sky, Jennifer is surprised at how much she's enjoying watching the bands perform with her kind young companion.

As they're laughing at something Jennifer said, an attractive teenage girl with shiny blond hair walks by, smiles at Emre, and says hello. Jennifer clears her throat, thinking that this is a good opportunity to set some boundaries.

"She's very pretty," Jennifer whispers to Emre once the girl is out of earshot. "Is she in your class? I think you should go and talk to her and maybe see if she wants to listen to the next band with you."

Jennifer takes a moment to consider what feeling this moment evokes in herself. Is it jealousy? She shakes it off—she can't think about her own feelings right now. They are so wrong but so hard to deny. He is so young. She studies Emre's reaction.

"She is one of the nicer girls in my class," he says. "But she is immature. She giggles and only talks about partying and clothes." He sounds hurt. "I would rather listen to the next band with you. Or, if you have to leave, I will walk you home and go home and read. Then next time we can talk about *Burning Daylight*." He breaks into a smile that looks a little bit sad. "Yes, I chose another London book."

Jennifer feels a bit bad, sensing she's put a damper on their day. He's been so kind today and seemed so happy. It may be best, Jennifer thinks, if she goes home. Today has brought them closer and Jennifer reminds herself she needs to shore up their boundaries.

Emre walks Jennifer home as promised. She says goodbye to him on the street in front of the restaurant, promising to discuss *Burning Daylight* with him tomorrow. Just before they part, Emre reaches his arms out for a tentative hug.

Jennifer tells herself she'll make it a quick hug, but is surprised by how effortlessly she melts into his arms. Emre's not that much taller than her, and Jennifer's chin rests comfortably on his shoulder. His arms are so warm. It's a really good hug, she admits to herself.

Suddenly she starts and backs away quickly, all but fleeing upstairs. Why is her body betraying her? Is she so touch-starved that a hug from a nice boy has her melting?

Still, Jennifer does meet him the following evening, and every evening for the next two weeks. With Anna sound asleep by the time the kitchen closes, she tells herself she is just using this time with Emre to wind down after work. But she can't believe how much her feelings toward him are growing every day. He is such an intelligent and mature young man—teenager, she scolds herself. Every night she pours her heart out to her journal, all the conflict she's feeling about Emre. She knows she shouldn't be having these feelings at all, let alone feeling them so strongly.

Two weeks after their Christmas market not-date, Jennifer all but stumbles out of the kitchen. These shifts are starting to wear on her—she still loves cooking, but after she hangs up her apron in a week, she won't want to see another tortilla for quite some time.

As her eyes sweep the restaurant looking for Emre—it's time for one of their after-dinner chats—she stops in her tracks, gazing out the windows. The ground is covered in a thick blanket of snow. It's still snowing outside—it must have been the whole time she was in the kitchen. Without grabbing her coat, she dashes outside. She hears Emre follow her, feels him throw his still-warm coat over her shoulders.

"What are you doing?" he asks.

"It's snowing!" Jennifer squeals. "It's the first snowfall since I've been here. I thought I was going to have to go to the ski resorts to play in the snow." He doesn't look as impressed as Jennifer, but she can see a slight uptick in the corner of his mouth. "Sorry," Jennifer says with a chuckle. "I always get super excited for a snowfall."

He gets a sly smile on his face and grabs a handful of snow. Jennifer barely ducks in time to dodge the snowball he throws at her. Before she knows it, they're locked in a major snowball fight, eventually dissolving into laughter so hard they can't even throw anymore. Emre uses both arms to scoop up a pile of snow and dumps it on Jennifer's head. She hasn't played like this since she was a little kid.

The laughter subsides as they realize their faces are inches apart. Jennifer holds his gaze. It feels like the rest of the world disappears as they stare into each other's eyes. It is like an electric shock, like their whole lives just melded together. Jennifer knows at once that it's the strongest connection she has ever felt.

It is only a moment but feels like eternity. Jennifer takes a deep breath and breaks away, turning and heading back to the restaurant. She mutters that she's tired and that they can talk about the book tomorrow. She just knows she can't be in his orbit at all right now.

When Jennifer reaches her room, she closes the door and leans against it. She has to get her emotions under control, clear her head. It's only a few more days—then she can be on her way. As she reaches for her journal, she realizes she still has Emre's coat on. Jennifer hugs it around her and feels tears gently roll down her cheeks.

The next day, Jennifer feels much more in control. She didn't sleep much last night, but steeled her resolve to keep Emre in the younger-kid friend zone. She gets through the lunch and dinner orders feeling surprisingly strong.

That night at their booth, she is able to keep the conversation solely book-focused. Over the past few weeks they had fallen into a pattern: book talk for a half hour or so, and sharing their thoughts and feelings about life for the rest of the evening. That is what must have caused the confusion in the snow, as Jennifer told Anna that morning over breakfast. Anna had no idea of the growing friendship between her best friend and her frequent customer—she thought Jennifer was helping Emre with a literature assignment. But she agreed with what Jennifer had been telling herself for weeks: It can't be anything more than a friendship.

"It's smart to put some boundaries around that," Anna had said between bites of brötchen. "You only have a few days and I know you can set things right, let him down easy and remain friends. I mean, you were the queen of doing that in college."

Jennifer had rolled her eyes at her friend, but Anna had a point. And over the next few nights, Jennifer is proud of how she puts distance between her and Emre during their chats. She stays friendly, yet professional; Jennifer is a kind teacher reviewing a student's thoughts on a book, she tells herself. She knows Emre can tell the difference. One night, he tries yet again to bring the conversation around to a more personal level and Jennifer continues to deflect. As usual, confusion flashes on his face.

"Ela, did I do something wrong?" he finally asks. "Have I upset you? You seem so different and I am so confused. If I did anything wrong let me know so I can make it better."

This is Jennifer's chance to be direct.

"No, you have done nothing wrong," she says, determined. "I sensed we were becoming close in a way I was not comfortable with. Maybe you aren't feeling the same way as I am, though."

He fixes her with a confident gaze, so direct it's hard to remember that he's not an adult who's used to women telling him they're enamored with him.

"I have felt the same thing, probably more deeply." His voice is steady. "But I do not find these feelings uncomfortable. I find them perfect, as they should be. I feel like we are one."

Jennifer has to take a moment before she can speak. His words have touched her heart in a way that has been missing in her life. After composing herself, she finds she is able to reply. "You are a wonderful person but you are sixteen, I am twenty-four. At this stage of our lives we are in different universes. You need to find a nice girl your age and I need to find a nice man my age. And that, my dear friend, is not open to negotiation." Somehow Jennifer forms these words while she melts inside.

Emre looks deeply into Jennifer's eyes and nods.

With only a few days left of Jennifer's stay in Germany, the restaurant gets a new set of regulars: a group of military guys who are on R&R from the American Air Force base in northern Italy. Jennifer guesses that the margaritas and tequila sunrises remind them of home.

They have also developed the annoying routine of trying to flirt with her. Jennifer avoids them like the plague. After weeks of intelligent, sensitive conversations with Emre, she knows these brash, obnoxious guys are exactly what she's not looking for.

On her last night in Germany, Jennifer swings through the kitchen door and joins Emre in their usual booth. She notices the servicemen sitting in the booth that butts up behind theirs. This is something they started doing once they realized Jennifer wasn't going to engage with them. They would sit there for hours, prattling away and making snide remarks here and there about the snobby bookish American woman.

After a couple of hours, Jennifer tells Emre that she had better call it a night. She hasn't even begun packing for her morning train out of Germany. Emre hands her a small box and smiles.

"An early Christmas present for you," he says.

Jennifer takes the box and opens it. In it is a gold pendant in the shape of a leaf, hanging from a simple yet elegant chain. The leaf is round with a slightly pointed tip and serrated edges, and etched on it is a nazar boncuğu, a Turkish evil eye symbol.

"This is so beautiful," she says honestly. "You shouldn't have, but I love it."

Emre stands and circles the booth, taking a seat next to her. "It is a hazel leaf. I know you love the grove and, although the names of the tree and your eye color aren't the same in my language, they are in yours. And the nazar boncuğu is used for protection in my culture. I had this made specially for you. It means that I will always be protecting you."

He takes the necklace from Jennifer's hands and gently places it around her neck. His hands brush the nape of her neck, sending an electric current through Jennifer's body. No one else's touch has ever caused that kind of visceral reaction in her.

Jennifer clears her throat and shifts away from him, trying to put some distance between them. She presses her back against the side of the booth and smiles weakly at him. "Thank you," she whispers. "It's lovely."

Emre suddenly gets a serious look on his face, his gaze boring into her eyes. "Wait for me."

It is so beautiful and sincere, but Jennifer knows she needs to tell him that won't happen. That she and Emre both have their lives to get on with; the age difference is just too much and will be for a while. But before she can say a word, a bark of derisive laughter rings out behind them. Emre's expression falls. He slides out of the booth and Jennifer follows awkwardly. They both turn to see the military boys hanging over the booth, not bothering to stifle their laughter, and with snide looks directed at Emre. Clearly they were listening to their conversation.

Jennifer is seeing red. Sure, she didn't want romance tonight, but these rude men have ruined a beautiful moment. Why do people in this restaurant keep underestimating this extraordinary, sweet, intelligent young man? Before she can stop herself, Jennifer does the only thing she can think of. She grabs Emre and kisses him.

The army guys' laughter dies but Jennifer barely notices. Emre's lips are so soft and warm—it just feels so right. Her knees become weak and her breathing shallow. No other kiss has ever made Jennifer feel this way. She can't bear it.

Jennifer breaks off the kiss and runs from the restaurant, sprinting up the stairs to her room. In the morning, she'll catch an earlier train, she decides, just so she doesn't run into Emre. How could she face him again? How could she tell him that kiss was just for show, to stop the servicemen from mocking him? How could she lie and say it made her feel nothing?

Luckily, she's already had a lovely evening with Anna and Tobias to celebrate her farewell, so she doesn't feel too bad leaving them a note when she slips out the front door the next morning. Jennifer writes most of the truth: She is catching an earlier train and is sorry she won't be able to come back for a visit after their busy season.

Jennifer just can't risk seeing Emre again.

Chapter Three

2009

Jennifer dances around her office, Flo Rida's "Low" blasting from her iPhone speakers. It's one of the two things she does before every lecture; the other is to learn something new about the topic she's about to present to those bright minds in her class. (Today, she delved into the relationship between the Native Welfare Act of 1905, commonly known as the Laws of 1905, and the problems Australia's indigenous population is dealing with in today's society.) This routine always gets Jennifer energized and piques her interest anew in whatever topic she's presenting.

Ten years ago, Jennifer would have never seen herself here in Western Australia.

Life's twists and turns take us to places we never thought we would be but deposit us exactly where we are meant to be. And Jennifer's twists and turns have been no exception. After her grand tour (a.k.a. the early-twenties worldwide heartbreak tour), Jennifer returned home to Los Angeles and couldn't stomach the thought of returning to the corporate grind. The conversations she had with Marietta, the professor she met in the restaurant in Germany, kept running through her mind. So by the time she set down her bags in LA, she had decided on yet another sea change. Following her passion for traveling and the quest for a deeper understanding of different cultures, Jennifer went to graduate school and got her masters degree and PhD in anthropology. During the grad student exploitation component (a.k.a., working as a teachers' assistant) she realized she actually enjoyed teaching.

There is just something thrilling about a classroom full of students representing the full spectrum of the college experience— from those who are excited to be there and want to learn everything they can, to those who are just fulfilling a requirement but have no interest in actually learning anything. Getting all of them so hyped on the subject matter that they actually show up and participate is a huge buzz. And Jennifer is hooked on that buzz.

Landing in Western Australia was part of another one of her great escapes from home—this time, from a four-year marriage. Jennifer met Steve in grad school, where he was preparing to become a corporate lawyer. That should have been the first red flag. Steve displayed all the textbook tendencies of a narcissist, but Jennifer couldn't see past his muscular six-foot-two frame, his dark russet hair, and crystal-clear blue eyes. And the love bombing, of course. He seemed too good to be true. But he swept Jennifer off her feet—or, she sometimes thinks, Jennifer allowed herself to be swept off her feet. That's when she learned that if the person doing the sweeping isn't a reliable catch, you will end up on your ass. And that's exactly where she landed.

Well, it's all over now. After the isolation and his serial cheating—cheating that he felt Jennifer should just accept, because she had the privilege of being married to him and the others didn't—she had enough. Jennifer knew she deserved more. So she turned and ran the other way.

During that time, while she was attached to an insensitive, careless man, Jennifer's thoughts turned often to her time with Emre. The way he spoke to her, always with kindness, and the respect he showed her. She hasn't ever removed the hazel leaf pendant—Emre's pendant—from her neck. She still touches it mindlessly from time to time.

Jennifer asked Steve for a divorce around the time she became a freshly minted PhD in 2008—not a great time to be looking for employment. Just like she had ten years ago, Jennifer decided it was time to run away. She focused her job search on places as far away from LA as possible.

Jennifer was excited when she saw a position at the University of Western Australia and knew she would have an advantage because of the one thing of value her mom gave her: dual citizenship with Australia.

Three months later Jennifer is settled into a cute unit in Nedlands, a nice suburb of Perth close to the university. Australian students are really great to teach. Unlike in the States, young people in Australia aren't all pushed to go to uni; Jennifer's theory is that as a result, the students in higher education are more well prepared and focused.

Still, the first few weeks of teaching were a bit rocky. Jennifer first tried to copy the lecture-based graduate classes she had taught in the States. She could tell her students were smart, but they were struggling to stay engaged. So Jennifer switched it up: She became much more of a storyteller, encouraging students to participate and add to the discussion. She focused on what she loved about the material, and helped them learn to love it, too. Since then, the weeks have zoomed by, and now there are only a few sessions left until winter break. She's still getting used to thinking of July as winter break.

Just as she's thinking fondly of the progress she's made with her students, she realizes the song playing from her iPhone has ended. Having lost track of time reminiscing, Jennifer grabs her notes and dashes from her office.

On her way to class, Jennifer continues the list she's been making in her head over the past week of places to take Anna when she visits during the break. The restaurant has turned into a real success since Jennifer's brief stint there. Now they have the funds to hire more help, which has given Anna and Tobias so much more freedom. It's good to see that all their hard work had paid off.

One of Jennifer's colleagues stops her as she's considering which seafood restaurant Anna will prefer. He's tall and slender with floppy Hugh Grant hair and the kindest eyes Jennifer has seen since she arrived. She knows she's passed him in the halls and seen him in department meetings.

"Hi," he says with a smile, extending his hand. "We haven't formally been introduced. I'm Ian Archer, I'm a senior lecturer here." After Jennifer introduces herself, Ian points to a notice on the bulletin board. "This is what I mentioned in the department meeting yesterday. There is a great opportunity to participate in an archaeological dig—and for once, they are extending it to us anthropologists."

Jennifer had seen it. It was a high-profile dig in southeastern Turkey, one that had already yielded a trove of artifacts.

"Maybe we could have a coffee and chat about it," Ian offers. "I'm the unofficial cat herder for this particular adventure."

Jennifer pauses. Is this a pickup line? Then again, it may not be anything but kindness to the new girl. A colleague trying to get her to participate more with the other professors. She's thus far avoided all the social Friday drinks and invites to watch Aussie Rules footy at the stadium nearby, Subi Oval. Jennifer has started to worry that her need for personal time and space is starting to make her look like a stuck-up American princess.

Jennifer pastes on a smile. "Thank you. That does sound interesting. I have a break on Thursdays at one o'clock—coffee then would work."

"Great!" Ian says with another big grin. "Meet you here then, and we can walk over together."

Thursday arrives and Jennifer couldn't come up with a way out of their coffee meeting, so she finds herself in the Catalyst Café enjoying an excellent cappuccino. Australians make some of the best coffee in the world, Jennifer has decided—second only to the Italians.

"Thanks for suggesting this," Jennifer tells Ian from across the table. "I haven't really let myself explore the campus and enjoy all of its nice shops and cafés. I pretty much stay in my office or classrooms."

"Well, I believe the fault for that lies with those of us who have been here for a while," Ian says. With one hand he stirs sugar into his coffee and with the other slides his vanilla slice towards Jennifer and hands her an extra spoon. "We forget what it's like to be the newbie. And not just new to campus but new to the entire county. So I apologize for not being more friendly from the get-go."

"No worries."

"Look at that, you're already sounding like an Aussie!" he chuckles.

"My mom was originally from Australia," Jennifer says, carving her spoon into the vanilla slice. "She moved to the States as a teen with her family. Her dad worked in the petroleum industry and was transferred there for what was supposed to be three years, but they ended up staying. Back then, it was much easier to immigrate if you had a sought-after skill set." Jennifer pauses and glances at Ian. He's listening patiently.

"I don't think it was the best time for my mom to make that move." Jennifer hears the catch in her own voice and hopes Ian doesn't notice. "She got in with the wrong crowd; I think it was her way of rebelling, being moved away from all her friends and extended family. Anyhow, that's how I ended up with dual citizenship, my dad is American—was American, I'm not sure if he is even alive anymore—and my mom is Australian."

Jennifer shrugs, keeping her eyes on her cappuccino. "TMI, I guess. You're just so easy to talk to."

"That's exactly what my husband, Scott, says about me," Ian says with a kind smile. "He says that no matter where we go, people just spill their guts to me. I don't mind. It's the best way to cut through all the bullshit and small talk and get to know someone. And I would like to get to know you."

Jennifer perks up. "When did you move here and where are you from? Did you meet your husband here or move here together?" She chuckles. "Sorry, I don't mean to interrogate you. I'm just a curious person."

"We moved here three years ago from Alberta, Canada," he says, with no hesitation at Jennifer's rapid-fire questions. "It has been a great move for us. The university even found employment for Scott. He was a human resources executive in Canada, so all he had to do to transfer his skills was to learn the employment laws. We are really happy here."

Jennifer's feeling pretty happy, herself. She's just made a new friend and she's relieved he's married—and even if he wasn't, he wouldn't be interested in dating her. They chatter on, Ian telling her all about the amazing places to go and things to do in WA. He even offers to help her with an itinerary for when Anna visits. Jennifer beams, relieved that she didn't cancel this coffee with Ian.

"And now, that dig in Turkey. It wasn't just an opening to introduce myself to the newbie," Ian says, folding his hands in mock-seriousness. "Would you be interested in attending the presentation by the archaeologist who is setting up the summer break team? It's next week during finals, so we won't be in class."

"Yes, I would be interested," Jennifer replies honestly. "Actually, I'm excited about it. I had a friend from Turkey and he got me interested in exploring it. I'll put it in my diary."

Another Aussie expression—"diary" is what they call their calendars here. But it reminds Jennifer of the journals she used to keep. When she gets home that afternoon, she searches through some boxes she has yet to unpack and eventually finds her old journals. She rubs her hand lovingly over the deep red, pebbled-leather cover of one volume, thinking about all that these little books have gotten her through. Jennifer would have kept journaling in recent years, except Steve would whine every time she picked up a notebook. He felt it took Jennifer's attention off him and he was always paranoid that she was writing mean things about him. So she stopped journaling to keep the peace.

As she leafs through the diary in her hand, Emre's name practically leaps off of one of the pages. Jennifer's breath catches for the second time that day. She can't believe that after ten years, such a brief time spent with someone still has such an impact on her. Jennifer makes a cup of tea and curls up on her new comfy reading chair with the journal. She finds the section written while she was at Anna and Tobias's and begins reading.

Those few weeks in Germany take up dozens of pages—Jennifer doesn't remember writing quite that much at the time. After finishing the entry from the night of her departure, she looks up, surprised. The sun is setting and Jennifer is sitting in the dim light with tears gently running down her face. She closes the journal and sits for another half hour, memories of Emre flooding back in vivid detail as she runs her thumb across the pendant he gave her so many years ago. She's still in awe that someone so young who had been through so much upheaval in his short life was so mature, kind, and intuitive.

It's been a decade since their brief encounter. Jennifer hopes by now that he has real friends, a woman who loves him, and continued business success. Not for the first time, she regrets that she didn't keep in touch with him. Jennifer glances at her computer across the room. Back then, everyone didn't have a digital footprint, but now …

Maybe it would put her feelings to rest to see the man he has become, rather than remembering a fairy tale from her youth. A little peek on the internet won't hurt, will it?

Jennifer settles into her new desk chair and switches on her desktop. As a research professor Jennifer feels pretty confident about her skills in the area of digital hunting. She considers herself a bit of a cyber creep and tends to research the shit out of anyone she meets. Some may think that's weird or paranoid—Jennifer just feels like it's playing it safe. If the information is out there, she reasons, why not use it? It could save her the time of starting to develop a friendship or romantic relationship and then realizing she's wasted a couple weeks of her life with some neo-Nazi or fascist.

She searches for the next two hours as her living room darkens, illuminated only by her computer screen. She looks at Myspace, Facebook, Twitter, and LinkedIn, then conducts a pretty thorough Google search. Nothing. Emre has zero digital footprint.

Jennifer sits back in her chair, staring into space. Could he have had some horrible accident? Is it possible he's dead? Jennifer shakes her head to clear it—her thoughts always go to the extreme. She knows she needs to stop this fantasizing and get back to reality. She has work to do, a real job. Dwelling on the past isn't achieving anything.

A few weeks later, Jennifer waits in the arrival area of the Perth airport, feeling like a kid on Christmas morning. Anna's flight landed on time, and she would have cleared customs in Sydney so she should be out any minute.

All of a sudden, there she is, smiling and waving. Jennifer barely contains herself from hurdling the barrier. As Anna reaches her, Jennifer takes her in her arms in a big bear hug. It all comes spilling out: all Jennifer's excitement to finally have her dear friend in these new surroundings with her, along with all the longing for the past that she's been holding on to so tightly. For the first time in a long time, Jennifer feels safe, like she's come out of a storm and into the shelter of the familiar. So much has happened in the ten years since they have seen each other, but neither time nor distance get in the way of true friendship.

"How the hell can you get off of a twenty-hour flight with your hair flawless?" Jennifer laughs and hugs her friend close. "Remember in college, when you would spend the morning straightening my hair, and no matter what, it would be all curly and frizzy before we got to campus? Yours was always perfect even after walking through fog or rain. If I hadn't loved you I would have hated you for that."

Anna flips her perfect bob dramatically, and Jennifer laughs again. It's so good to have her best friend back.

Once they are settled in Jennifer's apartment, Jennifer shoos Anna off to shower and unpack while she prepares dinner.

As Jennifer whisks a vinaigrette for the salad, Anna joins her in the kitchen. "That felt great," she says with a big yawn. "I may even make it until nine o'clock, but I'm still fading."

"We'll have a relaxing day tomorrow, maybe have a nice walk around Kings Park and then lunch on the beach in Cottesloe," Jennifer says, handing her a glass of red from Margaret River, a region in WA whose wines she had recently fallen in love with. "How does that sound?"

"Sounds great," Anna says. "What else do you have planned for us? I know you said you want me to see as much as possible while I'm here so I'm sure you have a great itinerary planned."

"On Tuesday I've invited Ian and Scott over for dinner. I really want you to meet them," Jennifer says. "Ian is my colleague at the university and he and his husband are my only friends here at this point. I think you will like them."

"As your 'only friends here' I'm sure I will like them. Why don't you make an effort to develop more friendships—maybe even a romantic relationship? You have been here a whole semester already."

Jennifer frowns as she pulls the lasagna from the oven. She's always preferred quality over quantity when it comes to friendships. *Or,* a voice in the back of her mind asks, *is that what you say when you can't bring yourself to put yourself out there and chance being let down?*

"I will or maybe I won't. I'm enjoying having time to myself and exploring a bit on my own," Jennifer says.

Anna gives her the side-eye and Jennifer laughs.

"I know that look. I promise, next semester I will make an effort to participate with the other faculty more," Jennifer wipes her hands on her apron. "Now if you are finished judging my reclusive life, let me tell you the plans for the rest of the week."

Anna's teasing makes Jennifer feel more at home than she has felt in years.

"Come on, you must have some juicy stories about Jennifer," Ian says to Anna. "I can just imagine the eighteen-year-old Jen partying hard on and off campus."

Anna laughs. "Jen always had her nose in a book and was a serial monogamist who had the worst choice in men," she says with a sip of her after-dinner wine. "They were, basically, all assholes."

"Anna is so right," Jennifer agrees from her spot in the comfy reading chair. "I think my man picker was broken at birth. Anyhow, Anna was the wild one. I lived vicariously through her antics. I could tell you about her night with this hunky baseball player that featured the skimmed fat from the top of some refrigerated chicken soup."

"Oh, pray tell!" Scott says while trying to look salacious and somehow just looking like he caught his hand in the car door. That, aided by good wine and single malt, makes the foursome dissolve into hysterical laughter.

"No," Jennifer says with a wink at Anna. "A promise is a promise even years later." Anna silently mouths "thank you" back at her.

Jennifer knew she and the boys would get on like a house on fire.

"Shit, look at the time!" Ian says with a start, setting his glass on the coffee table. "It's two a.m. and we are volunteering at Woodman Point at eight!" He and Scott stand for hugs goodbye. "Thank you for a lovely evening. Superb food, amazing conversation, and a new friend!"

"What's Woodman Point?" Anna asks.

"It's this really cool historic site that used to be the main quarantine station for Western Australia," Scott explains as they gather their jackets. "It's where all the people arriving on ships in the late eighteen hundreds through most of the nineteen hundreds had to wait out the quarantine period before they entered and interacted with the general community to ensure they wouldn't be spreading influenza or smallpox. There was a nurse there named Berty Poore who took care of the smallpox patients. It was amazing that he never caught it. The doctors wouldn't even enter the areas where the smallpox patients were housed, but good ol' Poorey would be there tending to their needs. His descendants played a big part in drawing attention to the historical significance of the place and now it is a protected historical site."

"You guys should stop by on your way down south. It's not that far from here," Ian adds.

"Sounds super interesting," Anna says. "Maybe we will if we have time. It was so great meeting you both. I hope I see you again before I head back to Germany."

After Ian and Scott leave, laden with leftovers (a habit Jennifer got from her grandma. Always make way too much so everyone can take some home), Anna tells Jennifer how much she liked them.

"Why don't you volunteer with them?" she asks while clearing plates. "Get involved in some community organizations, put down roots?"

"Hm, I don't think I will stay here," Jennifer says as she busies herself with washing dishes. "I mean, I love it. It's one of the most beautiful places I've ever been. But I don't know, it's like that U2 song about not being able to find whatever you're looking for. Anna laughs as Jennifer jogs her memory with some off-key singing.

"I don't know what it is in me, but I know I'm not going to be buried here," Jennifer continues. "I'm thinking maybe five years, then on to the next adventure."

Until this moment, Jennifer hadn't realized she felt that way. Maybe that's why she's kept to herself so much.

That night in bed, she can't sleep, distracted by questions like "What am I looking for?" "Why do I never feel satisfied or fulfilled?" "What is missing that leaves me feeling so incomplete?" Rather than wait for any great epiphany to come, Jennifer escapes into sleep.

"Wow, I can't believe how gorgeous WA is," Anna says on her last day. "I don't know what has impressed me the most. I mean, the Margaret River wineries were incredible. But Augusta was so quaint with its lighthouse and water wheel. And those caves—

amazing! Maybe Cosy Corner was my favorite. Such a beautiful cove with that lone fisherman catching all those whiting. That was special."

"What, no love for the eastern foothills and the old monastery at New Norcia?" Jennifer teases, watching her pack her suitcase. "And all the spectacular beaches? And of course, Fremantle and its Round House, and other sites like the asylum and prison—they have done a good job preserving all that history. And the Fremantle Markets have so much yummy produce, not to mention the great buskers."

"Okay, okay, WA has too much … spectacularism, is that even a word? But I must say that Woodman Point was a highlight. Actually, it brought a tear to my eye," Anna says. "I think ten days is way too short for a visit. But really it's all I could swing. Although we are doing really well, the restaurant needs me and so does Tobias. Maybe next time we can both come." She tilts her head in that way she does when she leaves a question hanging. "That is, if you are still here."

Jennifer just smiles. She can't tell Anna what she doesn't know.

As Anna is packing, Jennifer tries to build up her courage to ask about Emre. She wanted to leave it until the end of her visit so that Anna wouldn't make a big deal about it. They haven't talked about him since Jennifer confessed to Anna about the kiss on one of their late-night phone calls. Needless to say, she was shocked and a bit squeamish about the thought of her then twenty-four-year-old friend kissing a sixteen-year-old. Now, Jennifer tries to approach the topic delicately—if she seems too interested in what happened to him, Anna may suspect Jennifer's suppressed feelings all these years later.

"It seems a lifetime ago you had that broken leg and I was the temporary cook in your nascent restaurant," Jennifer starts. "Boy, has life changed. Who would have ever thought I would be here; I certainly didn't. It was thanks to talking to one of your regulars, Marietta, and hearing her stories of being a professor. It really inspired me. If she is still around, please tell her so."

"I wish she still was, but she and Larry moved to Munich about two years ago," Anna says, folding a sweater. "But I will tell her the next time we text, which isn't too often. We hit birthdays, Christmas, you know the main events of the year."

"Who else from the old regulars is still around?" Jennifer asks, trying to sound nonchalant.

"Good old Hans still comes around but not so regularly. His daughter, who never married, moved from Freiburg to live with him now that he is in his eighties. He stays home with her most nights. But I will tell him you said hello when he comes in."

It appears those are all the updates Jennifer is getting. She steels herself and asks, "What about that young Turkish kid I would discuss books with? Is he still in town?"

"No, about a year after my broken leg, he moved. I'm not sure where, someone said Switzerland. I heard some gossip that an uncle sent someone to fetch him from the couple he was living with. I guess after his parents died and he was sent to Germany, there was some family feud about who would raise him long-term. I guess the uncle finally decided he wasn't going to try to negotiate anymore and just took him." Anna carries on, checking the items in her toiletry bag. "It was the main town gossip for a couple of weeks. He just didn't show up at school one day and all his clothes and personal belongings were still at his family friend's house. Shortly after that, his family friends moved and no one ever heard from him again."

She turns from stuffing the suitcase. Jennifer must look stricken because Anna throws up her hands. "Oh please don't tell me you are still pining over him," she says. "He's a little boy."

Jennifer quickly masks her expression. "Of course not! It's just awful that someone who first loses both his parents in a horrific accident at such a young age is then used as a pawn in some demented family drama. I mean, he was just getting settled in his new home and then a couple of years later, bam! He is torn from it."

"Then why are you still wearing this?" She reaches out and flicks the pendant that has hung around Jennifer's neck since it was placed there by Emre so long ago.

"You know how paranoid I can be," Jennifer sputters. "I had good luck right after I first wore it, so my future luck will rely on me wearing it. Remember that train I was supposed to take that was delayed for something like four hours because of a mechanical breakdown, but I had taken the earlier train and missed all that mess? And what about when the group I met up with in France all got sick and I didn't? Your superstitious friend, moi, believes it does protect her. It's also really cool and it goes with anything I wear."

"Hm, the lady doth protest too much?" Anna softens, looking Jennifer in the eyes. "No one was able to find him. He could even be dead. I know that sounds cold, but I'm trying to be realistic. No one, not even the school, was able to find a trace of him. After about a year everyone stopped looking because they thought there was nothing left to find."

Jennifer feels a sadness deep in her heart. What Anna says is probably true. Jennifer needs to stop looking, too. She will get on with her life. She's thirty-four now—it's time to focus on her career and personal life. She silently tucks the pendant into her shirt, and tucks the memory of that kind boy into a distant corner of her heart.

After Anna disappears through the security gate the next day, Jennifer turns to head home. Anna is right—it's time to get on living her life. She will make an effort to be more social and become part of the community.

At work on Monday, Jennifer stops by Ian's office.

"I've decided to apply for the dig in Turkey, " she tells him.

"That's fantastic!" Ian exclaims, looking up from the papers he's grading. "I think that makes nine of us. I'll forward you the paperwork."

Jennifer takes a deep breath, to stop herself from saying *I would rather hide in my house during summer break than travel across the world with a bunch of strangers.*

This is her first step towards the new Jennifer.

Chapter Four

Two weeks later, Jennifer double checks all her document scans and all the paperwork for the archaeological dig. Satisfied everything is in order, she presses send—and can't believe she's actually excited when she receives the confirmation email. Ian will compile everyone's submissions and send them all off to the appropriate government departments so they can get the approvals and visas required to participate in a project that has to do with such historically important artifacts.

The excitement builds as the end of the semester and the adventure draws closer. The Culture Vultures, as the group of anthropologists going to Turkey refer to themselves, have been getting together once a week to plan and bond. Jennifer is surprised to find that she enjoys getting to know her colleagues on a deeper level. She even joined the others in requesting a few extra days on her visa so they could explore and have some fun together after the dig. Anna would be so proud of her.

Jennifer is proud of herself, too. She's always been a solo traveler. Always loved the freedom that went into going where she wants, when she wants. But this time, Jennifer is honestly looking forward to being part of a team and sharing experiences with her colleagues—*friends,* Jennifer frequently has to correct herself in her mind.

One month before the group's departure, Ian comes to see Jennifer at home.

"Hey there! What a good surprise. Come in, come in," Jennifer says. "Where's Scott?"

"Although I love to make spontaneous visits to my buddy, this has to do with work."

They get settled into Jennifer's comfortable sofa and take a sip of lemonade. Ian smiles uncomfortably at her.

"You were rejected."

"What?" Jennifer says. "Not that being rejected is foreign to me, but I'm not dating anyone at the moment."

Jennifer thinks that may get a laugh out of Ian but he doesn't even crack a smile.

"No, your visa application was rejected. I can't seem to get a straight answer as to why."

"That doesn't make any sense. I don't even have a parking ticket. There must be some mistake. Maybe there is another Jennifer Young who is a drug smuggler or international jewel thief."

Jennifer knows that she's grasping at straws, but she's incredulous. She finally let herself get excited about something, finally tried to throw herself into a new community, a new home. She's trying not to cry but not doing a good job of it.

"Can you try again to get some answers, or clear up any errors or mistaken identities?" Jennifer pleads.

"Sweetie, because it's you, I did," Ian says with a sad smile. "I went as high as I could. I personally went down to the Turkish consulate myself and spoke directly to the consul. There wasn't anything wrong with the packet you or the uni submitted, it was just a rejection. They didn't know why, but said that maybe it's because you are a dual national. That didn't make sense to me, but what do I know." He drops his voice to a whisper. "I'm so sorry."

Jennifer is devastated but can see that Ian feels bad enough.

"It's not your fault. I'm sure it's some dumb clerk who pushed the wrong button and now it will take an act of parliament to reverse it." She gives Ian her best fake smile.

He doesn't buy it but pretends to so they can both stop being embarrassed.

"Come on, I made some chicken piccata last night. Fancy some leftovers for lunch?"

Jen gets up and walks mechanically to the kitchen, hoping that doing something normal like sharing a meal will ease the discomfort of the conversation they just had. The last thing Jennifer wants is anything ruining her friendship with Ian and Scott. Especially now that the Culture Vultures probably think she's a CIA operative or evil Bond villain who is being denied entry into Turkey.

As they share the lemony, capery chicken, Jennifer and Ian fall back into their usual easy conversation, and all is right with the world. Well, all may be right between the two of them, but something is very wrong with this whole situation.

It's warm out and relieved students are chatting outside Jennifer's office as she sends off her semester grades. Jennifer exhales and settles back in her desk chair. That 'click' usually evokes euphoria, signifying the end of another successful semester. But this time Jennifer's mood is dampened knowing the Culture Vultures will be taking off next week, but Jennifer will be stuck here, more alone than ever. Scott is going to visit his family in Ottawa while Ian is in Turkey, so she will be at loose ends for the summer. She's already planning how to fill her time: getting through some research she's had on the back burner, getting a jump on next semester's planning, and enjoying the beach. Jennifer usually revels in exploring solo, but the thought of this summer alone disappoints her.

Jennifer looks up to see Ian standing in her doorway.

"For once, I got my grades in early. I'm sure you have," he says.

"I just submitted!"

"Want to grab a celebratory drink? Warning: The Culture Vultures will probably show up."

Jennifer takes a deep breath and forces a smile. She's been avoiding the bar where they all congregate—Jennifer figured everyone would feel uncomfortable talking about the trip in front of her. But today is about celebrating the end of another successful semester. "Sure, I would love to catch up with everyone."

They arrive at the Subi Hotel to find it popping. It must be the nice weather—everyone wants to be out and social. Jennifer forces herself to be both.

As they approach the table where the Culture Vultures sit, a hush falls.

"Now come on guys, no one died," Jennifer says. "Some clerk messed up and I can't come. I'm bummed but that's life. I'm still super excited for you all and I expect lots of photos and stories when you get back."

That seems to have its desired effect. Jennifer can feel everyone relax and the chatter resumes, with the group saying how much they'll miss having her join in. Maybe these can still be real friends, Jennifer thinks. As she settles in, she vows to continue to nurture these relationships.

After a couple weeks of summer break, all Jennifer has done is wrap up some research and clean out her closet. At least all her summer wear is front and center. It is a gorgeous day and she packs her beach bag and heads to Cottesloe.

The beach is sparkling, and with summer vacation in full swing, the sand is dotted with families and groups of people lounging or tossing a ball around. The intense turquoise color of the Indian Ocean still takes her breath away. Once she scopes out a position not too close to any of the other people, Jennifer lays back on her towel, enjoying the feeling of sun on her (SPF 50-covered) body.

She has no idea how much time has passed when she's startled awake by a footy landing about two inches from her head. As she brushes the sand from her face, she senses someone standing over her.

"Oh mate, I'm so sorry. Billy is a bloody awful aim."

Jennifer blinks up at a man—presumably the owner of the offensive ball—smiling down at her. He's got piercing blue eyes and shaggy blond hair.

"It's not a problem," Jennifer says. "Just one of the potential hazards of sleeping on the beach."

"Oh, you're a septic! Cool. I'm Brayden."

"Pardon me?"

"Septic, septic tank, yank," he explains. "You're an American."

"Oh, the famous rhyming slang. I've been here almost a year and I hadn't heard that one yet."

"So not a tourist. What are you doing in our fair land?"

"I'm working at UWA. I'm an anthropologist," Jennifer says. "Next semester I plan on researching the Noogar people's sacred sites and how best to preserve them. It would be a shame to be in a land with a people who have such a rich forty-five thousand-year history, and not try to learn from them."

Brayden's friends are calling him and he looks over his shoulder.

"I had better get back, I do have the ball and it's a bit hard to have a kick without it." He tosses the ball back and forth between his hands. "But I'd like to hear more about your research."

Jennifer stops herself from rolling her eyes at that pickup line. She's about to make up some excuse and brush him off when he tells her that he is working on a computer program that will archive and teach the Noogar language.

"I'm no anthropologist, just a simple programmer," he says, shaking the hair out of his eyes. "But working on this project has made me really interested in the Noogar culture."

Everything in Jennifer says *walk away and don't look back.* But she's a sucker for someone who shows an interest in another culture and wants to learn more about it.

Jennifer smiles. "Okay, I'm always happy to talk about my research."

He runs off without another word, leaving Jennifer stunned. *Well, okay arsehole*, as they say here. But a minute later he runs back with his name and number scrawled on an empty paper bag.

"Sorry, that's all I could find to write on," he says breathlessly. "Lucky for me, me mate had a biro." He flashes another smile and dashes across the sand with a wave. Jennifer blinks after him. Maybe she won't be alone all summer, after all.

Chapter Five

2014

Jennifer wakes early, as usual, and rather than getting out of bed straight away, she sits up and stares at the gorgeous man with his sun-kissed skin and saltwater-bleached hair asleep next to her. And as usual, she can't believe it has been five years. Brayden is a great guy, but in all their time together, her feelings haven't grown stronger. She cares for him, but it doesn't even approach true love.

Jennifer knows it's time to make some decisions about her future. If she stays any longer without a plan to leave, she will stay forever. And increasingly, Jennifer thinks that may not be such a bad thing. She stuck to her vow and made real community here. Jennifer has her hiking friends, her theater friends, her beach friends (okay, those are mainly Brayden's friends), and her academic friends. She, Ian and Scott still make sure to see each other socially at least once a week, which is usually dinner at Jennifer's house with excellent Margaret River wines that they bring.

It was over one of those bottles that Jennifer first told Ian and Scott about Brayden, after Ian got back from the research trip she was rejected from.

"He's nice, good looking, nice body, really nice body, smart," Jennifer told them. "But he's a snack."

Scott just laughed. "A snack? What do you mean by that?" Ian asked.

"I mean, a fun guy to hang out with and have sex with but not to get serious with," she explained. "A meal is what you get serious with—a snack just tides you over."

"Only you would use a food analogy for sex and love," Scott said, rolling his eyes.

Jennifer just smiled. She still believes that sex, love, and food all belong in the same column in life's spreadsheet. The one labeled "pleasure."

Ever since that first summer with Brayden, her life here has had a comfortable rhythm: It's easy, it's predictable, it's safe. But lately, as has been happening when she lists the things she loves about her life, that old U2 song plays on a continuous loop in her head. Will she ever find what she's looking for? What is she looking for? Sometimes she is afraid that when it comes to love, she likes the falling, but not the landing.

Jennifer gets out of bed quietly so she doesn't wake Brayden. She still has to finalize the latest paper she's co-authoring with Ian. Instead of daydreaming any more, she settles into her work so she can take the evening off for the lovely date night they have planned. Brayden has outdone himself with a gourmet picnic for them, plus Ian and Scott.

It's a lovely December evening as the couples settle on a blanket along the shore of the Swan River in East Fremantle. The sunset is gorgeous tonight. Summer is approaching, which means longer sunsets and twilight hours. They've always been Jennifer's favorite. As Brayden unpacks their meal of fancy finger food, Ian and Jennifer chat about how quickly this academic year has passed.

This reminds her that she has completed her sixth academic year here. And looking at her dear friends, this sweet, handsome guy, and this gorgeous setting, it's one of those moments when Jennifer thinks that she may just stay. Her life could be a lot worse.

Brayden interrupts Jennifer's thoughts by clearing his throat and getting on one knee. Her stomach drops.

"Jen, I love you. I want to spend the rest of my life with you and I wanted to share this moment with your best friends." He proceeds to pull a ring box out of his back pocket and opens it, smiling.

Holy fuck. That got her attention. Jennifer feels the panic rise in her throat, along with the tapenade and triangle sandwiches she just ate. She can't even look at the ring, and turns instead to see the mortified look on Ian's face.

A moment of silence passes. Brayden takes in her stricken look. He fumbles with the box and says, "If you don't like the ring, we can exchange it."

Jennifer just shakes her head, a look of both resignation and sadness on her face. Ian and Scott scramble up from the blanket and slip away down to the river's edge.

Jennifer looks deep into Brayden's blue eyes and shakes her head. "I care for you but I don't want this. I thought you understood. I was always honest with you about not wanting anything serious."

He looks confused and then angry. "After all this time. Are you kidding me? I thought you were just saying that so I wouldn't feel pressured into proposing. I thought you were just playing coy."

Jennifer bristles. "I don't kid about things as important as my future and I certainly don't play coy; I don't play any games in relationships."

Brayden narrows his eyes, their usual crystal blue turned piercing with fury. "You'll never find anyone like me," He throws up his hands and gets to his feet. Jennifer has never seen this look on his face before. "I can have any woman I want, and I've thrown away all of this time on you. Fuck's sake, you're a cold bitch." Without another look at her, he storms off.

Burning anger replaces Jennifer's panic. "I think that's the whole reason for dumping someone," she hollers at his retreating form, "to not *ever* have to be with anyone like them."

Alone on the picnic blanket, Jennifer shivers a bit in the evening chill. With the sun behind the horizon, she can't find the same magic in the air that she felt before Brayden's proposal. She should have broken up with him when she had the chance. Now his final words have cast some kind of curse on what she thought was a place she could see herself living forever. If she was so wrong about Brayden, what else has she been wrong about? Has she really found a home here, or has she been trying to force herself into a life that doesn't feel like exactly what she's been looking for?

Ian and Scott return to the picnic and offer to take her home. And though they make the short drive in silence, Jennifer hears that old U2 song blaring in her head, as though someone has just turned up the volume. By the time they arrive at her flat, she has made up her mind: Her time in Western Australia has run its course. She'll write to the university tomorrow and make her plans to leave. She knows Brayden's angry words to her aren't true—she's not a cold bitch. But Jennifer can't stop herself from wondering if the common denominator in her disastrous love life is … Jennifer.

Two days later, Jennifer hears a knock at the door and opens it to find Brayden. She listens stone-faced as he begs Jennifer to forgive him. He asks if they can go back to the way it was. He tries to explain that it was his embarrassment talking and he didn't mean what he said.

Jennifer stops him mid-sentence. "I understand how you must have felt but your reaction was pretty shitty. I can't unhear it. I don't go back once a relationship ends. Never have and never will." Jennifer holds Brayden's gaze as the hopeful expression falls from his face. "I am sorry. I enjoyed all the time we spent together and don't feel like I wasted my time. I hope you have a great life and find the woman you are looking for. It just isn't me."

To make sure it is final in his mind, Jennifer hands him the box she had packed the night she got home from the picnic, containing all his possessions that he kept at her apartment. He grabs it from her hands, turns and walks away without looking back.

Jennifer sighs. It's time for her to do the same.

Chapter Six

Marion pops the champagne cork and pours two glasses.

"Here's to your business's three-year anniversary!" she says.

"*Our* business," Jennifer corrects her with a smile. "I couldn't have done any of this without an executive assistant like you!"

Thank God she found Marion. Three and a half years ago when Jennifer arrived in DC, fresh off of that messy breakup, she knew she was ready to leave academia and be her own boss for once. And that there were plenty of opportunities for Jennifer's kind of work. According to all the research she'd done in Perth, there are many Indigenous communities across the globe whose rights are trampled on by large developers, oil companies, and others. A lot of people with qualifications similar to Jennifer's work for the developers, but there aren't many anthropologists working on behalf of the Indigenous communities. So that's exactly what she set up her very own business to do. Although she won a few generous grants that got her going in the first few months, Jennifer needed someone with Marion's skills to support the business side of her consulting operation if she wanted to keep afloat long-term.

Marion, a feisty, fifty-something powerhouse all packed into a five foot two super-fit frame topped with a salt-and-pepper pixie cut, is her right arm. She keeps all the plates spinning when Jennifer is on the road. She also organizes Jennifer's life outside of the office—although there's not much of that these days. Between ensuring there are jobs coming down the pipeline (almost literally—a lot of work goes into keeping those greedy oil companies from destroying heritage sites and the lives of residents), working on sites all over the US and Canada, and keeping meticulous records for Marion to file grant reports, Jennifer has little time for anything else. She does try to catch any performance she can at the Woolly Mammoth Theatre Company, usually by herself.

After all this time, Jennifer still enjoys doing things solo. And she still has her love of travel—she's actually leaving in June for a three-month trip alone through South America. Jennifer should have any open projects completed by then. Anything else she can leave to Sharon, a freelancer who assists on big projects and whom Jennifer has grown to trust. Between Sharon and Marion, Jennifer has confidence that she'll have a business to come home to. And if she doesn't, it won't be the first time she's started over. Jennifer has needed this break; she's been itching to feed her wanderlust. Working for oneself is a 24/7 commitment. Jennifer loves it, but has been thinking that she needs time to rediscover herself.

At home after the anniversary celebration, Jennifer sits at her computer researching places to visit on her trip when a message from Anna pops up. Jennifer starts to type a reply, then stops and picks up the phone instead.

"That was fast," Anna says when she picks up.

"I was just playing on the computer, looking at all of the wonderful places I could visit on my trip."

"Well, I would like to come and see you before you go. Would that work out?"

"Of course. I may have to do some work, but I could work from home while you are here."

"That's great, just tell me what days work for you. I could stay a week while Tobias keeps things going here."

"Will you two ever be able to come and visit together?"

"Yes." Jennifer can practically hear Anna's smile through the phone. "I'll tell you all about it when I get there."

Two weeks later, Jennifer is standing with a silly sign that she made that says "long lost BFF," waiting to see Anna come through the international arrivals doorway. She can hear her friend's scream of delight before she sees her. Anna runs wildly towards Jennifer and pulls her into a tight bear hug. Something feels different. Jennifer holds Anna at arm's length and starts her own delighted screams.

"You're pregnant! How far along are you? Why didn't you tell me!" Jennifer says all at once.

"Take a breath, Jen." Anna puffs out a laugh. "How can you tell? I'm not even showing yet!"

"Well, your boobs arrived five minutes before you did!"

"Well I must say it's nice to finally have some. Now you won't be the only one with an impressive set!"

Back at the house, the friends get settled in the living room. "I guess I won't be serving your favorite wine," Jennifer says, setting down a San Pellegrino in front of Anna.

"And I can't have any of that brie either," Anna says with a wistful smile. "But I don't care about all the restrictions. We never thought we would get pregnant. We stopped even thinking about it once I turned forty. But here I am at forty-three and one day I wake up and puke. I thought I had eaten something that was off but when it continued to happen every day, I went to the doctor. I was blown away when she gave me a pregnancy test and even more shocked when it came back positive. I thought Tobias was going to faint when I told him."

"You must be over the moon," Jennifer says. "When we were in college, you always talked about wanting to be a mom. I'm so happy for you." She's surprised to feel tears in her eyes at seeing her friend realizing a dream they never thought she would. Having children was a dream Jennifer never shared, but she understands what it means to Anna.

"Aw, come here," Anna says as she engulfs Jennifer in a heartfelt embrace.

Once Jennifer composes herself, Anna says, "You can't tell anyone for another month. We aren't going to let anyone know until I'm twenty weeks."

"Really? I promise I won't but won't that be hard for you to do?"

"No, I'm considered high-risk because—get this—this is called a geriatric pregnancy. It's like they think I need a walker and soft food or something." Anna sighs and pats her stomach. "But I don't want to take any chances or jinx this."

"Now, positive thoughts only," Jennifer says sternly "This baby will be healthy and so well loved."

"That brings me to my other news," Anna says. "We are selling the restaurant and moving to a lovely house near good schools. Tobias and I are concerned about me working so hard during the pregnancy and we've had inquiries over the past year from people interested in buying it."

Jennifer's head is spinning from all this good news. "I honestly can't express how happy I am for you both—I mean, for you *all*. You guys deserve this. You've done all the hard work and now can reap the rewards."

Anna sighs and settles back on the sofa, with the most contented smile Jennifer has ever seen on her friend's face.

"Okay," Jennifer says, standing and placing her hands on her hips. "Now I'm going to get some food you can eat, and after dinner you are to relax and then go to sleep early."

Anna laughs and teases Jennifer about being a mother hen. But Jennifer can tell she's loving every second of it.

Jennifer continues to pamper her friend for the entire visit. They visit the National Gallery of Art, the National Museum of African American History and Culture, and the National Mall, playing tourist around all the sites. And of course, Jennifer makes sure they eat well and relax. She even manages to squeeze in a couple of hours of work while Anna is napping.

On the morning of her flight back to Germany, Anna pulls Jennifer next to her on the couch. "I need to ask you two questions," she says seriously. "The first is: Will you be the baby's godmother?"

"Of course, you don't even need to ask!" Jennifer can't stop smiling. "It will be my honor."

Anna beams. "And the second question is, will you come to Germany for the christening? We plan on holding it when the baby is one month old, so if the little one keeps to the schedule, that should be seven months from now. Will that work? We don't want to interfere with your great escape."

Jennifer grabs her phone to check out her calendar.

"I think that would work out perfectly," Jennifer says, counting the weeks in her head. "It's the end of March now, and I leave the first week of June. I plan on returning at the beginning of September, so that would have me coming to Germany a month after I return. I won't be able to stay long, you know, after being back at work for only one month. But if I get too attached to this baby, I may end up staying forever!"

By the time the eve of her trip approaches, Jennifer has packed and repacked her bags at least five times. Deciding what to take on a long trip is always so stressful, she thinks, staring down at the explosion of clothes on her bed. You don't want to take too much because you don't want to be lugging around a whole bunch of stuff you won't use, but you also must plan for different activities and weather. And, as far as Jennifer is concerned, you don't want to have to waste time shopping. But she thinks she finally has it right.

Jennifer is feeling antsy. It's definitely been too long since she's had an international adventure. She had finally squeezed all her things into one carry-on, one small backpack, and one crossbody bag, which she left by her front door before heading into the office to wrap up a few loose threads. But she certainly hadn't planned on staying there so late. She sends her last email and sets her out-of-office automatic reply directing everyone to contact Marion for the next three months. That's everything. She's thankful she has no pets or houseplants so she can just lock her front door and call a Lyft to the airport tomorrow.

As she walks into the reception area, she is surprised by a little sendoff party planned by Marion and Sharon. They have a small cake, some champagne, and lots of goodbye hugs. *They are the best*, Jennifer thinks, not for the first time. If this works out, she wants to hire Sharon full-time, and possibly expand the business. But that is the future. She wants to be focused on the present. Who knows what her adventure will bring.

Marion checks her watch as Sharon tosses their paper plates in the trash. "Um, Jen?" she asks, waggling her eyebrows. "Don't you have a certain dinner you ought to be getting to?"

Shit. Jennifer says her final goodbyes and bolts out of the office and to her car. She grumbles as she merges onto the highway, regretting that she let Marion convince her to try online dating.

Marion wasn't exactly wrong: Jennifer hadn't had much romance since she moved to DC But apps aren't much better than being alone, in Jennifer's experience. She has wondered if the men on the app actually read the profiles because it appears most of the ones she hears from just look at the pictures and have nothing she's looking for. Jennifer's not cryptic at all in her profile—Marion made sure of that—but that doesn't seem to matter.

Jennifer sighs as she winds her car through the quiet residential streets on the other side of town. She knows it was stupid to set up a first date for tonight, just before her big trip, but she's already had to cancel on this guy twice because of work emergencies. She felt bad and said she would meet him for a quick dinner. He does seem nice and he checks most of the boxes for what she's seeking in a man. The light turns yellow and Jennifer breaks slowly. She feels an unexpected bump.

Damn it! Jennifer shuts her eyes in frustration. The light had been yellow for at least five seconds. At least he was going slow—it was barely a nudge. Jennifer is ready to just ignore the incident and carry on to her date when she sees the driver exit his car, waving what looks like an insurance card. Now he expects her to come to him? Jennifer scoffs. The cheek of him! *Oh well,* she thinks. *I'll just get this over with.*

Chapter Seven

2000

Emre's Uncle Ahmet doesn't look like the powerful man his lackeys have been talking about. Seated in his wheelchair and impeccably dressed, albeit with too much gaudy gold jewelry, he appears to be a once-strong man trying to hold onto his former self. Although, Emre can't get a read on what that former self was. Ahmet puts his arms out for a hug and has tears in his eyes.

Emre's not sure why this man he's never met is so emotional to see him. Emre was told that was why Ahmet sent five men to sweep Emre away on his way to school a week ago—he valued Emre that much. Now, Emre's about thirty-two kilometers outside Istanbul, as far as he can tell, and more confused than ever.

As Emre stares at this stranger, he wonders if Bridgit and Ralph are worried. His uncle's man Cemil told Emre that they didn't want to be burdened with him anymore. Emre doesn't believe it. When Bridgit and Ralph arrived in Turkey to collect him right after his parents died, they said that his parents had left written instructions with their lawyer stating that if anything ever happened to them, it was their wish that Emre would live with Bridgit and Ralph and that they would raise him as their son.

But Emre is here now. He goes to his uncle, hugs him, and tries to start asking some of his many questions. Uncle Ahmet smiles and just says, "All in good time."

Emre is beginning to feel like that is everyone's only answer to any of his questions.

Ahmet makes Emre sit through dinner before finally excusing all of his men from the room and bringing him closer.

"Emre, I am not a well man," he starts, leaning back in his armchair. "I have a large business empire and have amassed vast wealth. This all means nothing without health or an heir. I am going to be honest with you. Your mother—my sister—wanted nothing to do with me, my businesses, my associates, or my money. She didn't really know me, as I had left the family home when she was still a child. And she did not want to know me, or even let you know me. That saddened me, but I abided by her wishes. Until now," he says, then starts coughing.

Once the coughing settles he gestures for his water, which Emre hands him.

"You were sent away before I had even heard of the death of your parents. I would have come for you then. I had private investigators searching for you, and once they found you, I tried to reason with your parents' friends, but they were not willing to let you come and live with me. I am family, and who are those people? They do not even understand your heritage. They would raise you as a German. You are a Turk, a proud Turk!" he shouts to the mostly empty room.

He lowers his voice as he continues. "I need you, you are the only family I have left. You must stay with an old man at the end of his life."

Emre steels himself. "Uncle, I am sorry I did not get to know you when I was a boy," he says, speaking honestly. "I am a young man now and you are my only blood relative. But I don't know you, I don't understand your business."

"Emre, I will make sure you get what you need to succeed, but this isn't a question," Ahmet says, narrowing his eyes. "I am telling you what is required of you."

Ahmet looks serious, imposing. For the first time, Emre gets a glimpse of the man Ahmet must have been before his illness. But something in his eyes betrays remorse—maybe for kidnapping his nephew, maybe for something else.

"Okay," Emre says. "I will stay and help you until you are well again."

He's not sure why he is agreeing. There is obviously a reason his mother wanted nothing to do with her own brother, but Emre can't resist the chance to belong, to feel at home for the first time in a long time. To be part of his family, a blood relative who understands his love of his country and culture. Emre hopes his mother's spirit will not be upset with him.

Ahmet smiles at him and clasps their hands together, promising Emre he has made the right decision.

Chapter Eight

2001

There are some perks to being the eighteen-year-old heir apparent to a vast fortune. Emre's uncle has exquisite taste and wants him to appreciate the finer things in life—to have the comportment of one born into royalty. His words, not Emre's.

That's how Emre finds himself at a beautiful townhouse in Knightsbridge, London, with Geoffrey, an English personal butler (he calls himself a valet, but Emre doesn't see the difference) on a crash course in being rich. Emre is curious about this six foot four, broad shouldered man with chiseled features who appears to be in his late forties. Not your usual English butler type.

"This is a gorgeous home," Emre says, turning in place to take it all in. "Whose is it?"

"It's yours, sir," Geoffrey says. "Well, it was your uncle's, but the solicitor will be calling around tomorrow at ten o'clock for you to sign the papers, which will transfer the property into your name."

Emre stares at him blankly, dumbstruck.

"Come, sir," Geoffrey says. "I will show you around your new London residence, then you can rest before your evening meal. You will want to sleep early tonight as tomorrow is a very busy day. I have you for two years, then you must return to your uncle." He glances sideways at Emre, as though sizing him up. "We have a big job ahead of us."

When Uncle Ahmet called this "the next phase" of Emre's education, the young man wasn't sure exactly what that entailed. Up to this point, Emre had been learning most of the aspects of his uncle's business empire. The ins and outs of supply chains, negotiating, managing a global enterprise, and the like.

But Emre can't shake the feeling that Ahmet is keeping something from him. Emre may have only had a few small businesses in Germany, but he does have an excellent understanding of finance. The legitimate enterprises he has spent the past year learning could not generate the enormous wealth he possesses. When Emre has tried to talk to him about this, all his uncle says is, "All in good time, Emre, all in good time."

Ahmet has even had his lawyers change the structure of the umbrella company to list Emre as the owner. It's generous, but Emre suspects there could be an ulterior motive, which he assumes he will learn "all in good time."

Emre's first full day in London starts with Geoffrey drawing open the drapes, sending the sun shining right in Emre's face.

"Really? Ugh," Emre says, throwing an arm over his eyes.

Geoffrey smiles and brings Emre a tray with Turkish coffee, just the way he likes it, with lots of sugar. There are also today's newspapers, many of them, on the tray. Emre picks up the Financial Times. I *could get used to this,* he thinks.

"If that is all for now, sir, I will lay out your clothes and then review your day's schedule with you."

"Yeah, this is great!"

Emre catches Geoffrey hiding a smile at his casual reply. It sounds like ol' Geoff will have to teach him how to handle his enthusiasm to appear more refined.

Once he goes exploring, Emre is happy to find that the home has a well-equipped gym on the third floor and that his packed schedule includes an hour and a half per day for working out. Emre has always liked to keep his body in good shape, but this is going to make it much easier. He makes a mental note to talk to his uncle about building one at home in Turkey. Emre has had to improvise his workouts thus far.

Emre meets the solicitor in the office, which is on the first floor of the house (Emre has already gotten lost several times— thank goodness for Geoff). After the papers are signed and the solicitor leaves, a Savile Row tailor and his assistants show up. Geoff helps Emre pick out styles and fabrics for every occasion possible.

Over lunch in a stuffy formal dining room, Emre reads over the rest of his daily schedule. The afternoons are for his studies, which includes languages—Emre is already fluent in Turkish,

German, and English but must now add Italian, French, and Spanish. He must also study history, art, antiques, and design elements. In addition, sports such as horse riding, polo, cricket, squash, skeet shooting, and hunting are to be part of his education. Geoff will teach some sports and history lessons, but the rest are to be taught by tutors that Emre assumes must be handsomely paid by his uncle.

Emre leans back in his chair and takes stock of his new life. The last year has been all about becoming a better steward of his uncle's business. But this regimen is meant to make him a better man—a certain type of man, but a grown-up one, nonetheless.

He sees a postscript near the bottom of the schedule, stating plainly that there will be no entertaining female companions for the first eighteen months of his training. Emre smiles sadly. His uncle has hinted before that he wants Emre to marry and settle in Istanbul permanently. But Ahmet has no idea that Emre is in love with a hazel-eyed American woman.

It has been more than two years since Emre has seen Ela, but he thinks of her every day. Since they parted, he has regularly searched the internet for any mention of her. He even prints photos of her and uses them as bookmarks in whatever novel he's reading. Emre wants to forget her; their lives are so far apart now. But he can't. Maybe one day they will meet again, and she will see the man, and not the boy he was.

Di Toma

Emre looks again over the schedule of lessons. He has always been a quick study, but can only hope two years will be enough time.

Chapter Nine

2003

Because he has Sunday afternoons free for exploring, Emre has gotten to know the geography of London well over the last two years. It is an amazing city—a wonderful tapestry of the old and new. Of course, Emre's not quite alone; Geoff follows discreetly behind him. When he first did this, Emre balked, but Geoff, in his usual calm manner, said it was one of his uncle's rules and was nonnegotiable. It was then Emre realized Geoff was a rare combination of high-end valet and highly trained bodyguard.

When he started getting closer to Geoff, Emre began formulating the idea of building his own hand-picked team. Once Uncle Ahmet is gone, how does Emre know he can trust the old cohort? Emre has heard rumblings that some of them are none too pleased that Ahmet brought him into the fold and will be leaving everything to his nephew. Apparently some of them thought they had earned Ahmet's loyalty, and now feel betrayed. With Emre's return to Istanbul quickly approaching, he has begun the process of vetting and developing people who will comprise his inner circle, his own trusted team.

"With only a month remaining here, it is time for you to select the car you want," Geoff says on one of their city-spanning walks. "Your uncle said that if you rose to the occasion and were successful in all your lessons, that you are to select whatever you want with no restrictions, as a reward. You will order it here and I'll have it delivered to your uncle's compound."

Emre can't help but smile. Even with all the training Geoff has drilled into him, a twenty-year-old being given carte blanche to buy whatever car he wants pushes the boundaries of his ability to act refined.

After visiting many showrooms, Emre decides on a Mercedes-Benz SLR McLaren in metallic blue. In his wildest dreams Emre never thought he would own such a vehicle. Geoff gives his ward a nod of approval and handles the paperwork.

"What a difference two years makes," Emre says to Geoff over tea one evening.

"It certainly does, sir. You arrived an exuberant teen and leave a well-cultured man," Geoff replies. "I hope I am not overstepping by saying I am very proud of you. You are ready to begin your new life. Will you miss London?"

"Yes, there are many things I will miss but I am ready to get back to work," Emre says. "Back to running businesses, I mean. Ever since I was fifteen, I have enjoyed the many challenges and opportunities of the business world."

"Will you miss any of the young ladies you have entertained?"

Emre gives Geoff a wry smile. Even though he considers Geoff a friend now, he hasn't told him—or anyone—about Ela.

"Considering you only allowed me to start entertaining those young ladies six months ago, no. And we both know that was more about testing my skills in the right crowds to see if I would fit in. I felt like Pygmalion rather than a man on the town."

Geoff chuckles. "Well, you passed with flying colors and, might I say, will break a few hearts when you leave. I'm sure one or two of those ladies will miss you. As will I."

"Thank you, Geoff. That brings me to what I've been wanting to ask you." Emre sets down his teacup and leans forward in his chair. "I would like you to accompany me back to Turkey. Actually, I would like you to be with me wherever I go. I have come to know you and trust you and feel it's time for me to surround myself with my own team."

"I would be delighted," Geoff replies, looking relieved. "I was quietly hoping you would ask."

"Well, it's settled then. Get the caretakers in just before we leave and check to make sure my new car will be delivered after we arrive. I also want to find a penthouse in Istanbul. I can spend weekdays at my uncle's compound but want my own place in the city."

"Yes, sir. Gladly," Geoff says.

Chapter Ten

2015

Emre gazes out his favorite window, eyes on the horizon. The city lights gleaming on the river Bosporus always calm him. As does his home, and not his suite of rooms at his uncle's compound, which have never quite lost their jail cell aura. With the help of Geoff and a brilliant interior designer, he finally has a space that is 100 percent Emre. Muted tones, low profile furniture. Elegant, yet contemporary. Exactly what Emre envisioned when Geoff first showed him this penthouse.

Geoff got to work on the property search as soon as they got to Istanbul. Uncle Ahmet wasn't thrilled with Emre's decisions—both having his own place and installing Geoff as his private executive assistant. But he was also pleased to see Emre standing up to him and being his own man.

For months, Emre and Geoff worked carefully to identify experts in all of the areas of the businesses he oversees. Emre slowly folded them in, raising them up through the ranks until all of his direct reports and all decision-makers were his hand-picked team. It ruffled some feathers at first, but Emre was very generous with severance packages for those he displaced. Many were his uncle's old cronies, well past their prime. They couldn't keep up with the modern business environment and, after Emre began implementing processes and technology they didn't understand, they seemed relieved to move on with a sweet golden handshake.

Emre was sensitive to making too many changes all at once, but Ahmet grew used to his preferences after a time. These days Emre spends most of his time in Istanbul, but even now, twelve years later after setting up his own home, Emre makes a point of going to Ahmet's compound and having dinner with him at least two nights a week. Emre has grown sympathetic to his uncle in recent years. He now sees him as a lonely old man who has only sycophants surrounding him. Without him, Emre would have none of this luxury he has grown to love.

Behind Emre, Geoff loudly clears his throat, shaking him from his memories. Geoff tells him the car has been brought out front. Emre now has a stable of autos, which he updates every few years. Tonight he's chosen the red Ferrari F12berlinetta. (When he bought it, Geoff teased him about the cliché of a red Ferrari, but Emre couldn't resist it.) Emre smiles at his trusted advisor, checks his reflection in the entryway mirror, and heads out to meet Ayesha … or is it Naomi? It doesn't really matter. It's all just good fun. Although, Emre would like to find someone he could see himself settling down with eventually. Right now, he's taking Ayesha (yes, that's her name) to a big party at some nightclub to celebrate his thirty-second birthday. How can Emre feel like he's lived so many more years—lifetimes actually—than his age?

The following day, at the compound, Emre leans down and Uncle Ahmet clasps his hand. "Happy birthday, Emre. Thirty-two years. You are a fine man." He gestures for Emre to guide his wheelchair into his office.

Once Emre is seated, Ahmet fixes him with a stern look. "It is time. The doctors say I don't have much time left. The cancer has returned and is winning the fight. So you need to know all the businesses that you own."

"How can I be the owner of businesses that I have not even heard of?" Emre asks. But truly, Emre has been waiting for this moment, when his uncle would unlock something he has been keeping from him.

"Listen, Emre, and I will tell you. But you must let me finish before you speak." Ahmet takes a labored breath before continuing.

"There are a number of shell companies all over the world. You are the owner of the umbrella company that controls many entities: some that you know about already, and some that you do not. After the time we have spent together, I feel I have gotten to know you, to understand you. I know that you will not embrace these other entities, but you must. This octopus has many arms.

"I have two partners on this other side of the business. They are from the old neighborhood. We grew up together; I had the brains and they had the muscle. We went from petty crimes to getting into the drug trade. We started pretty low in the pecking order but between my business sense and their daring ... you have to understand, people were genuinely afraid of them, for good reason. We grew and moved up the hierarchy very quickly. We eventually took over international control of production and distribution.

"As my legitimate businesses grew and I had more wealth than anyone needed, I tried to leave the partnership. My partners would not hear of it. They knew as well as I did that they did not have the business mind to keep it going. They made many threats. I have no proof, but your parents' accident may have been a warning. This is what they do: They find the people you love and go after them. They know you may not care what happens to you, but you want to protect those you love. I didn't think they would find your parents; I had withdrawn from their life years earlier. Even though my baby sister had disowned me because of the drug trade, she always held a special place in my heart, and they knew that.

"After the car crash—I still don't think it was an accident— I stopped even thinking about exiting the business. I still had you to protect. So you have no choice but to continue the work."

Emre says nothing for a moment. He feels like he's just been sucker punched. A burning hatred for his uncle's partners is searing through him. They stole his parents, his entire life, from him. Emre knows that from this point forward, he will be singularly focused on destroying them and their empire.

"What exactly are the businesses you have been hiding?" Emre asks. Ahmet's little speech made it pretty apparent, but he wants to hear his uncle say it.

Ahmet pushes a button on his desk. Cemil and TD, the overseer of his empire, enter holding two large document cases. TD pulls out a large color-coded global map, setting it on the table.

"There is a large network of heroin producers and distributors who—" TD starts.

"What the actual *fuck*!"

Emre glares at his uncle. He stares straight back at Emre, stone faced, and waves Cemil and TD out of the room.

"I know I have been selfish bringing you into this life," Ahmet says slowly. "But I didn't want to die alone and have my life's work broken up and sold off to strangers. The vast majority of the ventures you own are legitimate." His voice takes on a pleading note. "You are my heir and have a keen intelligence, even greater than mine, and I know you can, and must, keep it all going. When you have children, they can inherit it all and there will be a dynasty."

"You have destroyed any chance of that," Emre spits out. "How can I put this burden on anyone I love?"

Emre storms out of the room. He makes for the front door, hearing rushed footsteps behind him. A hand—Cemil's—grabs his arm. As Emre turns to shake Cemil off, he sees his uncle's medical team racing for his office.

After the final guest has left, Cemil and Emre watch the dirt being shoveled onto the casket. Emre's emotions are swirling. Ahmet was Emre's blood, he was kind to him. He also left him a terrible burden.

Now that Ahmet is gone, Emre is solely responsible for his uncle's empire. Emre knows he must find a way to extricate himself from the heroin business and shut it down. He can't be responsible for the addiction and death of innocent people.

Emre thinks again of his parents, the car crash he thought was an accident for his whole life, but was actually the work of his uncle's business partners. At least, Emre thinks ruefully, he has no family left for these partners to harm. The only person he loves is Ela, and no one knows about her. Emre has been careful to use burner accounts to follow Ela's life on social media. On his public-facing accounts, he follows only the German national football team, DFB-Elf. They can't take out a whole football team.

As Geoff reviews Emre's schedule with him one evening, the butler asks if he may be blunt.

"I've noticed a pattern," Geoff says carefully, closing his portfolio and setting it on the desk between them. "You date models, actresses, and socialites, right?"

Emre nods.

"Well, two things, sir. You are in your thirties and may be wanting to think about settling down, having a family. Are these the right sort of women to be dating?" He gives Emre a soft look. "And secondly, I've noticed that over the past couple of months, you never have more than three dates with any one woman. It seems odd. I'm curious: Do they all do something on date two or three that is off-putting?"

Emre looks at Geoff and shakes his head. "No, they don't. I am just having fun," Emre shrugs. "You told me to get out there and meet some women."

"I meant with an endgame of finding one you will marry. All this playboy stuff is no good. The paparazzi are starting to be as interested in you as they are with the steady stream of models, actresses and socialites you are seen with."

"I've never used my real name with any of these women, and to date, not one photo of me has appeared," Emre counters. "I'm a ghost to the world at large."

"You said you don't want to be highly visible. That you don't want to be a nouveau riche cliché," Geoff says, averting his eyes. "I just think you may be falling into that trope."

"Three dates is my limit," Emre says bitterly. "My uncle made sure of that."

Geoff looks confused and Emre sighs. His uncle's funeral was only two months ago, and Emre has barely had time to process the news Ahmet delivered on his deathbed about the empire.

"Geoff, I have not been totally truthful with you. But it's time you know everything."

A couple of hours later, Emre and Geoff stand over the penthouse's large dining table with a myriad of documents spread out. Geoff just stares at the array, shaking his head.

"I knew there had to be more," he mutters. "I knew this immense wealth couldn't be amassed from the businesses that I knew you ran."

"I'm sorry, Geoff," Emre says quietly. "I honestly didn't know the extent of this side of the business when I asked you to leave London and come and work with me. I've only known since the day the old man died.

"You can leave. I won't hold you to your promise to stay by my side," Emre continues, before Geoff can interject. "I'll set up an account for you so you will never have to work again. But if you choose not to, you can help me dismantle that disgusting trade. That's why I'm glad that I've worked so hard to grow the legal businesses. We will have the money and power to bring down my uncle's brutal partners and, with luck, come out the other end of this with our lives."

Geoff doesn't even hesitate. "I'm in. I want to destroy these criminals." He fixes Emre with a fierce look. "My little sister, my only sibling, got in with a worthless boyfriend when she was only sixteen. By eighteen, she was dead. Heroin overdose."

Emre had never heard his old friend sound so resolute. He exhales, and the two start to devise a strategy.

Chapter Eleven

2018

Emre takes a final look at the spreadsheets and gives a nod of satisfaction to his accountants. The leadership team he put in place has done very well. Over the past few years the business—at least the legitimate side of the business—has doubled in value. Emre's uncle was a good businessman, but was stuck in the past. And now, finally, as Emre approaches his thirty-fifth birthday, three years after discovering his uncle's dark secret, he and his confidantes are ready to take it down.

The first thing Emre did once he and Geoff began plotting was move permanently to London. Hasad and Mazhar, the muscle of the illegal enterprises, rarely travel beyond the greater Istanbul area. Although their network is far-reaching, Emre knew it would be safer to begin the dismantling operation far from its headquarters in Turkey. He has found over the past few years that the adage "out of sight, out of mind" has some merit.

It took a year or so after Ahmet's death for Hasad and Mazhar to settle down. The partners thought that if Emre was going to do anything to damage their heroin operation, it would be immediately. So they tried to intimidate Emre for a while, who in turn played the meek little nephew who would honor his uncle no matter what. Ahmet was right when he said they weren't the sharpest knives in the drawer, but they certainly know how to elicit fear in everyone around them.

Since Ahmet's death, Hasad and Mazhar have kept the heroin syndicate far from Emre's reach, which is fine by Emre. He's spent those years turning the wheels on a long-term plan toward the partners' destruction. Phase One: Grow the legal side of the business until it's thriving.

With Geoff's help, Emre established a contact at Interpol, Nigel Payne. Geoff has connections at MI6 from his years before he became a private valet and bodyguard. As Emre has come to learn, Geoff's father was a personal valet to some earl. Geoff learned the trade, and used that skill set as camouflage when Ahmet wanted a bodyguard for Emre without his knowledge.

Emre laughed when Geoff first told him the truth about three months after Emre first arrived in London. Geoff felt they had developed enough trust that he could be honest with Emre. Emre had to agree his uncle's subterfuge was smart. He wouldn't have wanted a bodyguard, but was very open to having a valet and tutor to prepare him for his new life. And now, Emre is glad he has both sets of skills on his side as he prepares to take down an international drug operation.

"Do you have family or loved ones who will need protection?" Emre asks Geoff as the accountants exit the office.

"Remember, the partners go after loved ones." Emre thinks of his parents when he says this.

Geoff shakes his head sadly. "My parents retired to South Africa. They are in their eighties. We lost touch when I was twenty, right after my sister died. They were so angry with her for becoming an addict and embarrassing them that they didn't even want to have a funeral. They had disowned her and even in death wouldn't relent." He gets a faraway look in his eyes, lost in the memory. "I scraped together what I could and provided a simple funeral for her. After that I had little regard for my parents and never saw them again. I didn't even tell them when I graduated from Oxford, or when I got my first job at MI6. There is no way anyone would associate them with me. And there is no one else." Geoff shakes his head a little. "In my line of work, I learned it was best not to get attached to anyone or anything."

"I'm sorry." It's the only thing Emre can say. "I'm sorry for your sister, your parents, and you. A family should not be torn apart, but that is what heroin does and it's why we have to stop Hasad and Mazhar. I know it won't rid the world of it, but it will make a huge dent."

It's on to Phase Two of their plan.

Emre wanders around the Lürssen yacht and has to admit—it's perfect for him. It looks like his Istanbul penthouse on water, all decked out in his quietly elegant style.

"And why did I need to buy a yacht?" Emre asks Geoff. "I'm not in the mood for R&R."

"I'm serious," he says, examining the paperwork. "It's the best place for secure meetings."

The whole transaction was conducted by a broker, who was unaware of the buyer's identity. An intricate web of shell companies was also established to hide Emre's ownership. It would take decades for anyone to unravel the web. Emre purposely stayed out of the picture until now. He boarded via the helipad in the dark of night for this tour of his new vessel and then will take the helicopter back to dry land when it's over. No one should even know Emre left Knightsbridge.

Weeks after taking ownership of the yacht, Emre and Geoff sit with refreshments on the main deck. Phoebe, an actress on some BBC limited series, is lounging in her bikini reading a magazine. She is lovely, Emre thinks, and then sighs. This will be date number three.

Geoff says he has some contracts for Emre to sign in the office downstairs, and they excuse themselves. She smiles and waves then gets back to her magazine. The small team of trusted staff onboard know they are to ensure she has everything she needs and stays put while Emre and Geoff are below deck. She has no idea that she is providing a cover story for them to be on this vessel.

As they enter the soundproof office, freshly swept for listening devices, Emre shows Geoff the card he had received by courier the prior day: a summons from Hasad and Mazhar. It doesn't say they would like a meeting, just that Emre should come to see them in Istanbul.

"This could be a trap," Emre says, pacing the room. "If they have any inkling of what we are doing, once they have me there they can torture me for details and then murder me. If I don't go, they will know something is up. They need to believe I am still the obedient boy my uncle took under his wing."

Geoff says nothing from his seat in one of the leather armchairs. He knows this is Emre's call.

"Pack my bags," Emre says finally. "I want you to stay in London so one of us can quickly execute the plan if I am compromised."

"I would not advise that," Geoff says with a frown "If you are compromised, you will need me to help you escape. Also, there is no 'quickly' in the execution of this plan—at least not until all the pieces are in place."

Now it's Emre's turn to stare silently at Geoff. Emre is resolute, and Geoff knows it.

"Well, if you are going to be a horse's ass about this, let me get you a few things that may come in handy," Geoff huffs.

Emre perks up, genuinely intrigued. "Really? like James Bond stuff? It may be worth being on the receiving end of the partners' unique form of justice just to be able to play 007 for a day."

Emre's attempt at lightening the mood is less than successful, as Geoff gives his boss a steely-eyed look.

As they return to the main deck, Emre sees Phoebe asleep, her magazine next to her on the ground where it fell. The crew member nods, letting Emre know that Phoebe hadn't moved during his absence. Emre looks down at her peacefully sleeping on the deck chair, and realizes he will actually miss her. She is smart and fun—and unlike some of the other women he has dated, they actually share some interests. Then again, Emre thinks, he may have purposely chosen the company of women he would tire of by the third date. Maybe all of that will change if their plan—*when* their plan—is successful. Maybe he'll even try to get Phoebe back.

Emre knows he is his best self around women of substance. He believes it all started with Ela. She is somehow both a distant yet constant memory for him. The way she made him feel ... so seen, so validated, so valued for who Emre was as a person and not for what he had.

By the time the yacht docks back in Knightsbridge, Emre makes his usual excuses to Phoebe, explaining that he must travel on business for the next few weeks. Phoebe just smiles impassively. "It has been great knowing you," she says. "Have a nice life."

Emre is a bit taken aback. He's usually the one saying goodbye for good, not the other way around. "What makes you say that?"

"Well, my darling, this is our third date," Phoebe says, gathering her things into her bag. "I've done my research and I have never heard of you having a fourth date with anyone. I'm a proactive woman."

"And so many other wonderful things." Emre smiles sadly. She shrugs her shoulders, kisses him on the cheek and gives him one last resigned smile, then turns and leaves.

As Emre watches her go, Geoff emerges from the shadows. He was clearly waiting until that farewell was over. He hands Emre a pair of sunglasses, a lighter, and a watch.

"Um, thanks?"

"These sunglasses have small cameras built into the frames so I can see whatever you are seeing, and the watch has a microchip that enables me to follow your movements via satellite GPS. Let's hope this is just me being overly cautious. We have no reason to believe you have been compromised."

"What about the lighter?"

"Whatever you do, don't light a cigar with it. It is a flamethrower. Use it in only the most dire situations. Don't let it fall into anyone else's hands, it's too dangerous. Understand?"

"Yes, believe me when I say that I take this shit very seriously," Emre says. "The only way I can have the life I want, free of this horrible business, free to settle down with a woman I love"—*a woman like Ela*, Emre thinks—"is to make it through all of this alive."

Emre's visit with Hasad and Masar is in two days. Geoff's spy contacts are trying to find out any information they can about the purpose behind the meeting. Emre has flown to Istanbul with a number of burner phones, each of which he will not use more than once. In case of emergency, Emre will send them a code—a phrase he chose from *Martin Eden*. It makes Emre feel that Ela is with him, and she would never let anything bad happen to him. Thinking of her now, on the eve of a dangerous operation, Emre is still amazed that their brief encounter almost two decades ago has stayed in his heart so long.

On the day of the meeting, Hasad calls, saying they will send a car to the penthouse for him. Emre explains that he will be meeting some friends after the visit, and will need to take his own vehicle. To Emre's surprise, Hasad readily agrees.

Emre prepares a coded message detailing this update to Geoff. He notes that it must be a good sign: Hasad would have insisted on having control of his transportation if this was a trap—at least, Emre thinks so.

Rain slashes the windows during Emre's drive out of Istanbul. He has an hour alone to get his head on straight. Emre must appear open and relaxed—even happy—to see his uncle's oldest friends, and now, his partners in the unsavory business of heroin.

By the time Emre arrives at Hasad's home outside of Istanbul, he is completely immersed in the role of adoring nephew and young subservient business partner.

Emre enters the main room and sees Hasad and Mazhar. He approaches and greets each individually and formally, showing deference and respect, before taking a seat on the sofa across from them. They look like caricatures of old-time gangsters. Beady eyed, dressed in expensive, but tacky, suits, with thick cigars held between sausage fingers. Quite the picture they paint.

It's clear why Emre's uncle sent him to London to become a gentleman: He didn't want Emre to turn out like these two.

Mazhar looks smug but Hasad smiles at Emre. "We are very pleased that you have graced us with your presence. We have not seen you since your uncle's funeral. We realize that your London playboy lifestyle keeps you very busy, but you should not neglect your partners as you do."

Mazhar, clearly the bad cop of the duo, spits out, "You must pay more attention to the business. This business, not just your other businesses."

It is so difficult for Emre not to just tell them both to fuck off, that he couldn't have supported the drug trade with Mazhar and Hasad holding tight to the wheel. But this is exactly why Emre is here, he reminds himself. He's playing the long game.

Emre, Geoff, and Nigel have been trying to think of a way to put together a complete organizational chart with all players in the heroin trade identified, so they could be apprehended. Emre knew that suddenly wanting to be involved in the business would throw up warning flags. But this is perfect. They are not just asking, but demanding that he do so. They obviously have heard that Emre has more than doubled the value of his legitimate businesses. And they want him to do the same with the illegal ones.

"Uncles," Emre says, using the term they prefer him to call them. They believe it keeps Emre in his place. "I will become involved in our partnership. I will use my business acumen to streamline the operations which will help exponentially grow the profit. I am sorry I neglected it, and you, for so long."

Mazhar and Hasad glance at each other with a wicked grin, clearly pleased at a job well done. Emre tries to look sufficiently penitent.

Emre joins the partners for lunch and endures their crude comments about the women their lackeys have told them Emre has dated. *God, they are neanderthals,* Emre thinks. But he smiles and jokes along with them. He makes sure to thank them for their guidance, saying he has missed the wisdom of elders since his uncle passed away. They seem to buy it.

As Uncle Ahmet always said, they are not the brains of the operation.

Back on the yacht later that week, Nigel gazes out over the water from the main deck as he processes what Emre has told him about the meeting in Turkey.

"I don't think we could have hoped for a better outcome," he says in his clipped British accent. "Not only are you alive but it seems you have been given the keys to the castle. Good job, man!"

"Simply put, I was lucky and they were dumb," Emre says, placing his hands on the railing. "Now I must tread carefully as I delve into their network and begin to put faces and names on that company chart. Before, we only had general knowledge of roles and responsibilities."

Geoff ascends from below deck to tell them that the office onboard is now fully kitted out as their headquarters. "While you are working your way through each layer of the drug syndicate and gathering the intel necessary for that network to be destroyed, Nigel will be at another site that is networked into our operations center here on the yacht. He will be using the information you gather to fill in all the pieces of this puzzle. Once all the pieces are in place, we can finally execute the plan."

Emre just looks at him, not sure if he should verbalize his doubts.

"What is it, Emre?" Geoff says. "I know that expression."

Emre takes a deep breath, then the words just tumble out. "I know the pieces are all coming together and that being asked to improve business operations of the drug syndicate was a big win for us. I just have doubts about the ability of the authorities to execute the entire plan with perfect synchronization. If one tactical unit is out of sync, it leaves us vulnerable to serious retaliation. Geoff, you and I only have ourselves to worry about, but Nigel has a wife and son.

"Also," Emre keeps on going, even as Nigel and Geoff open their mouths to interrupt, "I have serious concerns that once we inform a wider circle of law enforcement agencies, a leak could happen. And that could ruin our chances of finally bringing down the bastards."

"We have answers to these questions," Nigel says, putting his hand on Emre's shoulder. "Let's go see this operations center that Geoff has put together. I must say, a luxury yacht is a much posher office than where I'll be working."

Emre can't help but smile at what is probably the understatement of the year. Because only a few people can know of their plan, Nigel will be working out of a secret center that MI6 and Interpol set up in an old warehouse.

Emre loves British understatement, he thinks as he descends below deck. It is in direct contrast to Turkish hyperbole. Although the drama of his people is endearing, it can be exhausting. The day with Hasad and Mazhar was draining, not just because Emre had to playact as the obedient nephew, but because they overreacted about everything. The temperature of the soup was too hot, the bread was too soft, the yogurt was too runny. For two murderous gangsters, they certainly have delicate palates and demanding attitudes.

Emre has thought before that they should maybe just wait it out, and Hasad and Mazhar's staff will lash out and kill them. But it's unlikely to happen. Hasad's staff showed unquestioning loyalty and Emre believes Mazhar is becoming increasingly paranoid as he ages, and would never let his staff turn the tables on him. At first, Emre thought the paranoia could be driven by drug use, but these two are old-school; they never get high on their own supply. They never get high *period*. As they told Emre at lunch, they believe it shows weakness, and the last thing they want to do is appear weak. Their brutality is their only strength.

Emre doesn't do drugs either, nor does he drink—he wants to be in control of his actions at all times. His business success relies on being able to think on his feet. When he was young in Germany, his friends would drink alcohol every night and Emre would drink orange soda. They all thought it must be his religious beliefs, but Emre wasn't raised religious, he just always wanted to keep his senses sharp.

Honing his senses over the years ultimately gave Emre an edge on his competition.

Thinking about Germany always brings Emre back to Ela. No one before her or since has made him feel the way she did. He may just look her up again tonight. Last thing Emre saw was that she had moved back to the US and is living in DC running her own business. Her eyes were so beautiful, her—

"Hey, hello, Emre. You haven't heard a word I've said," Emre hears Nigel say, as if from far away. They've made it down to the office while Emre was daydreaming.

"Where were you? It certainly wasn't here," Nigel teases. "Which model were you fantasizing about, hm? You probably won't have time to squeeze in those three dates any time soon."

"Oh Nigel, you should quit your job as a spy and go into standup," Emre says, then pats him on the back.

Down in the new operations center, a large electronic board takes up the whole of the inner wall. On it is a chart representing the members of the drug syndicate; most spaces are labeled with only the role or job title. Everything is color-coded, including the lines that connect one branch of the organization to another.

"Impressive work, Geoff, as usual," Emre says.

Nigel points to the board. "You see only the first two layers of roles have names attached. Mazhar and Hasad and their direct reports. Emre, your job will be to obtain the names for the remaining layers. We are only targeting the producers and main distribution networks. Don't worry about the kids on the street buying or selling. Even if we sweep that layer, those dealers are much too easy to replace. It's the big players that we want. That's the only thing that will make a meaningful impact.

"This board is synchronized with the one I have at the warehouse. When you update this board, it will automatically update mine. This way we will be working in real time without risking face-to-face meetings."

Geoff jumps in. "Once the information on the board is complete, Nigel will be ready to execute the next stage of the plan. You will need to convince Hasad and Mazhar that each of the offices of the network must install a specific audiovisual conferencing system. We will provide you with the exact model. Sell it as a vital business tool to ensure secure communications. Make sure you oversee each installation personally. The equipment is above board, but we've installed each set with software of our own design that will send out a beacon providing their exact location at our signal.

This is the only way we can ensure that we don't have to let the authorities know each criminal's site prior to the moment Nigel orders the raid. We're pretty sure some of the local cops have been compromised and are on the syndicate's payroll, we are just not sure which ones."

"You will need to get Hasad to call a meeting that requires participation of all of the players whose roles are identified on this board," Nigel says, picking up where Geoff has left off. "Tell them it will be held remotely and that they must use their secure conferencing system to log into the meeting. Once everyone is in the meeting, local law enforcement in each jurisdiction will be deployed at the same time, which means we can arrest every single person at once. We will also arrest you, which should provide some protection for you. Timing and secrecy are vital to the plan's success."

Emre nods. "I understand. I'm sure I can get Hasad to call the meeting. I will have to show some successes as I streamline the operation. If I can show him that he gets more money in his pocket, he will support my requests. He is driven by greed, never knows when enough is enough." He turns to Nigel. "How can Interpol ensure that they can synchronize the teams on the ground and make the arrests all at once?"

"We have local law enforcement teams on notice. They don't know what they are ready for, they just know that they'll only have about thirty minutes to deploy once they are given the word. At this point, we are hinting that the operation has to do with human trafficking to throw them off."

Nigel levels Geoff and Emre each with a steady look. "If you don't have any more questions, I will take my leave. If I need to reach you from now on, I will have an encoded message added to the lower right-hand corner of the board. Be well, you two. And all the best for a successful mission."

Emre walks Nigel to the main deck then returns to the office. He looks across the desk at Geoff, his closest confidante and now his partner in a life-or-death drug bust.

"Well," Emre says. "This shit just got real."

Chapter Twelve

2019

As Emre prepares to leave Knightsbridge, he checks for the fourth time that he has the three nicely bound reports: one each for Mazhar, Hasad, and himself.

Geoff gives Emre a slight push on the back. "They are all there. You are ready. And just think—when it is all over, you will be free and clear of any association with those dreadful people and abhorrent business. You can go back to being a respectable businessman and, quite possibly, be able to even go on a fourth date with some lucky lady."

"From your lips to whatever power you believe in's ears, my friend."

On the jet heading to Hasad's compound near Istanbul, Emre gets himself into character as a junior partner awaiting the words of wisdom from his elders. This is the most important play of the match. He must get them to think calling the meeting is their idea. That all along, this is what Mazhar and Hasad planned. Emre cannot be seen as advocating too hard to call a meeting of all the senior officers in the drug trade—they may start to suspect that something underhanded is going on. Mazhar is paranoid enough without any red flags being waved in front of him.

After freshening up, Emre meets Hasad and Mazhar on the back patio. They welcome him, smiling for once.

Hasad slaps Emre on the back and looks at him with something akin to pride. "We have received dozens of positive reports about you from the network. You have done a good job and treated everyone with respect. They not only liked you, but they also believed you could make a positive impact on the business."

"You are lucky, boy," Mazhar barks. "If you had embarrassed us, you would not be standing there looking so pleased with yourself—you would not be standing at all."

That may constitute the longest sentence Mazhar has ever uttered to Emre. Granted, it was to spew out a threat.

Emre takes a seat in a lounge chair and asks if the three of them may enjoy some refreshments on the patio, as it is such a lovely day. They look surprised and pleased. If Emre's time in the field with the syndicate members over the past several months has taught him anything, it is to not rush into doing business. Take some time to connect before addressing the main reason you are there. Pretend that spending time with them is also a reason you are there. This makes it appear that you aren't hurrying them into anything.

Emre enjoys a refreshing iced tea while they slosh bourbon over rocks in their tumblers. This is good. They will be relaxed and, if it is possible, even less sharp than they are naturally. After about a half hour of discussing football and politics, Hasad suggests they head into his office.

"Let's finally see these plans you have to make us more profitable."

As they gather around the conference table, Emre hands them the reports. "I can promise I will do just that," he says, hoping he sounds confident, not cocky.

Emre must have hit the right tone because the two men look suitably impressed by the personalized reports. Why is it that simple men always like seeing their names embossed on the cover of a document?

Emre clears his throat, pulls his shoulders back up to his six foot two height, and begins. He outlines a plan that would expand their heroin empire, reaching into new markets and strengthening existing ones. Emre projects that his proposal would more than double their profits. It doesn't matter that he doesn't mean any of it—Emre just needs them to believe he's worthy of getting closer to the heart of the business.

An hour later, after thoroughly reviewing every recommendation, Emre asks if there are any questions. Hasad and Mazhar each ask a couple of simple, seemingly rehearsed questions. They must have asked someone for a couple of questions to ask at the end of a business meeting so they would appear intelligent. Emre suppresses a chuckle as he smoothly answers their queries. Then the

114

men say they would like to speak privately, and direct Emre to step out of the office for a moment.

As he sits outside of Hasad's office, Emre bounces his knee a little, then stops himself from seeming nervous. After about ten minutes, he begins to worry. It should not be taking this long. Maybe they don't want to implement any changes. What then? There would be no reason to call a meeting. Emre doesn't have a Plan B. The thought that he and Geoff and Nigel wasted all those months plotting would be too much to take. Just when he is about to panic, Hasad opens the door and ushers him in.

"We like your ideas," Hasad says once the door is shut behind them. "We support most of them—"

Mazhar interrupts. "But not all of them. I do not agree with your third recommendation. I will not fire an entire layer of leadership. I don't care if it creates 'redundancies,' they are loyal people and I will not do away with them just because you say so." He crosses his arms, looking defiant, ready for a fight.

Emre lets out a breath. He was expecting this. "Respectfully, all I did was make recommendations. I identified where savings could be realized, but it is your call. You should think of this document as a menu. You may select what you want to do, and then I will make it happen."

Mazhar grunts as he sits back down, looking pleased that he has a win on his side. He and Hasad exchange a look and Mazhar nods.

"Very well then," Hasad says finally. "Mazhar and I support the other recommendations. It feels like each day you are becoming more valuable to us. We still don't consider you a full replacement for your uncle, but this work has moved you much closer to that esteemed position."

Emre breaks out his widest, most earnest-looking grin. "I cannot tell you how happy that makes me. I will strive for you to one day see me filling the big shoes of my uncle." Sometimes it is hard for him not to puke when he says these things. If Emre ever gets tired of business, he can always go into acting.

Hasad looks at this watch. "It is late. We will have dinner and tomorrow we will discuss how to make this happen. Will you stay as my guest tonight?"

"That is a very kind offer, I wish I had known before I finalized my plans," Emre says. "I have promised to meet with the caretaker of my penthouse. There are a few issues he needs my guidance with, and I must sign some papers having to do with some remodeling I've requested. I want to get my home here perfect, as I believe I will be needing to spend more time in Istanbul because of the anticipated growth of our mutual business interests."

This seems to soften Emre's refusal. In all honesty, he wants some time to breathe. Emre will need a good night's rest and all of his skills to pull off tomorrow's finale.

Before he leaves, almost as though it is an afterthought, Emre places the invoices for the conferencing systems in front of the two of them.

"Here are your copies of the invoices for the conferencing systems. Everyone was very open to accepting them and appreciative of your generosity in purchasing them. They are enthusiastic about being able to virtually meet and work together soon."

The following day, Emre arrives in time to share a drink with Hasad before dinner.

"No alcohol still?" Hasad asks, pouring himself a healthy dram of whiskey. "That is good. Keeps a clear head for business. At my age, I can handle alcohol, it does not affect me at all."

Let him keep thinking that.

"You are a good boy, Emre," Hasad continues. "I am glad that you have come around to our way of thinking. Now you just need to marry a nice Turkish girl, settle down, and have babies. And I mean settle down in a secure compound, like me and Mazhar. Your uncle's home is a good solid place to live and raise a family."

Just then Mazhar comes in and the conversation stops. Emre has learned it's best to gauge his mood before speaking to him.

Di Toma

Today, as the three of them head into the dining room, Mazhar slams his chair back from the table. He seems to be in a sour disposition. This is not out of the ordinary for him; he has one of the most unpleasant demeanors of anyone Emre has ever known.

Hasad sighs deeply and gives Emre a look that means he has also sensed Mazhar's mood. Emre needs them both to be on board and open to suggestion before he proceeds. He racks his brain, trying to think of what to say before the thick silence undermines everything.

"Mazhar," Emre says slowly. "Hasad and I were just talking about the time you single-handedly held off that band of muggers when you were just sixteen. I remember my uncle telling me how brave you were, and that the prettiest girl in your group of friends was so impressed that she fell head over heels in love with you."

Hasad perks up, egging on his friend and filling in the details of the story. He embellishes it as much as Emre did, but it doesn't matter. Mazhar's mood perceivably lightens.

"Oh yes, and I married that girl," he says smugly, leaning back in his chair. "She said she wanted the strongest and bravest man as her husband. It's a shame she didn't stay that young and beautiful, but as men, we can find our pleasure elsewhere." Mazhar huffs and begins musing on his glory days. For the next half hour he regales Emre and Hasad with stories of his youthful exploits.

As painful as it is for Emre to sit there and nod enthusiastically as Mazhar recounts horrid things he has done to people who crossed him, it does the trick. Mazhar is in a fine mood as the three move to the patio for cigars and the uncles' tumblers of single malt.

After a few moments of discussing the garden's fruit trees and the expensive lighting setup for them, they appear ready to get down to business. Hasad places the report Emre presented yesterday on the table and asks how it will be possible to introduce the plans to such a vast operation of officers around Europe.

"Well, it is vital that we introduce it to everyone in leadership at the same time," Emre says. "If one finds out before another, it could create jealousies and infighting. And you want everyone to know these proposals come from the two of you—that it is your brainchild born of information I collected at your direction. I don't think it will be accepted as well if it appears to come from me."

They look at each other and from that one glance, Emre can see that they had planned to take credit for the plan anyhow. What Emre just did was make that very easy for them. He's given them the chance to appear humble and even gracious.

"Well, if you think so. We would hate to take credit for your work, but if you think it is best, Hasad and I will present it as our own ideas and recommendations."

Their acting skills are on par with their intellectual abilities. Emre, on the other hand, continues his Oscar-worthy performance. He taps his chin with his finger, as if in thought. "Now if we could figure out how to make a major presentation like that happen …"

Mazhar jumps in, eyes wide. "I've got it! I've figured it out. That expensive conference system we generously supplied for everyone. That is how we can do this!"

"Yes, we just got the invoices for those expensive conferencing systems," Hasad adds. "We can make good use of them with the rollout of our plans."

Emre makes himself appear to think this over. "Yes, I think you are right. That would be the best way to get your recommendations to everyone at the same time. Let me know if I can do anything to help."

"Earn your keep, boy," Mazhar snaps at Emre. "Work with our secretaries and get it all set up!"

Emre tells them he'll follow their orders and have the meeting scheduled as soon as possible. In spite of all the planning he and Geoff have already done over the past fifteen months, this may actually take a while. There are close to ninety-four people across eight countries who will be taking part in this meeting. That's a lot of schedules to synchronize.

On the eve of the big meeting, Geoff is finalizing the conference setup in Emre's Knightsbridge home office. It seems unreal that this nightmare is finally coming to an end. The meeting is set to start first thing in the morning London time; the police raids on each site will follow thirty minutes after. The plan is for the conference systems to go offline a moment before the raid so if there is any delay in any location, each member of the drug ring won't see what is happening everywhere else.

The tech team at Interpol has been working on this for months. It should go off without a hitch. For their crimes distributing heroin on a global network and for their countless acts of violence against their enemies, the businessmen and businesswomen will be held under constant watch because they are all flight risks. And with their assets frozen, their power and influence over authorities will be greatly diminished, if not totally nullified. Emre will be swept up in the raid, too, although only as a way to not make it obvious he was the architect of the plan. They've already greased some palms to release him within hours of his arrest. Nigel says Emre will have to lay low for a while and then he can report some procedural misstep by London police, resulting in Emre's case being thrown out.

With any luck, Emre can resume a somewhat normal life in about three months. He's pleased Geoff has outfitted the Kayıp Aşk so well, and kept it so well removed from Emre's name. He'll likely be living and working there for quite a while. It's the one place Emre can disappear to without fear of being tracked down.

Around nine o'clock p.m., as Geoff is nearly done with his double and triple checks, they hear a pounding on Emre's front door. Both men turn to the screen to the right of the desk: Nigel is in the entryway, waving at the security camera. Geoff rushes to let him in and they share hushed whispers as they enter Emre's office.

Seeing Nigel look panicked is unsettling. Mr. Cool, James Bond's more chill brother, doesn't ever look panicked. Until now.

"What's going on, you two?" Emre demands.

Geoff and Nigel exchange an indecipherable look. "Remember I said if ever something becomes a concern, we will discuss it with you?" Nigel starts.

Emre is unable to speak as a sense of terror creeps through his whole body. He shakes his head so Nigel knows he understands.

Nigel takes a deep breath. "Who is Jennifer Young?"

The creeping terror now becomes all-consuming. "Why? What does this have to do with anything?"

"We were testing the equipment a couple months ago and the techs picked up chatter from a couple of guys in the syndicate's office in Serbia," Nigel says, letting the words tumble out. "They said that their boss wants to push you out of the business and take your place. He is concerned you are wielding too much power with Hasad and Mazhar. But he doesn't want it to appear that he used force; he wants you to step down. So these guys were told to find your vulnerability. At the time I didn't think anything of it. You've never seemed to have any vulnerability, and you never mentioned a Jennifer Young to Geoff, so we figured it must have been a mistake on their part that they would clear up," Nigel says, looking abashed.

"But today we picked up more of the chatter," he continues. "They said you have a particular interest in this Jennifer woman. It sounds like they had their tech guy hack into some system and found that you have been seeking information on this woman for almost twenty years. They were able to place her in Germany at the same time you were there."

Emre's heart is in his throat.

"They plan on grabbing her in a few hours," Nigel says flatly. "They set up one of their operatives as a blind date she will meet tonight. They were saying that they were frustrated because she had rescheduled twice already but were confident she would show tonight. Once they have her, they plan on using her to force your hand."

"The good news," Geoff interrupts, "is that they never seemed to be suspicious of you, just concerned and jealous that you have earned Hasad and Mazhar's respect."

Emre collapses into the chair behind his desk, stunned. "I haven't seen or spoken to her in two decades," he says in a near whisper. "The last thing I want is to put her at risk. She is the only woman I ever loved and trusted completely. Everything I have done is so one day I will be worthy of her." A sob gets caught in Emre's throat and he looks from Geoff to Nigel.

"Help me."

Geoff and Nigel instantly agree: They need to bring Ela here for her own safety. Even if they stop tonight's abduction, the takedown of the syndicate could place an even larger target on her back. Emre can't risk that.

Thirty minutes later, MI6 operatives based in DC are tracking Ela's phone and pinpointing her location. Emre should go to bed and rest before the meeting tomorrow, the culmination of their months of work to bring down the syndicate. Instead, he is up at midnight, watching it all take place on his laptop screen via a camera in the agents' SUV. They follow until her car is on a dark, empty street, then gently tap the back of her car. No one would ever know it wasn't an accident.

And then, there she is, emerging from her car, looking as beautiful as ever, even as a fierce anger burns in her eyes. Emre knows he needs to keep focused until this operation is completed, but seeing Ela brought back all of the feelings he had as a besotted teen. Emre has suspected it for years but now knows it with sharp certainty: No one has compared to Ela and no one ever will. It breaks Emre's heart to see her grabbed and drugged, falling into an agent's arms. But at least he can exhale. They will bring her to Geoff in London and he will fly her to the *Kayıp Aşk*.

The next morning, the video conference meeting goes as planned. Even as the arriving police officers burst into his office, lead him into a cell in handcuffs, and then begrudgingly release him under Nigel's watchful gaze, Emre barely notices. The image of Ela being drugged and swept into an SUV keeps swimming before his eyes. Emre only shakes himself back to the present when Nigel explains in the car that the two men in Serbia were not among those arrested. They are still under orders to hunt down Jennifer Young.

After the arrests, Emre meets Iserate, another trusted member of his inner circle, on the *Kayıp Aşk*. Once Geoff brings Ela on board, they'll head farther out to sea.

Emre has instructed the medical team that is accompanying her on the transatlantic flight to ensure she doesn't wake until midafternoon. That should give Geoff time to get her safely ensconced in her suite onboard. Iserate has instructions to make sure she is comfortable and to bring her to Emre once she has had time to realize she is not in harm's way.

For now, all he can do is wait. To say Emre has grave concerns how she will react about being plucked from her life by someone she hasn't seen for twenty years and probably doesn't even remember, is an understatement. *Shit,* he thinks, pacing the main deck, *why did I keep researching her*. Ela will think he's some kind of stalker.

Emre felt less nervous bringing down an international heroin syndicate than he does waiting for Ela's arrival.

Chapter Thirteen

Jennifer feels that she must still be a bit drugged. None of this is computing, her brain is in a fog. It can't be, but when she looks into his eyes, she sees it is.

"Emre," she breathes. "I can't believe it's you."

She moves toward him, some subconscious force propelling her into his arms. After a pause, he holds out his own arms to welcome her. Just before she reaches him, her head clears and she stops herself. Jennifer slams her hand on Emre's chest, holding him at arm's length.

"What in the hell is going on!" she cries. "Are you insane? Maybe a phone call or email reintroducing yourself before you kidnapped me would have been a more chivalrous way to handle seeing me again. Or possibly, an invitation, rather than sending thugs to drug me and kidnap me."

She paces around the main salon, her anger fully returning to her. "My car, is it abandoned? What day is it? I was due to fly to South America the morning after this happened."

"Breathe, Ela," Emre says. "I will answer all your questions." He doesn't take his eyes off her face, even as he asks Mr. Blue Eyes, who has been hanging back by the doorway, to have some refreshments brought in. Then he asks him to leave Jennifer alone with him.

"I will ask him to stay if you prefer," he says softly to Jennifer.

Jennifer takes a shaky breath. "If you wanted any harm to come to me, I believe it would have already happened."

They settle on the sofas across the coffee table from each other. She can tell that each of them doesn't want to crowd the other. And he tells her the story of the past two decades. Arriving in Istanbul, thriving in London. Learning the truth about his uncle's sordid business dealings, plotting to take them down.

As he speaks, Jennifer studies him. She has to admit to herself that he appears to be the same endearing person she met twenty years ago. Only now he is, obviously, a successful, confident man. And Anna was right: The sweet teen has grown into a stunning man.

When he explains how she was drawn into this dangerous situation, she can tell he is embarrassed to say that he has been following her life online all of these years. It's not like she didn't try to do the same. Clearly she's not the only one who has thought of their time together since they parted.

To ease his embarrassment, she lifts the chain around her neck so that it frees itself from the dress's neckline. On the end of the chain is the pendant Emre gave her so many years ago.

He begins to speak but she just shakes her head. It is going to take some time to process the danger she is in, her need to leave her life for an unknown period of time, and the knowledge that they both held a flame for each other way past the time it should have fizzled out. A flame that may just end up burning them both.

"I think that is all I can take in right now."

"Yes, I think you are right," Emre says quickly. "It is too much, actually. I just wanted you to understand that I had no choice. There was no time to explain it all to you. You were on your way to meet with the person who had been hired to kidnap you." He grimaces. "I mean the bad kidnapping, not this one. Okay, I'm going to stop talking now. Let me show you around the *Kayıp Aşk*."

"Yes, I would love to see it all," she says, standing. "By the way, what does *Kayıp Aşk* mean?"

"It is Turkish for 'lost love.'" He says no more. The way he looks at her says it all.

As they stand on the main deck and look at the endless sea, the tension between them seems to fade a bit. Jennifer tries to get her thoughts in order.

Still shaky, but beginning to feel more like herself, she says, "This is a beautiful place to be held captive."

Emre blanches. "I don't want you to feel like—"

She interrupts him. "That was supposed to be a joke. I guess it's a difficult time for humor. Anyhow, you said that my car was locked in my garage at home. And everyone thinks I'm in South

America. So, basically, no one will know that I am missing for at least three months. Right?"

"That's right. If need be, we can always have a message delivered to your assistant saying you have extended your trip. Maybe say that you are unwell and unable to travel home for a while."

"One thing your spies didn't find out is that I have to be in Germany in four months for Anna's baby's christening," Jennifer says. All that seems so far away now. "So you have four months to clear this up. I will not miss being there, being a godmother to my best friend's child." The last thing Jen wants is to appear hysterical, but the tears start to fall, and she just stands there softly sobbing.

She was so stoic while Emre told her about the drug syndicate and the danger she is in. But the thought of not being there for her best friend is her tipping point.

Emre seems unsure what to do, seeing her distress. He opens his arms to invite her to step into them. Jennifer just shakes her head and walks away. She needs to be alone with her thoughts right now. She also feels like she needs a good cry, something she would prefer to do alone.

It takes Jennifer a good five minutes to find her way back to her suite. She notes that along with the bedroom, dressing room and bathroom, there is a door that leads to a sitting room. Inside, the bookshelf has many of the books she and Emre shared in Germany.

There is also a small writing desk, inlaid with an intricate design. She sits in the elegant chair in front of it and begins looking through the drawers. There is a beautiful leather-bound book with 'Ela' embossed in gold on the cover.

Intrigued, she lovingly caresses the fine leather and gold-edges pages. She opens the book to find it blank. A journal. Now she is blinking back tears again, amazed that Emre is still the kind, thoughtful person she had known all those years ago. But how does that match up with this tough businessman who worked with criminals? Granted, he worked with them to bring them down— Emre never would have gotten involved with them at all if his uncle hadn't basically tricked him. No wonder his parents' wish was for him to be sent far away from that horrible man. It's just a shame that his uncle took Emre from that kind family.

Clutching the journal to her chest, she crawls back into bed and cries herself to sleep.

She is awakened a couple of hours later by a knock on her door. Jennifer pads to the door, opening it a crack, and peeks out. There is a tall, powerfully built man who, in a very cultured British accent asks, "Did you have a nice rest, ma'am?"

"Um, yes thank you. Who are you?"

"I'm Geoff, Mr. Sydin's personal assistant."

"Oh yes, the ex-MI6 spy who ferried me out here on the helicopter."

"I can see Mr Emre has brought you up to speed on the events of the past couple of days," Geoff says with a chuckle. "He would like to extend an invitation to join him on the main deck for dinner. It is a beautiful evening and the stars are brilliant tonight; you might enjoy some fresh air."

Her stomach growls loudly, as though it heard about dinner. "Um, I could eat. Yes, that sounds like a good idea."

"I will send Lizet in to help you dress for dinner, ma'am."

A moment later a very sweet young woman with what sounds like a French or Middle Eastern accent arrives at Jennifer's door. "May I come in ma'am?"

"There is no need," Jennifer snaps. "I am perfectly capable of dressing myself." She really didn't mean to sound so harsh, but it's been quite a day already.

"Please ma'am. I am to be your personal maid. If you do not accept me, I will be shamed."

Jennifer stares at this tall, toned young woman, maybe in her late twenties or early thirties with lush, silky dark brown hair past her shoulders. Her flawless tanned skin sets off her brown eyes flecked with gold and framed with thick black lashes and carefully arched brows. She should be modeling, not dressing Jennifer.

"Oh, all right," Jennifer sighs. "I'm sorry, I didn't mean to be rude. I still don't think I am comprehending what is going on. I keep feeling like I'm going to wake from this wild dream."

In the time it takes Jennifer to shower, Lizet has remade the bed, and laid out an outfit: a gorgeous little black dress, Christian Louboutin heels, an exquisite diamond necklace, and teardrop diamond earrings. She can see the look of surprise on Jennifer's face and says, "Mr Emre has ensured that you have everything you would need."

"This goes way beyond 'need,' but I'm not going to complain."

"If you please, may I dress your hair now? I think with such lustrous, curly auburn hair, we should just simply pull it to one side and let it cascade."

"Sure, whatever you think. I don't tend to do much with it because it is such an unruly mess," Jennifer shrugs. "But I will leave it in your capable hands."

When Lizet finishes, Jennifer looks at her reflection in the mirror, stunned. "Wow, I didn't think my hair could ever be wrestled into submission. But somehow, Lizet, you did it!"

As Lizet begins to secure the diamond necklace's clasp around her neck, Jennifer stops her. "No, I love what you have done. The clothes, shoes, hair, everything you have selected for me is gorgeous. But I will just stick with my simple pendant," Jennifer smiles softly at Lizet.

Lizet nods her agreement. "Yes, that is perfect. Simplicity is elegance. Will that be all then?"

"Yes, thank you so much. I am happy that you will be with me. It will be nice to have some female company. There is an awful lot of testosterone on this vessel." Jen can't help laughing—maybe for the first time since she arrived on the yacht.

Lizet just smiles. As she opens the door to leave, Jennifer asks, "I'm just curious—you have a beautiful accent. Where are you originally from?"

"Israel, ma'am."

And without thinking, Jen blurts out, "Mossad."

Lizet gives a slight tilt of her head and softly responds, "Ex," before slipping through the door.

As Jennifer emerges onto the main deck, she notes that it is a perfect evening. The moon is reflecting off the water, the stars are blanketing the sky, the temperature is ambient. The sight of Emre's figure leaning against the railing takes her breath away. He is resplendent in a dove gray suit impeccably tailored to highlight his perfectly sculpted body. Broad shoulders, narrow waist and hips, long legs. *Not much to find fault with here.*

He turns to face her, and it is obvious that she has the same effect on Emre. For a moment, they just stand and stare at each other. Unable to move, unable to speak.

They are both startled out of this trance when Mr. Blue Eyes—who Emre addresses as Iserate—enters with a bottle of Juglar Cuvée, 1820.

"Champagne, ma'am?"

"Yes, please. And please stop calling me ma'am. It makes me feel like a granny," Jennifer laughs to release some of the tension engulfing her. She shakes it off and accepts the glass he offers.

"Sorry, ma'am," Iserate says. "What would you prefer to be called?"

Emre says, "Ela. Please call her Ela." He looks towards her for permission.

"Yes," she breathes. It does feel right, somehow. "This is all so unreal, so not the life of Jennifer Young, you might as well call me Ela."

"I will personally be taking care of you both this evening," Iserate continues.

"Why is that?" Ela says. "I know you and Geoff are the top dogs of Emre's personal staff and his personal security. With your skills set and expertise, isn't serving drinks and dinner a waste of your talents?"

"Oh, Ela, you haven't changed," Emre says, laughing. "Just as direct as you were decades ago."

Iserate, unruffled by the direct question, explains that he chooses to do these things because he takes the safety of both of them very seriously.

"If I may speak freely in front of Dr. Ela," he waits for a nod from Emre. "Until we have a final report of everyone from the syndicate arrested and their current status in the legal system, we will be taking every precaution. We are also waiting for word from our informants to ascertain if all the players believe that Emre was swept up in the raid and that there is no suspicion cast his way. And, might I add," he continues, straightening his posture proudly. "I see nothing in my service to Emre as a waste of time nor talent, as you call it. Mr. Sydin is more than an employer. I consider him a valued friend and, by extension, consider you to be one as well."

With that, the remaining tension evaporates and Ela takes a sip of the absolute perfection contained in the glass she has in her hand.

"Oh my God, this is amazing. I'll have to be careful not to overindulge. Don't you think it's incredible?"

Then she notices Emre's flute is filled with what appears to be sparkling water.

"Oh, you still don't drink? I mean that's a good thing, a very healthy choice. Would you prefer if I didn't?"

"Of course not." Emre shrugs. "It's just a habit now. For so many years I needed to have an edge, keep my wits about me while others relaxed theirs. But, you know what." Emre gets a mischievous sparkle in his eyes. He really does seem thrilled to be with her "I'm going to have my first drink right now so I can share it with you."

"Oh, please, I didn't mean I wanted you to drink. I'm just surprised at thirty-six you still don't drink. Obviously from your body, you take good—I mean, great—I mean. … Oh shit, I'm rambling, talking about your Adonis body and—see there I go again." Ela gives a nervous chuckle that she hopes sounds endearing. "Shit. I guess I'm nervous. And you know how I used to get when I was nervous? Yup, still get like that. I think I'll shut up now."

Ela is about to take a drink when Emre places his hand on hers. He looks deeply into her hazel eyes and whispers, "Wait."

He dumps his sparkling water over the railing and gestures for Iserate to fill his glass from the champagne bottle. He clinks his glass gently against hers.

"To yesterday's memories, today's adventures, and tomorrow's fulfillment," he says softly, holding her gaze. "Ela, may you someday find what you are looking for."

Ela is taken aback by Emre's choice of words. She shakes it off, smiles, and takes a sip along with him. Then she turns and walks to the railing. Watching the dark abyss of the sea she can only wonder if he can read her mind. Or is he just so in sync with her still, after all these years, that he anticipates her thoughts and needs? Would he still want her to wait for him, like when he was a boy, or is he just protecting her from the danger he put her in?

Just then, Iserate comes out with the first course, and they both stop their musings and sit across from each other at a small candlelit table under the stars.

"Well, what do you think of the champagne?" Ela asks, filling the empty air. "I guess you have nothing to compare it to, but do you like it?"

"Actually, it is very good. To think I have been missing out on this for all these years." He gets suddenly serious. "I feel safe with you. I feel if I let my guard down, nothing bad will happen. I don't think I have felt like that since you left Germany."

"You deserve to feel safe. You deserve all of this—this amazing life you have made for yourself." Ela pauses, steeling herself as she asks, "Do you have a family to share it with?"

"My uncle was the last family member I had, for what that was worth. We wouldn't be in this predicament if he stayed out of my life."

"No, I mean, a wife, kids, family dog. Something like that."

"Oh no, I wouldn't be cosseted away with a woman, I … I mean no, I have no wife, kids, or family dog." Emre's face reddens and he clears his throat. "I wonder what's for dessert. If I remember correctly, tiramisu was a favorite of yours."

"It still is. And I guess you don't need to ask about my personal life. Did your spies provide you with a full dossier on me?"

"That's not fair," Emre says, feigning hurt. "I made my own dossier of your life for the first twenty years. I only got help from professionals a couple of days ago."

At this they both can't help but laugh.

"Seriously, I wish I hadn't," he continues. "Not because I didn't want to know what your life was like after you left Germany, but because my need to feel connected to you has placed you in harm's way."

As Iserate places the tiramisu on the table, the candle's flames flicker in their glass enclosures as the breeze picks up. Ela rubs her arms in the chill, and Emre gets up and places his suit jacket over her shoulders. As he sits down, she says, "All we are missing are the snowballs." They share a shy smile.

They decide to take a stroll around the deck after dinner. As they finish a full lap of the vessel, Ela looks quizzically at Emre.

"So you've never had a drink, and tonight you have champagne and wine with dinner, followed by a lovely port, and you are walking around like you are completely sober. I'm even a bit wobbly and I'm used to drinking. How does that happen?"

"Well, my dear Ela, I am feeling quite warm and fuzzy, with an emphasis on fuzzy. I just have the ability to appear to be completely sober. It must be the acting ability I honed while playing double agent with the syndicate."

With that said, Emre stumbles slightly. Ela reaches out to steady him and they find themselves face to face, chest to chest. She can see every fleck of gold in his dark brown eyes. As if by instinct, she moves her arms around him, circling her hands around his neck.

Just when he pulls her close, he whispers, "No, not like this."

He pulls away and says he should go lay down. "I will see you in the morning. I hope you sleep well."

And with that, Ela finds herself standing alone, pulling his jacket more tightly around herself, and feels the breeze drying her tear-stained cheeks.

That night in bed, Ela can't sleep. Finally, she gives up, goes into her sitting room, and takes out the journal. She finds a beautiful gold nib MontBlanc pen and green ink. Her favorite color. Of course. What hasn't he thought of?

Is she reading his signals so wrong? Maybe, now that she is here in the flesh, a real woman in her forties, she can't live up to the woman he created from memories. Journaling used to help her sort out her thoughts and emotions, so she curls up on a comfy chair and begins to write a stream of consciousness dump. She isn't even aware of what she is writing. When she finally looks up, she can see the sky is lightning to the east.

She decides she will read back what she has written after she shuts those blackout blinds, goes to bed, and gets a few hours of sleep. She knows that whatever tomorrow—well, today—brings, she will need her wits about her. It could be another kidnapping, maybe a murder attempt, or even unrequited love. She's just not sure which frightens her most.

Chapter Fourteen

Emre stumbles into his room, waving off Iserate's offer to help. All he wants to do is climb into bed and, possibly, scream. Ela far exceeds his every memory and fantasy. The ideal he has held onto all these years is eclipsed by the real woman. He can't believe his luck in finding her again. He always dreamed of this moment, albeit under different circumstances.

And what does he do? He decides it's time to have alcohol for the first time. He yells to the empty room, "If I want her to see me as the man I have made myself into and not the boy she said was too young, stumbling around drunk wasn't a good first move. You idiot!"

A tap on the door and Geoff enters. "Are you alright? I thought I heard you yelling at someone."

"Yes, I was yelling at the big horse's arse."

"Huh?"

"Me! I am the big horse's arse! Did you see me stumbling around?"

"Emre, are you … drunk?"

"Yes, old man, exactly," Emre says miserably. "I decided to try drinking tonight. Not the best way to impress the love of my life. The only woman who has ever meant anything to me. The one woman I have dreamed about and pined over for twenty years. I think I've totally fucked it up."

Geoff can't help laughing. "No, no. You barely stumbled. It could have even been the movement of the ship. Really, I could see you from where I was stationed. And she did put her arms around you. I thought she was going in for a kiss. But then you walked away."

"Really?" Emre asks dubiously. "I wasn't an embarrassment?"

"No, not at all. And you know I would be delighted to tell you if you were. You've seen me stumbling around after a good night out. You are just overreacting because you were not in total control for once. You let your guard down. And that's outside of your comfort zone. You just need to sleep it off and all will be right in the morning. I promise."

Just before Geoff leaves the room, he turns and asks, "Why didn't you kiss her?"

Emre stares straight ahead. "I wanted to," he sighs. "I wanted to hold her and never let her go. But I want both of us to be 100 percent in our right minds with all our faculties. I want the kiss to be the beginning, not the end."

The next morning, Emre sits alone at the dining table, his eggs congealing on the plate. He keeps stealing glances towards the door. Geoff leaves the room and returns a few minutes later. "Lizet

143

said that when she went to lay out Ela's clothes, she was sound asleep. Lizet said she will ensure Ela gets some breakfast when she wakes."

Emre grimaces.

"Don't look like that, Emre, she is just tired."

Emre pushes his chair back from the table and goes to the office, shutting the door firmly behind him. A moment later Geoff enters.

"Does a closed door mean nothing to you?"

"It means you need a friend to tell you some home truths, old boy."

Emre just scowls at him. Geoff throws his hands up.

"Who are you and what have you done with Emre? Even the very young man who graced my doorway in Knightsbridge for the first time had more confidence than you are exhibiting."

"Fuck!" Emre drops his head in his hands. "I don't know what it is. I feel like that sixteen-year-old who fell madly in love with a woman. A woman I knew felt the same way about me but who refused to acknowledge it because of my age. All I wanted was to prove to her that I would be worthy of her someday, and that the age difference would be meaningless when that day finally arrived."

"If I may say, I agree that she is a remarkable woman, but you are more than worthy of her," Geoff says, frowning at his friend. "You have grown a legitimate business empire to a level of success no one could have predicted, while playing the pivotal role in destroying a syndicate that was the scourge of so many communities. You employ thousands of people and, from what I hear, are considered quite a catch by the opposite sex. So what in the bloody hell is wrong with you?"

Emre sits with his fingertips tented against his mouth. After a few minutes he smiles up at Geoff.

"It is somewhere between comical and sad that years of growth can be wiped out in a moment as soon as we are confronted by a trigger from our past. Ela met me when I was at my most vulnerable. My parents had passed away, I was in a foreign country, and, other than the kind friends of my parents who took me in, was surrounded by false friends. Seeing her again brought back all those untamed emotions."

"Do you think that you are truly still in love with her? Or is it the memory, the emotion from your past, that you are feeling?"

Emre allows the question to hang in the air. " I suppose I've just allowed myself to get caught up in this emotional tsunami without questioning what I am really feeling and, more importantly, why I am feeling it."

"I'll have some breakfast sent to your suite," Geoff says firmly. "You can regroup, then come out to face the day. You don't want your crew losing confidence in you."

"Excellent. I will see you later. Oh, and Geoff?"

Geoff stops, his hand on the doorknob.

Emre smiles. "Thanks for being the friend who will kick me in the arse when I need it."

"We all need it sometime in our lives. Just happy to help, *sir*," Geoff says with a smirk.

Chapter Fifteen

At the first moment of wakefulness, Ela takes a luxurious, catlike stretch, enjoying the feel of the sheets—*Sferra Giza 45*, she thinks, *impressive*—against her skin. She feels serene and rested in this moment. The moment when we first wake, before our awareness and memories surface. That split second when there is nothing but joy to fill our senses. Then that sweet sense of serenity is shattered in an instant as reality comes flooding back. And with awareness, her feeling of dread returns. What was she thinking throwing herself at someone, only for him to reject her so abruptly?

She looks at her clock and notes that she would have missed breakfast by now, which is for the best. Ela can just picture the embarrassing silence that would hang like a wet curtain between her and Emre while she tried to choke down her breakfast.

The smell of coffee and cinnamon draws her to her sitting room. There on the table is a tray holding the most mouthwatering, gooey cinnamon roll, dripping with icing, alongside a delicate silver coffee pot. She sits down and takes a sip of the rich, perfectly roasted Italian coffee and tears off a piece of the cinnamon roll, licking her fingers after she pops it in her mouth.

Lizet taps at the door and pokes her head in. "I hope that's okay, ma'am. I wasn't sure what you would feel like. You obviously didn't sleep well. I was led to believe you were normally a very early riser."

"I am, and I did have an awful sleep," Ela says, swallowing another bite. "But somehow you knew just what the doctor ordered. You are a godsend!"

"Thank you," Lizet says with a soft smile. "I am a woman, and know that carbs and coffee are the cure for just about anything that ails you. I am also an ex-spy—that makes me able to read people fairly well. If you need to talk, I'm a good listener."

"That is kind of you, Lizet, but right now I don't feel like I would be very good company. I would just like to have some time alone. I have so much to process. I feel a bit overwhelmed." Lizet nods.

"Although," Ela starts, setting down her coffee cup. "I have been wondering why you left Mossad. You seem so young to have already had a career as a spy."

Lizet nods again, smoothing an imperceptible wrinkle in her crisp white shirt. "I went through all the training but the more I learned about the organization, the more disgusted I was. I couldn't see myself being a part of it." She looks back up at Ela. "I left, and now use my skills to keep women safe."

Ela crosses the room and gives Lizet a spontaneous hug. She turns before the tears that had been brimming in her eyes fall slowly down her cheeks.

As Lizet slips out, Ela notices the journal she placed on the desk early this morning. She wipes the remaining icing from her fingers and picks up the journal, thumbing its spine. Ela curls up in the comfy reading chair—her comfy reading chair now, she supposes—scrutinizing her words from last night.

Well, tonight I made a real fool of myself. I rambled on like a teenage schoolgirl who has never spoken to a cool boy before. Geez, I am cringing right now just thinking about it. The man Emre is so much more than the teen Emre was. He is still the same sensitive, intellectual person, but has a refinement and finish about him that either I hadn't seen or that he has acquired in adulthood. And he is gorgeous. Those huge dark brown eyes fringed with long, lush lashes, thick, wavy black hair, and a smile that would melt the glaciers.

Of course he has outgrown his teenage crush. Back then, I was kind and he was lost. He has probably had any woman he could want. I'm sure some divorced forty-four-year-old who doesn't travel in his jet-setting circles, would not be exactly what he is looking for.

He is just being kind and helpful. He feels responsible for me being on some gangster's hit list. So he is helping me out of a sense of obligation.

Now that I've got that straight, I need to know why I am acting like some swooning woman who has a case of the vapors:

1. *I met Emre when I was twenty-four.*
2. *I had just gone through a bad breakup and had my heart broken.*
3. *My grandma had just passed away.*
4. *I wasn't sure what career path I wanted to take.*

All these factors made me feel vulnerable and insecure. Maybe seeing him again brought those long-suppressed feelings to the surface.

I hadn't truly worked through any of those issues. I just do what I normally do: move on to the next adventure. I'm like a magpie, always chasing shiny objects.

Sure, that perpetual state of motion has led me to see amazing places, earn my doctorate, start my own business. But it has kept me from being grounded and finding whatever it is I'm looking for.

Moving forward: I am not that vulnerable, insecure person anymore. Although I still have many things to work through in my life, I am a successful, confident woman. I don't need anyone's validation. These are truths I know.

Emre isn't even the boy I knew. He is a man I have known for a couple of days. Probably hours, if I count the time we have spent actually talking. I will not allow myself to be anything but the strong woman I am.

Okay, wow. She presses the call button and Lizet joins her a few minutes later.

"Yes, Ela, what can I do for you?"

"I feel much better after the sustenance and my quiet time," Ela says. "I think I was just exhausted—or maybe my body was still eliminating the drugs they had me under for so long."

"I'm so pleased you feel better. And I believe you are correct; it takes a body some time to recover from what yours has been through. We are sorry for that, but we could not risk you fighting us or escaping until we had you safely aboard."

"I understand. Emre told me the whole story. I appreciate what you all did. Now I would like to freshen up, then I will have …" Ela pauses. "Um, what time is it?

Lizet looks at her watch. "It is almost eighteen thirty. Dinner will be served at twenty-one hundred hours. Will you be dining in your room, or shall I lay out dinner clothes for you?"

"Yes, please lay out something, I will be dining on the main deck, weather permitting."

Lizet rewards Ela with a smile and leaves her to shower.

As Ela steps out of the shower, her hair dripping down her back and over her full breasts, she looks at herself in the full-length mirror. Her body is still in good shape—stomach still flat, bum and breasts still firm and high, legs long and well defined. *Yes,* she muses to herself, *not bad at all.*

She slips on the emerald-green mulberry silk robe hanging on the back of the door, enjoying the sensuous feel of the fabric against her skin, still warm from the shower. Lizet taps on the door and asks if she would like to wear her hair straight tonight.

"That's a great idea," Ela says. "And I would like to wear something in a striking color tonight, nothing black. Nothing like last night."

"I believe I know exactly what will fit the bill." Lizet's expression turns serious. "I haven't yet broached the subject because you seemed rather fragile before, but now that you seem to be … what I assume is your old self, I will need to schedule some time to review safety and extraction protocols with you."

Ela shrugs. "Of course. I don't know how much safer we can be than on a luxury yacht constantly on the move. But I'm sure you all know much better than I do how to keep people safe. Let's schedule it for after breakfast tomorrow. How much time will we need?"

Lizet gives Ela a nod of acknowledgement. "Let's plan for two hours. That will give us more than enough time. I will have a briefing paper for you, but you must commit everything to memory and we must destroy any documents related to our plan."

Ela salutes Lizet, then smiles and gives her a brief hug. "I am sincere when I say that I feel very safe in your care. And I thank you for being more than a minder. I feel that you are a dearly-needed friend right now."

"Thank you. I feel the same."

"Although you would say that even if you didn't."

"True, but that is not the case here. Did you used to be a spy? You are very perceptive."

"Just an anthropologist. But that helps me look at behavior and artifacts and draw pretty precise conclusions."

Thinking of her academic past gives Ela an idea. "I just thought of something. Would there be any way you could find out why I was denied entry into Turkey about a decade ago, when I was working at the University of Western Australia? We were sending a team to work on an archaeological dig and everyone on the team was granted visas except me. We assumed it was a clerical mistake and we didn't have time to really challenge it, but I now think that someone I know may have had something to do with it."

"Once again, very perceptive," Lizet says, mouth flattening into a tight line. "I would suggest you speak to Mr. Sydin about that."

Ela takes one last look in the mirror. "Lizet, you are a magician. If you are half as good at this clandestine stuff as you are at taming unruly hair, I will have nothing to worry about."

The image reflected back at her is clad in white linen pants tailored to accentuate her small waist and full hips, a sage-green fitted summer sweater vest that provides just a hint of cleavage. Her auburn hair is so straight and silky, cascading down her back and over her shoulders, that she hardly recognizes herself.

It's perfect, Ela thinks. So removed from the way she looked last night that she can almost believe that she is a totally different woman from the one who made such a fool of herself. With a deep breath, she turns and they head out of her suite.

"Good luck Ela," Lizet whispers. "All will be well, just relax and be yourself."

Ela gives her a quizzical look.

"I saw what happened last night. I have to keep an eye on you whenever you are out of your suite."

Before Ela can express her righteous indignation, Lizet holds her hand up to stop the tirade before it begins.

"It is necessary. Right now, your safety is my priority. Your privacy and your love life come a distant second and third. You could easily be taken from this vessel: Emre is not the only person in the world who owns a helicopter. Small fast boats can be lowered from larger vessels, and a hostile team could be here in no time. I'm going to keep you alive." Lizet fixes her with a firm stare. "You can question anything but never how I do that."

"I'm sorry, you are right," Ela says with a sigh. "This is just all very new to me. I trust you. I promise, when it comes to your professional judgement, I will never question you."

"Thank you, Ela. It is so much better when I am not having to treat my charge as a hostile at the same time I am working against the true hostiles." She pauses, glancing to see if anyone else is in the hallway they're walking down. "And speaking as the friend you mentioned you needed: He is into you, you are into him," she says matter-of-factly. "You are both awkward because of two decades without a word between you and, most importantly, the insane way you were reunited. Give it some time."

Ela blinks at this frank assessment. "Thanks," she says honestly. "I don't agree with you though. He is most certainly not into me. I don't think I'm the model type he would likely normally be with. But there is no reason I can't eat dinner with the man. He is just trying to keep me out of harm's way. Then again, he is the one who placed me there to begin with."

With a shrug of her shoulders, Ela pats Lizet on the arm and heads out to the main deck where the small dining table sits again under the canopy of stars. She is alone on the deck for a few moments, until a crew member with sandy hair brings her a glass of champagne on a silver tray.

"Thank you. Where is Iserate?"

"I am not sure, ma'am, but I am happy to serve you in his stead. I am Henri."

"Thank you. Lovely accent."

"I am from Paris, ma'am. I am the newest crew member. I take Sven's place."

Ela vaguely remembers Lizet telling her during her makeover that a young man had been helicoptered earlier that day. Apparently it was appendicitis.

"Oh, welcome. What—"

Ela stops mid-sentence as Emre approaches.

Chapter Sixteen

"That will be all, Henri. I need a word with Ela. Thank you." The new crew member bows and departs.

"Good evening," Emre says to Ela.

He forces himself to tear his eyes away from the sensuous vision she is. He can't help questioning how Ela could be the embodiment of Aphrodite wearing what, on anyone else, would not even be noticed.

He digs his nails into the palm of his hand to bring him back from his thoughts and focus.

"You look lovely, Ela. Green certainly is your color."

"Thank you," Ela says, taking a sip from her glass. "You did an excellent job filling my closet with everything I could ever need or want."

"I supervised, but had some help."

"Oh, that's good," Ela says, narrowing her eyes. "I'm sure you have plenty of *friends* who helped. You must know lots of … stylish people."

"Sort of. Geoff, along with his many other qualities and skills, has a distant cousin who is a fashion consultant and stylist. She was a great help, but I did make the final selections. I'm glad you like what we selected. We only had a day to get everything arranged."

"Geoff is full of surprises, and lucky for me, excellent contacts."

Ela takes another sip of wine. She seems a little nervous, in a different way from last night. But so is Emre. They could talk about the weather, her clothes, and other neutral topics all night but …

"Ela, we need to talk."

She blanches. "What about?"

"Us."

Ela's eyes go wide.

"No need to look like a deer in the headlights," Emre says, trying to act like his own heart isn't thudding in his chest. "Last night was a disaster. I am sorry for the part I played in it. I was awkward and uncomfortable."

"I'm sorry I made you feel that way. I —"

"Please let me finish."

Ela, looking hurt, nods.

"I don't know you. You don't know me," Emre says bluntly. "When we met, you were a twenty-four-year-old on an adventure and I was a displaced sixteen-year-old finding my footing in a foreign land. You were kind to me. I believed something was happening between us, but because of my youth, you did not. That's fine, the adult me understands it completely."

"So far, you are correct," Ela says, closing her eyes. "Except I did feel something was happening between us, but because of your youth, I would not allow it to manifest."

Emre feels warmth bloom in his chest. "Thank you. The boy I was appreciates your honesty and for validating his feelings. But the man in front of you, that is a different story."

"Yes, I know," Ela says quickly. "I'm not your type, not a glamorous jet-setter, and I certainly don't look like a model or socialite and —"

"Please Ela, let me finish!" Emre snaps, then softens. "I'm sorry, I did not mean that to sound so harsh. I just really need to get this out."

"Okay." Ela lifts her right hand to her tightly pressed lips and turns an imaginary key.

Emre smiles and continues. "How do you know what my type is? You haven't heard from me or about me for decades. That's the point I'm trying to make. We need to get to know each other. We have to know if what we are feeling is just some sort of muscle memory, or some fantasy we have built up over time and distance, or if it is real and has a chance to grow between us."

Ela blinks at him and twists that imaginary key again to unlock her lips. "Did you sneak into my suite and read my journal?"

Emre hadn't realized he was holding his breath, but finally exhales.

"Really, you were thinking the same thing?"

"As they say, great minds do think alike." Ela lets out a breath, too. "Maybe that earlier connection is still there. But I agree completely, we need to take a step back and get to know each other as we are today, not as we were in 1999."

They stand there for a minute and just smile at each other. Then Ela sticks out her right hand and says, "Hello, I'm Jennifer, but I picked up a nickname I am partial to. Please call me Ela."

Emre gives a sweeping bow, then takes her hand and brings it gently and briefly to his lips.

"So pleased to meet you. I am Emre. Would you care to join me for dinner? There seems to be a lovely table set and it would be a shame for it to go to waste."

"Thank you, that would be wonderful."

The next three hours pass in a flash, as they share a five-star meal and stories from their lives. Emre hears about Ela's marriage, her divorce, her business in DC, her academic research. All his reading online over the years is nothing compared to hearing the pride in her voice about the life she's lived.

"Oh my, it's midnight," Ela says, glancing at the watch Lizet must have dressed her with. "It feels like we've only been out here for a few minutes." They stare at each other for a few moments, soft smiles on their lips.

"Emre, your rise through the business world is truly amazing," she says finally. "I am not surprised—I mean, back when I knew Emre the boy, he was quite the entrepreneur at sixteen. It's no wonder that Emre the man leads a huge business empire at the age of thirty-six. Not surprised, but I am impressed."

"Thank you, Ela," Emre says, warming to her praise. "And I am impressed with the successes you have achieved. Your doctorate, your academic and business success …"

"Oh, that reminds me," Ela says, setting down her wine glass, her gaze hardening for the first time all night. "What, if anything, did you have to do with me not being allowed into Turkey?"

Emre's smile fades. "Um, that—"

"You stopped me from experiencing one of the great adventures of my life, with friends I worked hard to make."

Ela's anger and indignation are simmering just below the surface. The last thing Emre wants is for this promising evening to be ruined.

"Please understand," Emre pleads. "Please. At that time I did not know what my uncle's illegal businesses were. I originally thought he was doing some dodgy hedge fund or something. But I knew his partners were thugs. And I didn't know how much of my life they knew about—I just couldn't put you within their reach. The fear of anything happening to you made me act irrationally."

Ela just shakes her head and Emre's heart sinks. He can't believe he upended Ela's life twice, and through no fault of hers.

"Okay, it's water under the bridge," Ela says, sighing. "But it hurt, really hurt, to be excluded. My friends were good about it and played down the whole adventure they had without me. I hate when people pity me, and that's how it felt."

"When this is all over, and we are safe to live our lives," Emre says earnestly, "I will fund an entire dig for you and your friends, anywhere in the world."

Ela begins to laugh, which seems to stem her anger.

"Thank you, but that won't be necessary. I just needed the air cleared if we are to move forward with getting to know each other."

"Ask me anything. I will be honest with you," Emre says, leaning back in his seat. "I want to continue this *adventure* of getting to know the remarkable woman sitting in front of me."

Ela smiles her captivating smile at him. "This was a lovely first date, Emre," she says. "Thank you for the invitation to dine with you. Now, I need to try to catch up on some much-needed sleep."

Emre stands, walks around the table and pulls Ela's chair out. When she stands, he takes a step back to avoid her body brushing against his. *A man must know his limitations,* he thinks to himself. He wants to take things slowly; he wants her to control the speed with which they progress.

Di Toma

He leans forward and lightly brushes his lips against her cheek.

She smiles. It's as though they are reading each other's minds again. Emre watches her return to her suite.

Chapter Seventeen

Lizet is all business now. Gone is the sweet personal assistant and in her place is the well-trained, highly focused ex-Mossad agent.

"Now our hope is that we will never have to execute this plan but we must be prepared for the worst possible case."

Realizing the necessity and seriousness of this briefing session, Ela is focused on Lizet's every word.

"If our people on the ground—informants, undercover agents—alert us to a possible threat against you or Emre, we must react immediately. There will be no time for questions, challenges, or doubts. You must—and I mean must—do exactly what I say without delay or questions. Your life, all our lives, will depend on it."

Eyes wide, Ela nods.

"We will not be unpacking the alert to determine the exact details of the threat. It is like the Buddhist parable of the poisoned arrow. When it's go-time, we are not here to try to figure out where the threat is coming from, why it is coming, or how they discovered our location. We are here to act quickly and minimize any threat to you by removing you to safety. Once you are at the safe house, we will have plenty of time to discover answers and those answers will inform the next phase. If you don't agree to this, I will wash my hands of your security detail right now."

"Yes, yes, you had me at 'all of our lives will depend on it.'" Ela says. "I promise, I will do whatever you say without question."

"Okay then. When I say 'Plan A,' that means that all of what you will be committing to memory over the next couple of days, has been triggered into action. There will be no drills, no rehearsals. It will be real. Do you understand that?"

"Yes. I will see it as a very real event when I hear you say Plan A." Ela nods.

"Right. We have two escape routes, depending if the threat is approaching from air or sea. As you know, the *Kayıp Aşk* is equipped with a helipad and will always have a helicopter ready. What you don't know is that in its depths, the boat has a docking chamber that leads to a DSRV and—"

"Excuse me, what's a DSRV?"

"That stands for deep-submergence rescue vehicle. It's a small submarine that can be used to transport us to another vessel from which we can take a helicopter to a waiting vehicle and head to the safe house."

Lizet pauses. "But now I've gotten ahead of myself. The first step will be to determine if I extract you by air or sea. That will hinge on where the threat is coming from. It will be more efficient to use the helicopter, but if the threat is coming by air, it would be too dangerous. If we have threats coming by air *and* sea, then the DSRV is the plan. So, threat by air, or air and sea, we withdraw via DSRV. Threat via sea only, we withdraw via helicopter. Understood?"

"Yes. Three options, one by air and two by sea. Sounds a bit Paul Revere-ish."

Lizet frowns. "This is not the time or place for jokes. This is deadly serious."

"Sorry, understood."

Two hours later, Lizet has provided details on every aspect of getting Ela off of the *Kayıp Aşk*, but little past that.

"Okay, I fully understand how we get off of the *Kayıp Aşk*. I can even operate the DSRV if necessary and fly the helicopter, maybe. But I have no idea what happens or where we are going once we leave the yacht."

"That's right. You cannot know where you are going for a number of reasons."

"Please share those with me."

"I don't think you want to know. But one of the reasons is that where we are taken has to do with where we are when we realize we have been compromised. As you may or may not know, we have been cruising around the Mediterranean, the Ionian, and the Adriatic seas. We may alter that but, for security reasons, no one knows too far in advance where we will be next. Okay, now let's move on."

Ela holds up a hand. "You said that was one of the reasons I cannot know the rest of the escape plan. I need to know what the other reason is."

"Are you sure?"

"Yes," Ela says. She's an academic. She's never believed information can hurt her. "Positive."

Lizet stares at her for a moment before continuing. "The main reason is, if we are not successful in escaping and you are captured, you will most likely be tortured for information. If you know the location of the safe house, you would be a risk to the safety of anyone who does escape."

Ela's blood runs cold. She didn't know what she was expecting, but it wasn't this. "Tortured," she says, voice trembling.

"I am not cut out for this." Ela can hear her shrill voice still reverberating in her own ears. "I'm a simple anthropologist. I study cultures. I don't know how to deal with torture. I can't even handle a paper cut."

Ela's interest in the briefing is now replaced with panic. Of course Emre had told her on the first day that she was in danger. But she realizes now that the danger she'd been visualizing was out of a PG-13 movie: some menacing by a mysterious villain before her handsome, dark-haired hero swooped in to rescue her.

"This is why I felt it best to leave that information out of the briefing," Lizet says, carefully watching Ela's expression change.

"The chances of you getting captured are near zero. Everyone on this ship has been put here for your safety. We would all give our lives to protect you."

"No!" Ela cries. "I don't want that either!"

Iserate bursts into the office, looking from Lizet to the hysterical Ela.

"What is going on here?" he demands. "I thought we were under attack and no one bothered to tell me."

Lizet walks over to Ela and takes her in her arms, soothing her. Ela is happy to see that she's back in her role as friend. Lizet holds a finger up to Iserate, motioning for him to wait as she sweeps Ela out of the room and returns her to her suite. Lizet gives her a dram of single malt, then tucks her into her bed, tells her to rest.

"I'll be back to check on you shortly."

Ela hiccups into the cloudlike pillows, feeling a little embarrassed. She's lost count of the number of times she's burst into tears over the last few days. Just when she seems to get a handle on the situation, she learns something new that makes her lose her cool. The truth of her kidnapping, her complicated feelings for Emre, and now torture, and the knowledge that these near-strangers would give their lives for her—it's all just too much.

Thirty minutes later, Lizet knocks on the door, bearing a tray of dolmades, hummus, olives and pita.

"I've brought you a snack," Lizet says gently. "You missed lunch and I don't want you to go hungry."

Ela looks up from her journal. "Thank you. And, um, Lizet," she says, fidgeting with the pen in her hands. "I'm sorry for my meltdown. It was just a bit overwhelming. I realize that you are just doing your job and preparing me with facts."

"Wow," Lizet says, looking impressed. "It didn't take you long to come to terms with everything. Thank you for being so understanding."

Ela lifts the journal from her lap. "Journaling has always helped me get my head on straight. I don't know why I haven't done it in so long. But Emre had this beauty waiting for me when I arrived and it was just so enticing, I've started journaling regularly again."

Lizet smiles, and Ela takes an olive from the tray she holds out.

"I must say, Lizet," Ela continues, chewing on the olive. "Your Jekyll-and-Hyde act back there, when you went from torture to tucking me into bed? It was jarring. But I understand that you, Geoff, and Iserate all are highly trained, professional ex-spies, and also have roles to play in order to stay close to your charges and be as unobtrusive as possible."

"Yes, quite right. But trust me, when the shit hits the fan, you will appreciate the ex-spy much more than the lady's maid." Lizet gives Ela a wink. "Now, have a bite to eat, then a shower. I promise you will feel better. Tomorrow, we will be back at it. I have to ensure you are completely briefed by the end of the week."

Before Ela can even voice her next questions, Lizet shakes her head. "And, no, we don't anticipate any trouble anytime soon. I am just a believer of sticking to a plan, and the plan states all briefings are to be completed by the end of the week."

"Okay, okay, what are you now, a mind reader?" Ela teases. "Go, shoo. I will eat and freshen up, ma'am." Ela salutes and smiles to soften her words.

The food and shower do the trick. Ela is feeling more like herself; she even does some yoga. But she still wonders if she is up for dinner with Emre. Her emotions went through the spin cycle today and she doesn't want anything to go awry with him. Their 'first date' went well. She recognized so many positive traits in him that she first saw years ago, but his depth and what he has achieved and experienced is miles deeper than she first noticed.

Lizet taps on the door and pokes her head in.

"Mr. Emre would like to know if you would join him on the deck for dinner this evening? The aft deck this time."

"Um, yes, that's different."

Lizet goes to the dressing room and comes out with a casual pair of denim capris, a lilac polo and a pair of buttery soft leather flats in ivory. "This will do, then."

Chapter Eighteen

When she enters the aft deck that evening, Emre is waiting for her, clad in jeans and a t-shirt. He's laid out a simple picnic on a blanket on the ground, and surrounded the scene with twinkling fairy lights.

"Oh my, Emre," Ela says, eyes wide. "This is beautiful. It's like we're sitting in the clouds right among the stars. And a picnic!" She claps her hands together with childlike glee.

Emre smiles, very pleased with her reaction.

"I remember you said you liked picnics, and I figured that by now you are probably getting tired of fancy dining. I know I am."

"This is exactly what I needed after today."

"Yes," Emre says uncomfortably. "Iserate told me that Lizet was a bit direct with you today. She sometimes forgets that not everyone is hardened to these types of situations. I'm sorry you were so distressed. Is there anything I can do?"

"Well. A picnic under the stars is a good start."

They take their seats on the blanket and Emre pours her a glass of wine. It's nice not having staff hovering at their elbows. Emre feels like they're just normal people on a normal date.

"Sometimes I feel like the more success I have had, the less my life is my own," he says, continuing his thoughts out loud. "That's something I admire about you, Ela, you have made your life your own. You have reinvented yourself—moved where you wanted to go, pursued the career you wanted. You are a self-made woman who isn't afraid of remaking herself when it suits her."

Ela beams. "I appreciate you saying that. Some people would see the same things and label me as flighty, unable to stay focused or commit to a path. It's nice to have someone see my qualities as positive." She plucks a grape from the bunch in a glass bowl. "Not to change the subject, but I have a question for you."

"Yes, ask me anything."

"It's nothing earth shattering. What do you do all day? I never see you until dinner."

Emre laughs. He was expecting some deep inquiry. "I work. I still have to keep my businesses running. I have great people on the ground, but I am still needed for the major decisions and to approve deals, you know, that kind of stuff. The high-level operations that my team is not authorized to do yet." He thinks for a moment. He hasn't said this next part out loud to anyone yet. "I am thinking of stepping back. But I am still a young man and need the day-to-day challenges for my mental health."

"What would you do?" Ela asks with a thoughtful look. "That is, if you stepped back from leadership of your empire?"

"I'm not sure," Emre says truthfully. "Maybe that's why I haven't."

"Okay, let's play a game." Ela claps her hands together. "Let's say that you were forced to step away from all your high-level roles tomorrow because of some world order change, and you had no choice—"

"Okay, what kind of world order change would force me to do that?"

"Oh, geez, just play along. Imagine an alien invasion. Everything else on earth stays the same except you must step down."

Emre rolls his eyes, but happily plays along. He enjoys this playful side of Ela.

"Let me think," he muses, fixing his gaze on the fairy lights. "I would open a small, beautifully appointed bookstore, with walls covered in art from local artists, the finest coffee and pastries served in the morning and aperitivo served in the evening. It would open at nine and close by seven. No more late nights of work." He sneaks a glance at Ela. "Maybe someone who loves reading with me would be there by my side making this little dream a reality. Laughing, loving, and enjoying the small things in life, together. That would be heaven."

"Sounds like it." Ela's eyes are bright, eager to tease him. "I would have never pegged you for a small bookshop owner. How would you find it possible to not grow it into a huge multinational enterprise?"

"Oh, that would be that special someone's job. Keeping me grounded. Maybe they would have to keep extra copies of *Burning*

Daylight around to remind me, or maybe just to bop me over my head with."

They both laugh at that. Emre can tell they both remember sharing that novel so many years ago.

For the next few hours the conversation flows seamlessly. Sharing stories about their friends, their feelings, hopes and fears. It feels so natural, Emre thinks, as though they've been together for years.

Ela yawns. "What time is it?"

"It is one o'clock, Dr. Ela. Way past your bedtime. But an hour with you feels like a minute. I am truly amazed that we can talk for four hours and I still want more."

They're flirting, Emre realizes. Have they been flirting this whole time? It feels so easy with her. Ela breaks his gaze and studies the pattern of the blanket.

Emre ducks his head to find her eyes. "Did I just lose you? Are you nodding off on me?"

"No, just thinking."

"About?"

"How safe I feel with you. No games, no emotional booby traps."

Emre exhales, relieved. "That makes me very happy. I hope you always feel that way." He moves to stand up. "But for now, let's get you off to bed. I don't want to be the reason you won't be able to concentrate tomorrow when Lizet finishes your briefing."

As soon as the words slip out of his mouth, he senses a shift in Ela: Her smile falls and she shuts down a bit. It's as though steel shades, like the ones on the yacht's windows, begin to descend. Emre could kick himself. Why did he bring that up? It was such a perfect evening.

"Hey, did you see that shooting star?" Emre says desperately. "Make a wish, anything, but make it fast!" Emre didn't see a shooting star, but hopes refocusing will help Ela shake off her dark feelings.

"Oh, I didn't. Sorry."

That didn't work. He tries honesty this time.

"This time spent reacquainting ourselves has been some of the happiest of my life." Emre says, softening his gaze. "It's right up there with when I first met a gorgeous American who took pity on a displaced teen."

That brings a smile to her face. "Who would have ever guessed that a chance meeting so long ago would bring our two worlds colliding now."

As Emre walks Ela to the door of her suite, he reaches for her hand. It isn't planned, it just feels natural. She links her pinky finger with his and leaves her hand there until they reach her door.

Emre's heart is pounding all of a sudden. "May I kiss you goodnight?"

"You did last night."

"No, that wasn't a proper kiss. That was a touch on your check." He takes a step back. "But if you do not want me to, or do not feel comfortable, just forget I asked. I don't want—"

Ela places her finger over his lips and whispers, "Hush." Then she leans in, closing the distance between them. And for the first time in two decades, she kisses him. It's chaste, but filled with promise. Emre feels passion bloom between them. Then Ela turns and disappears into her suite.

Chapter Nineteen

During the next three weeks, Ela's days take on some routine. After breakfast, she writes in her journal then works out in the well-equipped gym followed by a swim in the pool. The afternoons consist of self-defense lessons from Lizet, then reading time. She was delighted to find a well-stocked library onboard.

Then the evenings are spent with Emre sharing amazing dinners and hours of conversation. It's usually the only time they spend together, after Emre's workday. One morning, though, Emre joins her for her swim. She almost gasps aloud when he takes off his shirt. His body could be a statue, carved to perfection by the most skilled artisan.

Later that day, after their lesson, Ela decides to confide her feelings to Lizet.

"I am growing so close to Emre," she says, as they walk from the deck towards her suite. "I have never been able to spend every evening with someone and never run out of things to say. And it's not like my days are full of interesting and unique happenings to share. We talk about our feelings, our lives, ideas, everything."

"How does that make you feel?"

"It's so different from anything I've ever known. I'm still processing it. Do you think that whatever I am feeling is real? I mean, would I feel the same in the real world. I'm unsure if my …

romantic feelings would grow the same way if I weren't cosseted away on the *Kayıp Aşk*, if we weren't in fear for our safety." Ela doesn't say Stockholm syndrome, but that's certainly what she's thinking.

Lizet thinks for a moment, studying Ela. "Maybe not. But how do you know you couldn't also grow to feel the same about Emre under different circumstances? Maybe it would just take longer."

"So … um, is that a yes or no?" Ela says with a laugh. She never should have expected a straight answer from Lizet on this particular topic.

"Very funny. If I had all the answers on relationships, I could retire and buy a luxury yacht of my own." Lizet winks.

A few nights later, as Ela steps out of the shower, she glances in the mirror and is taken aback by the muscles she sees taking on a level of definition she never had before. She was always fit, but in a softer way. She thought she would be getting sloppy with all the good food and drink, but the workouts, swimming, and lessons with Lizet have sculpted her muscles while leaving her curves in place.

She runs a hand over the soft skin of her stomach, her breasts, wondering how it would feel to have Emre's hands on her, his exquisite body pressed up against hers.

A tap at the door interrupts her daydreams. "I'm assured everything is ready for you in the galley," Lizet calls out. "Geoff and Iserate promise to keep Emre busy until the appointed time."

"Thanks, you're the best," Ela says, pulling a robe over her shoulders. "I'll be right out and you can do something special with my hair. And how about something sexy to wear?"

After dressing, Ela heads to the galley, grabs the biggest apron she can find to protect her curve-hugging, bias-cut floor-length dress in midnight-blue. The subtle thigh-high slit on the right side tips the dress just over the line into the "sexy" category. Ela told Lizet that she always prefers to allude to sexy rather than flash an inordinate amount of flesh.

Lizet ties the apron around Ela and asks what else she can do.

"Please just make sure the table is set to my specifications," Ela says, clasping her hands together. She hatched this plan a few nights prior, wanting to do something to surprise Emre, like he had for her with the picnic. Preparing a meal for him was the perfect gift.

"I am so excited to be back in a kitchen," she gushes to Lizet. "I mean, the chefs here are incredible, but I love to cook, and I really want tonight to be special and personal. Feeding people is my love language—um, how I nurture people."

"I will totally forget you used the 'L' word."

"Great." Ela says matter-of-factly. "Now shoo, I have to get started."

A few hours later, Ela is waiting on the main deck next to a table laid with a set of china she had picked out herself (because of course, there was more than one set of china on this yacht.) She watches as Geoff leads a blindfolded Emre to her. Geoff gives her a conspiratorial wink and leaves them alone.

As Ela removes Emre's blindfold she smiles as he takes in the setting. She staged an intimate, romantic cocoon for their dinner this evening. He meets her eyes, and she asks him to take a seat.

"I will be your server this evening, sir," she says, with a mischief in her voice. "Oh, and your chef." She can't keep the smile off her face as she heads to the galley, affecting her most sensuous walk. One thing she knows without looking is that his eyes are glued to her retreating form.

She returns a few minutes later with their first course, one of four she lovingly prepared. She wanted to keep his tastes in mind — and keep it light so they can enjoy what she has planned for after dinner. While they feast, they talk about everything and nothing: their childhoods, the grief they share for their parents. All the travels they've each been on, and all the places they still want to see. *Together,* Ela can't help but think. *We could see the world together.*

"Wow," Emre says at last, placing his napkin on his empty plate.

"Is there anything you don't do well? That was the best meal I've ever had."

"Thank you, kind sir. With the meals you have eaten in your life, I doubt that to be true," Ela says, feeling her heart pounding faster in her chest. This was the moment. "But I can tell you it was cooked with … love."

Ela realizes she is holding her breath waiting to see his response. He slowly reaches over and takes her right hand in both of his. Looks deeply in her eyes. They are frozen in this moment, each afraid to break the spell by moving or speaking. Finally, Emre takes a deep breath and squeezes his eyes shut for just a moment, then looks at Ela again.

"I have loved you from the moment I first saw you," Emre says, all in a rush. "Even before you came over and asked about the book I was reading. I dreamt of this moment, never believing it would happen. That you would love me, too." His voice catches in his throat.

A wave of relief washes over her. It's been the same for her, she realizes—for two decades, she's been waiting for them to find each other again. A bone-deep desire she couldn't even admit out loud to herself.

"Shh, no need to speak," Ela whispers. Now that they've said it, she doesn't want to waste any more time. She stands, still holding his hand and leads him inside, down the hall until they've reached the door of her suite. Before she opens the door, she turns, looks deeply into his eyes. Without another word, she brings her face to his, then kisses him slowly, passionately, deeply.

She breaks the kiss when they're both breathless. As she turns to reach for the doorknob, Emre puts his hand over hers. "Are you sure, Ela? This must be about what you desire." He's desperate, almost panting. "Having your love is more than I ever hoped for. I only want to nurture that love—if you're sure this is what you want."

"Oh yes, I am beyond sure," Ela says, dizzy with desire. "Actually, as long as you are in agreement, I don't believe I could wait another day. I want you. I want your heart, your mind, and your body. I want to be yours and I want you to be mine."

With that, Emre snakes his arm around her back and pulls her body tightly against his. He kisses her again and a moan escapes from Ela's mouth into his. Nothing else in the world exists except the two of them and their undeniable need.

Just as they fall through the doorway, Ela hears the sound of pounding footsteps. She doesn't want to, but she opens her eyes, stops Emre's mouth with her hand. They both turn to see Iserate, Geoff, and Lizet running down the corridor.

"Plan A, stat!" Lizet yells.

When Ela begins to ask a question, Lizet snaps, "No words, only actions."

Then it hits Ela—shit just got real.

Chapter Twenty

Ela's panic is loud in her brain, like blaring alarm bells, but she summons Lizet's instructions from her memory. Lizet tosses Ela one bag with a set of all black clothes, and another backpack that Lizet told her she's had assembled for her since Ela arrived on the *Kayıp Aşk*. Ela turns back to look at Emre as Lizet pulls her toward the helipad.

Emre's eyes haven't left her face, and stay locked on her even as Iserate and Geoff grab Emre and bundle him off in the opposite direction, practically dragging him backwards. She has a thousand things she wants to say in this moment. *Don't go. Hold me. I love you.* But Ela watches as he's led down the hall, until he disappears around the corner.

Once they are on the helicopter, Lizet gestures for Ela to put on the headphones so they can communicate above the roar of the blades. Lizet is in the pilot seat and Ela wonders why Geoff isn't piloting.

"Where is Geoff? Iserate? And Emre? Shouldn't they be here by now? Aren't we ready to take off?"

Lizet reaches across and holds Ela in place with her right arm. "They will not be coming with us," Lizet says, not meeting Ela's eyes. The helicopter's blades begin to whir. "It is important that you are transported separately. I'm sorry I couldn't tell you."

Ela's heart sinks into her stomach. Trembling, she tries to free herself of her safety restraints and Lizet's ironhard grasp, to no avail. All she can do is silently sob as the *Kayıp Aşk* gets smaller and smaller in the distance, until she can't see its lights on the water's inky surface any longer.

When the helicopter touches down after about forty-five minutes, Ela finds that they are in a field among rolling hills that appear to have rows upon rows of grape vines. They exit the helicopter and jog out of the field to a dirt road, the moon illuminating their way. After walking a few miles, Ela notices a blue van parked on the side of the road with a couple enjoying a picnic nearby. Ela frowns. An early dawn picnic?

As they approach, Lizet begins whistling a tune that isn't familiar to Ela. The woman on the picnic blanket whistles what appears to be the next part of the tune. Then the man does the same. The couple gathers up their picnic and loads the car just as Lizet and Ela reach them.

Lizet slaps the woman on the back and says something in Hebrew that Ela doesn't understand. The man joins them and they speak for a few minutes before the man runs off down the road from the direction they just walked.

Lizet turns to Ela and gestures to the other woman. "This is Sara, she will be with us going forward. She knows where the safe house is and will stay with us since there is need for additional security now."

Ela exchanges a nod with Sara. " "Who was that man and where is he going?" she asks.

"That was Frank," Lizet says. "He is going back to move the helicopter to a third location. We don't want anyone who may be tracking it to find us." Lizet's eyes are steely, she's all business. "Get in the van, Sara will drive."

No one is attempting small talk, and Ela remembers that she cannot ask any questions until they are safely at their destination. Curled up in the backseat, she keeps her eyes on the horizon, but all she can see is her last moments with Emre in her head. He loves her. And what's more, she knows she loves him. Ela never thought that love would bring her such a feeling of peace. There's something right about them loving each other, after all these years. And now, she doesn't know when she will see him again. Ela knows she is safe in Lizet's care, but she won't feel completely secure until she's in Emre's arms again.

About an hour later, after passing only a few cars this early in the morning, the van turns from the paved road onto a dirt path. At the end of the path sits a classic Tuscan villa. It looks to Ela like something out of a movie, with stone walls, terracotta roof tiles, and green shutters.

So they're in Italy, Ela realizes. Under any other circumstances, these accommodations would feel luxurious. As they pull up to the villa, Lizet opens her door and barks at Ela to stay in the car, jolting her from her thoughts. She's not on some tour of the wine region, she is running from possible torture and death.

Lizet returns twenty minutes later and ushers Ela and Sara inside. "I've checked out the entire place, initiated all the surveillance and security systems," she says, running a hand through her hair. She looks as exhausted as Ela feels.

Lizet assigns them rooms, pointing Ela to a suite located through the door adjacent to Lizet's door. No one will be able to get to her without getting past Lizet first. Ela smiles ruefully to herself as she notes that the interior of this home is elegantly appointed in Emre's design style. Did he pick out these furnishings himself? She'll have to ask him when she sees him again, she forces herself to think.

"You need to rest, Ela," Lizet says softly. "I will answer all your questions after you have slept and we've had something to eat. I need you strong and nourished."

Sara, stationed in the hallway outside Lizet's room, looks up from the bag from which she is removing a number of weapons. "Lizet, you've been up as long as Ela has. I'll take the first watch." It's more than Ela's heard her say all morning. Lizet nods. "See you in five hours. Come on, Ela. I will be right outside your door."

After a heavy sleep, Ela stirs when she hears Lizet on the other side of her door. She crosses the room and taps on the door gently. There's a whirring sound as Lizet unlocks it.

"I would like to be able to ask some questions now," Ela tells her.

Lizet opens the door to let Ela exit. "Just sit quietly for the first ten minutes or so. Sara will have to brief me on her shift."

"Understood." Ela can't believe how compliant she is being. It's amazing how being confronted with your own mortality can get you to start being polite. She waits while Sara and Lizet murmur outside in the hall. Sara crosses in front of the doorway to get to her room to rest. She stops when she sees Ela watching her.

Sara just looks at Ela and shakes her head. "You must be very important to someone. I haven't seen this level of security in place for heads of state."

Ela's eyes brim with tears as she slowly nods.

"That's not open for discussion, Sara," Lizet says, giving her a hard look. Without another word, Sara turns down the hall. Lizet stands in the door with her hands on her hips. "Now Ela, you said you had some questions."

"Yes." she says, letting it all tumble out. "First of all, why isn't Emre here? And how long will we be here? And, what happened? I mean why are we even here?"

"Emre will be here soon. I am expecting them at any moment." Lizet averts her eyes. "He is the one who insisted that you be extracted separately. He believed he would be the main target, and he didn't want to put you in further danger."

Ela nods, tucking that detail away to unpack later.

"I'm not sure how long we will be here. But we are not to be in any one location for more than a month, so we'll move before then." Lizet sighs before continuing. "And as for what happened on the *Kayıp Aşk*, I don't have all the details. We received an encrypted message via the emergency satphone that just said our location had been breached. We sprang into action and implemented Plan A without asking questions. So I don't know much more than you. Although, sometime in the next twenty-four hours, I should receive more details."

But Emre doesn't show up that first day, nor the next. On day three there's still no sign of him, Geoff, or Iserate. Even though Lizet tells Ela morning and night not to panic, Ela can see the worry in her eyes.

In the wee hours of the morning, Ela is awakened by a steady beeping outside her door, almost like an alarm. She gets out of bed and uses the biometric lock, and opens the door to find Lizet and Sara arming themselves.

"What's going on?"

"Ela, get back in your room," Lizet says brusquely. She looks up to level Ela with a grave stare. "If anyone but me comes to let you out, use the escape tunnel under the armoire like I showed you."

"Shit, is someone here? Are we in danger?"

"We will find out. When we know we are in the clear, we will come and get you. *Go.*"

With one last grateful glance at Lizet, Ela locks herself in her room. She crosses to the tall armoire against the opposite wall and shoves her shoulder into it. The armoire slides a few feet to the right, revealing a stone larger than the other ones in the floor. Ela places her hand against it as Lizet showed her. It slides open, exposing a ladder down into a subterranean tunnel. She stares into it, breathing heavily.

What seems like an eternity later but in reality is probably only fifteen minutes, Ela hears heavy footfalls heading towards her door. Ela can feel herself shaking—she pictures herself opening the door to some strangers, Lizet and Sara dead on the ground behind them. What if she's tortured to give up Emre? At least she doesn't know where he is. At least she won't be able to betray him before she dies.

Ela knows she can't withstand being tortured. Even just the thought of it during her briefing made her totally lose it. The footsteps get closer—her heart is beating so loudly but they sound too heavy to be either Sara or Lizet's footfalls. Could someone else get in this room?

Ela steadies herself, and makes a snap decision. She's tired of being complacent and following all commands to the letter without the chance to question. She can't wait for Emre, her handsome hero, to save her anymore. Ela lowers her body down the ladder, into the tunnel. Once her head is below the surface, the stone door slides shut above her and motion-sensor lights flicker on to illuminate her descent.

Ela follows the ladder until it reaches the concrete floor below, the tunnel now turning horizontally before her. Her only option is to go right and follow that tunnel until she can go no farther. Lizet was going to give her a full briefing on escape routes tomorrow. So much for timing. But Ela tells herself she is an intelligent, educated woman and should be able to find her way out. The lights behind her dim then turn off after she passes, so she keeps moving forward.

After an hour of walking through this tunnel, Ela gets to another dead end. In the stone wall before her, she spies a flat stone curiously similar to the one that was under the armoire in her room. Ela hesitates, and places her hand tentatively on it. A metal plate spirals open and Ela finds herself outside, emerging from a secret door embedded in a rock face. It is still dark outside but the sky is that steely gray that comes just before sunrise. Panting, heart pounding, she spins around, trying to orient herself.

It appears she is deep in what seems to be endless rows of grape vines. The adrenaline that was surging through her in the safe house has begun to wane and she is overcome with exhaustion. Ela sets off down one of the rows. *Just one foot in front of the other, just one more foot in front of the other,* she tells herself. Not too far in the distance, out past the end of the grapevines, she sees a small outbuilding. She drags herself to it and peeks inside. It is empty except for some tools on a workbench. She slips in and sinks to the floor. She will just rest for a few minutes. Just rest her eyes and still her pounding heart.

Chapter Twenty-One

Emre is panting, charging down the hallway of the safe house he set up ages ago in a Tuscan villa. They landed moments ago but he had to see her before he debriefed with Lizet. Just a few more steps and he'll be with Ela. He's reaching for the electronic keypad next to the door when a strong pair of arms grabs his, pinning him back. He's dragged backward down the hallway, away from the door to Ela's room.

Sara kicks open the door to his office and deposits him on the floor inside. He blinks to find Lizet, Iserate and Geoff seated around the conference table.

"He was about to go charging into Ela's room," Sara says, out of breath. "We need to debrief before she joins us."

Emre looks at Lizet, then Iserate, and finally Geoff for support. He wants to go to Ela now. He wants her to know they are all safe and that he loves her and will always protect her.

"Besides," Sara says when Emre opens his mouth to argue. "Lizet should break it to her gently that you made it here safely first. We need to have answers for her before she joins us, or she may get hysterical again."

Emre furrows his brow. Hysterical?

The others agree to begin debriefing.

"So guys, what went wrong?" Lizet asks. "Ela and I made it here exactly to plan. You should have arrived not long after we did."

Iserate stands and begins to explain. "We executed the first phase of the plan without issue. Once the DSRV docked with the receiving vessel, we pretty much thought we were home free. The trouble started after we reached land and transferred to the vehicle.

"After about twenty minutes, when we are away from the dock and town, the man in the passenger seat turns, holding a very large gun pointed right at us."

Lizet mutters "Shit" under her breath.

"They lined us up on the roadside and stripped us of all our weapons. I sensed an execution coming. If our intelligence was correct, they only needed Emre alive; Geoff and I were expendable. I'm thinking that this is it, the end of the road. But then, what do I see from the corner of my eye? Emre slowly raising his hands like he is surrendering. But no—he flicks a lighter in his hands and, well, basically torched the driver and the guy pointing the gun."

Emre speaks up as he takes a seat at the table. "When I ran back to grab Ela's journal from the *Kayıp Aşk* before we fled, I also ran to my rooms and grabbed a couple of 007-type gadgets I got from Geoff and his MI6 mate."

Lizet beams, impressed with her boss. "Emre, excellent work! I would hate to think what could have happened if you hadn't decided to play James Bond. But how did you guys get so beat up?"

Geoff rolls his eyes and says, "Where those now-crispy guys failed, a wild boar almost succeeded. We were racing down the road in that damn van when this huge wild boar runs out in front of us. Iserate swerves to miss it, hits a big rock, the van rolls down an embankment and, well, we got a bit beat up. At least all the noise scared off the wild boar, so we didn't have to contend with him.

"We knew it wouldn't be long before whoever sent the torched guys realized something was amiss. So we used all the tactics necessary to ensure no one could follow us here and walked the whole way, avoiding established roadways. That's why it took us so long to get here. We knew you would be worried but could not risk contacting you."

Lizet drums her fingers on the conference table. "But we still don't know who initiated the original breach on the *Kayıp Aşk*, or how Plan A was compromised."

"I'll take this one," Iserate says grimly. "Remember the crew member who had appendicitis?"

Lizet looks stricken. "I always thought he was a good kid."

"No, not him. His replacement, Henri. He wasn't actually Henri. It turns out the real Henri was murdered and this operative was swapped in. He was only there to collect information. It looks like he told his bosses that grabbing us on the *Kayıp Aşk* would be a losing proposition. We were too well guarded and one man could not take on all of us."

Lizet fills in the gaps. "So the intelligence we received about the planned attack on the *Kayıp Aşk* was just a ruse to dislodge us from our citadel at sea. Smart, I'll give them that. But how did they know how to intercept you on the road?"

Sara, who's been fiddling with her belt while the rest of them talked, suddenly stands to her full height. Before anyone can react, Sara removes her gun from her waistband and points it at Emre's head. "I assume that any second now you would figure out I was the only other person who knew the details of the plan."

The barrel of the gun is cold against the side of Emre's head. His eyes dart to the rest of his team. Lizet is shaking with shock and rage, eyes wide. "But why? Why betray us?"

Emre can't see her clearly from his position completely at her mercy, but senses Sara shrug at this. "I'm a gun for hire. The other guys offered more. Now that Emre has shown up, I have everything I need. But enough about me. Let's reunite him with his little bit of crumpet. You are worth more as a complete set, you know."

Sara swiftly switches her aim to Lizet and cocks the gun against her temple, then warns them all that any sudden movement will result in Lizet's brains being splattered on the wall. She hands Lizet zip ties and instructs her to immobilize Geoff and Iserate's hands and feet, and bind Emre's wrists behind his back. After they are secured, she hauls Emre to his feet and marches him and Lizet out of the conference room. "Once we have your girl, we're leaving," she mutters to Emre. "The van's parked out back."

When they arrive at Ela's door, Sara prods Lizet and instructs her to open the lock.

With his heart in his throat, Emre watches Lizet raise her hand for the biometric reader. But he sees that she places it almost imperceptibly off-center, as though to distort her handprint. "Oh damn. I think when the alarm went off it shut off the biometric reader," she mutters.

Sara angrily elbows Lizet aside, removing the gun from her head to point it at the lock. In one swift motion, Lizet grabs the other woman's left shoulder with her right hand and sweeps her feet out from under her. As Sara hits the floor, before Emre can process what he's seeing, Lizet grabs her gun and shoots her in the stomach.

Sara stares up at them in shock as the red stain on her shirt front begins rapidly spreading. Lizet ignores her and opens Ela's room—her hand is shaking, Emre notices. He pushes past her to get inside, imagining Ela shocked by the sound of the gunfire. Inside, the bed is rumpled from where Ela must have been sleeping, and the armoire is slightly to the right of its usual position. But there is no sign of her.

While Emre stands frozen in the doorframe, Lizet remains focused. Striding over Sara's bloody body, stopping just long enough to take the knife off her belt, Lizet runs down the hall to free

Geoff and Iserate. Emre can hear her telling them that Ela is gone. He truly loves these people, they have always been loyal to him. But in this moment, he wants to blame them for not keeping his Ela safe. He sees genuine rage in Lizet's eyes when she returns with the others. She aims her gaze down at Sara, who is still still alive, barely.

Lizet places her booted foot lightly on Sara's stomach. "Now listen here you piece of shit. You are going to die. It can be peaceful and painless or I can make every last moment a living hell." She presses down with her boot and Sara cries out.

"Okay, okay, what do you want to know?" Sara rasps out.

"Who are you working for?" Lizet barks.

Sara starts to lose consciousness and Lizet slaps her. "I don't know who I'm working for," Sara slurs. "I'm just supposed to find Emre and Ela, both alive so …"

Lizet waits a moment, then feels for a pulse. "She's dead," Lizet spits out. She turns to the men, suddenly all business. "I'll go through her pockets, you guys go to her room and we'll gather whatever we can to see if she left any information that may be useful to us. Then get armed and we will head out to find Ela."

Emre opens his mouth to protest, to insist that they leave immediately to find Ela. He stops when Geoff places a hand on his shoulder.

"Ten minutes now can save us hours or even days in our search," Geoff says firmly. "I will arrange transport for us."

When they regroup, Iserate reports that Sara's room is clear. Lizet shows the trio what she has found: a small notepad, pen, and what appears to be some sort of listening device.

Geoff puts his finger to his lips and motions for them to not speak. "Lizet, is there anything to eat here? We've been on the road for days." As he talks, he grabs the notepad and pen and starts to scribble. He passes the note to the others: *If the other end of that device is in range, they know our every move. Our transport will be here in five.*

They silently acknowledge and follow Geoff's hand signals. "Let's make something to eat," he says loudly. "We can think better on a full stomach." Then they quietly make their way to a back entrance.

As soon as they emerge outside the villa's walls, they run to the cover of nearby pear trees.

"Geoff, are they really going to believe we are going to cook now?"

"Maybe, Emre, just maybe it can buy us a couple of minutes."

They hear the whirl of helicopter blades and Iserate says, "Let's hope this is ours and not theirs."

As it touches down and the pilot inside waves to them, Geoff smiles in relief and leads the others to the relative safety of the passenger seats. A moment after they are in the air, a huge explosion rocks the helicopter. As the pilot steadies them, they see the rubble that was the villa.

Emre looks at Geoff and says, "I guess those couple of minutes did help."

Geoff stares at the ruins of the villa. "I'm not so sure. Why wouldn't they have detonated those earlier? I think they knew we were leaving, and detonated those just to let us know they mean business."

Lizet nods. "Sara was there for a few days before we arrived. She must have planted the explosives then. She said she was 'readying the villa for us.'" She laughs bitterly. "Now we know what that means. But I agree, they want us to tread carefully. If they wanted to kill us, Sara and her companion could have done it on the road when we rendezvoused with them."

Geoff turns to his boss. "Emre, I'm afraid whoever is behind this is vindictive. It appears they want you and Ela alive. Unfortunately, that usually means they want to inflict as much pain on you as possible."

Emre is silent. He looks back up at Geoff, and knows his old friend can see the fear in his eyes, fear for Ela. Geoff presses a button on his headset and speaks to the pilot then taps another button to speak to his associates as the pilot passes a laptop to him.

"The helicopter is equipped with thermographic cameras," Geoff says. "He will sweep the area and we can watch in real time what the devices pick up."

Geoff powers up the laptop and they all stare transfixed at the screen. Nothing of significance shows up for a while. Emre doesn't blink once. Then the pilot banks far left.

"There!" Emre points.

It's an orange blob, the heat image of a person who could be Ela. Emre cranes his neck toward the windows, but can see nothing but trees below. Just as Geoff asks the pilot to land near the heat image, they hear bullets smashing into the body of their helicopter. The pilot ascends to avoid serious damage.

On the screen, they all watch in horror as thermal images of at least a dozen or more people converge where the one figure was.

Geoff bellows to the pilot, "What are you doing? Follow them, man!"

"Sir, we were hit by their artillery and are rapidly losing fuel," the pilot says gruffly. "We will crash if I don't land. I have called for another helicopter to meet us but, I'm sorry to say, by the time it arrives, your target could be anywhere."

Chapter Twenty-Two

Ela comes out of what feels like a drug-induced sleep and is met with the headache from hell. When she gingerly explores her head, her fingers find a very tender lump and something that feels like dried blood. Now she remembers: waking up in the shed to gunfire, camouflage-clad people rushing in, being struck in the head by something hard.

She begins to take in her surroundings. She is in a clean, nondescript room. There is a bed, a small table, and one chair. The interior doorway is open to show a clean, white-tiled bathroom. She cautiously enters it and sees soaps, shampoo, and clean towels.

When she tries the door on the other side of the bedroom, it is locked. She hears a voice from the other side giving some command in a language she doesn't totally understand; she can only pick up a few words. It's Turkish. Between the little she learned a lifetime ago when she was preparing for the trip she never made, and the words Emre was teaching her during their time on *Kayıp Aşk*, she thinks he has told someone she was awake. Then she hears a set of heavy footsteps heading away from the door.

She begins to panic; her breathing is so shallow and fast she is afraid she will pass out. She forces herself to take long, deep breaths. She counts to eight on her inhale, holds it for a count of four, then counts to ten on the exhale. After a few rounds of mindful breathing, she feels herself begin to calm down.

A few minutes later, the footsteps return and she hears another muffled exchange. Then, in accented English, the voice on the other side of the door tells her to step away from the door. She sees a shadow in the crack under the door. She does as instructed and backs up. As the door slowly opens, she sees a young man pointing a handgun at her.

She doesn't want to appear frightened, so she forces out a shaky laugh. "Is that really necessary?" she says with feigned nonchalance. "You have at least seven inches and, I'd guess, sixty pounds on me. Oh yes—for you that would be about eighteen centimeters and twenty-seven kilos. But if it makes you feel happy, by all means have your little gun pointed at me. But my guess is that if it somehow accidently went off and you killed me, your boss wouldn't be very happy with you."

At first, the young man is taken aback. Then he smiles and lowers his weapon with a sigh. "Ma'am, please come this way," he finally says.

"I'm Ela. And you would be?"

"I am Yigit."

He follows closely behind as he directs Ela down a maze of corridors. They stop before a large wooden door. He clears his throat then raps on it. A gruff voice responds and Yigit opens the door for Ela to enter.

In a cavernous room filled with dark, heavy wooden furniture and very little natural light, Ela sees an unattractive, heavyset man in a poorly fitting suit sitting behind a massive desk. He gestures for her to approach.

"So this is the famous Ela," he growls out. "You have been quite the mystery. We didn't even know you existed until your boyfriend betrayed us. I am his ex-business partner, Mazhar. Actually, thanks to him, I am the only member of our enterprise still free."

Ela just silently stares at him. His heavily accented English is difficult to follow but she gets the gist of it.

"You are beautiful, I suppose," he continues, more to himself than to her. "I thought the boy only dated models and actresses. You are not famous and certainly not built like those skinny models. What is it that you have that so intrigues young Emre?"

At the sound of Emre's name on this monster's meaty lips, Ela cannot help but gasp. Mazhar grins.

"Oh, so you are not made of ice. You hear his name and it melts you. That is good to know."

Ela silently berates herself. She can give nothing away. She only wants to protect Emre.

Another man enters the room and hands her a newspaper, guiding her roughly to stand next to Mazhar. Once she is by his side, Mazhar grabs her upper arm and digs his fingers into it. She recoils in disgust at the feel of his hand on her. The guard instructs her to hold the paper, front page facing outward toward the cell phone he has pointed at them. Yigit points his gun at her to ensure her compliance.

Mazhar tells her that Yigit will escort her back to her room. "Make yourself presentable. You will have dinner with my mistress, Feya. She speaks Turkish, French, and her native Russian but is now learning English. You will provide conversation."

Ela is dumbstruck. "You bashed me in the head and kidnapped me, all so I can help your mistress improve her English? You have got to be kidding me."

A sardonic smile spreads across Mazhar's face, making it seem, if possible, even more menacing. "No, my dear. You are bait. The bait that will bring that rat to me so I may slowly torture the life out of him. That is, after making him watch me do the same to you." He seems to enjoy the look of horror dawning on her face. "You helping my mistress improve her English is just a side benefit. Now go!"

After washing the blood out of her hair, Ela stands in the shower hoping the hot water will soothe the horrible ache she feels in her heart. She cannot allow that man to get his hands on Emre, not because of her. How will he even find her? If she's in Mazhar's domain, they most likely took her somewhere in Turkey. She must stay calm so she can think. She will play the game: Talk to Feya, keep her head down, and try to plan an escape. Seeing what a disgusting man Mazhar is, she anticipates even worse from Feya.

An hour later, Ela is led to a nicely appointed dining room. Obviously, this room has felt a woman's touch. Gone are the heavy woods, dark fabrics, and depressing lack of natural light. In it sits a white-washed oak dining table with chairs upholstered in a faded chintz fabric, a hutch displaying Villeroy & Boch French Garden dinnerware, and walls painted the slightest hint of pale yellow. Fresh flowers adorn crystal vases. Opposite the door, a wall of French doors leads out to a charming patio and garden beyond. This is certainly Feya's domain—just the thought of Mazhar in this room makes Ela chuckle.

A beautiful woman who must be Feya enters the room from the French doors carrying a basket of fresh flowers. She sets it down and strides across the room on long, slender legs and hugs Ela.

"Thank God, a woman for talk to."

"Hello, I'm Ela," Ela says stiffly. She takes a step back, not comfortable with this sudden affection from one of her captors.

"Oh, me am sorry," Feya says slowly. She sounds like she's concentrating on each word carefully. She must be very new to learning English. "I am Feya. Pleased to know you, Ela. Have food with me now. I am happy to speak English with you. Mazhar wants me better English and have you work for him to happen."

Ela stares. This beautiful young woman with full, slightly pouty lips, big blue eyes framed with lush lashes, and brows two shades darker than her blond hair is too exquisite to be with Mazhar. This can't be her choice, Ela thinks as she follows Feya onto the patio. There's more to this story.

Chapter Twenty-Three

From that moment, Ela spends nearly all of her time with Feya, just practicing having conversations. After two weeks, Ela is amazed at how proficient, almost fluent, Feya's English has become. Feya was already multilingual, which always makes learning a new language fairly easy. She had already had the vocabulary down, she just needed to adopt the general cadence, sentence structure, and common usage. But Ela notices that Feya only speaks fluently when they are outside. She falls back into her broken English when they are inside or whenever Mazhar or any of his men are around.

"Ela, come here, please. I want to share with you something." Feya pats the spot next to her on the bench up against the fountain. They are enjoying the garden, as it is the only place Ela can be outside.

"Share something with you. That flows better." Ela hardly ever has to make these minor corrections with her anymore. "You speak English so well. I don't think you need me anymore."

"No!"

Ela turns to Feya, seeing her eyes wide, real panic behind them.

"I'm sorry, are you alright?"

"Yes," Feya begins to sob. "These have been my happiest weeks. I even pretend my English has not improved when I am around Mazhar, just so I can continue to spend my days with you. Please don't let him know I can now speak English good. Don't go, don't leave me."

"Feya, I can't go. I am a prisoner here," she says, pleading with Feya. "Please don't tell Mazhar I told you."

Feya looks up, tears in her eyes. "You're not a teacher?"

Feya starts to shake, then cry. Ela has grown to feel almost motherly towards her in these two weeks, and takes her in her arms to soothe her.

"What happened, Feya?" she asks gently. "Why are you here? You are too kind to choose to be with a man like Mazhar."

Eventually, Feya calms enough to tell Ela her sad story.

From what Ela grasps between hiccups and sobs, Feya's father was a Russian businessman. He wasn't very good at business, nor at being a husband and father. Feya was only a baby when her mother left him. Sadly, she left Feya behind. When Feya was sixteen years old, her father wanted to do business in Turkey. He struck up a business arrangement with Mazhar, which left him in serious debt. About six months later, Mazhar called in the debt, knowing there was no way Feya's father could come up with the money. So Mazhar made a deal with him: He would forgive all of his debts, plus give him enough money to return to Russia and start over. All he had to do was give Mazhar the teenage Feya. She has been Mahzar's captive for three years.

"He bought this house for me to live in so his wife, and basically everyone else, would never find out about me," Feya says between sniffles. "Of course, he makes it all so ugly I didn't like it. He is disgusting. Last year he let me change, um, redecorate, a few rooms so I would be happy. I am still not happy but at least I have a few rooms that make a more attractive cage for me." Ela remembers the charming dining room where she first met Feya.

"He often tells me many women are happy with this arrangement. He forgets, I did not choose this. I was basically sold like a slave to him."

Ela's heart breaks as Feya stops talking and looks at her with her big blue eyes.

"Feya," she says slowly. "Mazhad is using me as bait to lure the man I love here so he can torture and kill him. Well, me first then him."

Another tear falls down Feya's cheek. "Oh Ela, I am sorry. Here I was thinking I was the only prisoner here. You are right, he would not let anyone know about me if he was planning on letting them live."

Ela nods. "I think we may be able to help each other. But for now, we can only discuss this outside while sitting on this bench that is up against the fountain."

"Why is that?"

"I learned a thing or two from my spy friends. Sitting near running water distorts voices so anyone listening to you on eavesdropping equipment can't understand what you are saying. We will need to—" Ela stops speaking as she hears Mazhar enter the dining room.

"Oh, there you are," he calls to Feya from inside. "I need you to come in and help me pick out a gift for my wife's birthday."

Feya nods and goes inside. Mazhar turns to Ela.

"You can go back to your room now," he says, looking bored. "I think you should rest."

Ela knows that means she will be locked in her suite until it is time for her to dine with Feya tonight.

As Ela enters the dining room that evening, Feya clasps Ela's hands in hers, slipping a piece of paper into them. "I hope you had good rest. I find gift for Mrs. Mazhar. She will like."

Ela surreptitiously tucks the piece of paper into her pocket and they eat while Feya purposely butchers the English language and Ela provides corrections.

Back in her room that night, Ela reads Feya's note. It confirms what Ela suspected: Feya's rooms are bugged. Moving forward, the utmost caution must be taken. But Ela can't help feeling the first stirrings of hope she has had since arriving here two weeks ago.

Two weeks. That's plenty of time for Emre's team to find out about Mazhar's secret home where he keeps his prisoner and mistress tucked away. According to Feya, no one knows about this place, but Mazhar must have leaked the whereabouts as part of the trap he is setting for Emre.

The last thing she wants is for Emre to find her. Her time to escape is running out. But now she may stand a chance. Feya has been allowed to wander around the house unaccompanied and to spend as much time as she likes in the courtyards and gardens. After three years, she must have a good lay of the land.

Ela can barely sleep that night for all the possible escape plans running through her head. Then, thoughts of Emre creep in. She has tried not to think of him; it is just too painful. They grew so close. Starting from scratch, reintroducing themselves as adults. They "dated" and let their feelings grow organically. And grow, did they. She loves him. And now, here she sits, wishing Emre doesn't find her. If he were to be captured because of her, she would never forgive herself. And where does she go after this? Back to the *Kayıp Aşk*? Back in hiding? She loves him, it's true. But he has irrevocably changed her life. She'll never be the woman she was before all this.

The next morning, Ela is awakened by Yigit pounding on the door. "Get up. Feya says you are to meet her in the kitchen. I will escort you. Be ready in five minutes."

Feya is waiting, aproned up in the massive kitchen off her dining room. Ela has never been in this room—they are always served meals that the resident cooks make.

Feya starts speaking in Turkish to Yigit, sounding playful and seductive at the same time. After a few apparent refusals, he smiles and leaves the women alone.

"What did you say to him?"

She winks. "I told him he can leave us and go call his girlfriend." Feya mimics her suggestive tone from earlier. "'I'm sure she is missing you. You never get a chance to talk to her in the morning. You know, she will be all snuggly, probably naked, under the sheets and is thinking of you right now.'" She rolls her eyes. "Men are so predictable. Sex has been used against me, so I figure, why not wield it against men. Play to their ego and lust."

"You are wise beyond your years, Feya. Why was he planning on staying here? We are usually left alone."

She smiles a wicked smile and holds up a large chopping knife. "Because there are sharp tools in the kitchen."

"How did you get them to agree to let us in here?"

"Ego. And necessity. Mazhar said we could not sit out in the garden near the fountain. He's so obvious; he should have just said 'we couldn't eavesdrop on you out there.' So, I thought, where else can we have running water and other noises?" She points to the sink, holding a huge stock pot being filled. "Then I said all we were talking about was cooking and that you said you are an amazing cook and that I demanded you teach me so I could cook for Mazhar. I went on and on that I wanted to cook for him and serve him so we could have some time just for us, without all of the staff around. I laid it on pretty thick. If he wasn't so dumb and egotistical, he would have seen right through me."

Feya hands Ela an apron. "So we can talk here and also, try to take weapons. Did I do good?"

"Oh, I would say better than good."

Feya beams.

On their third day of "cooking lessons," Feya bounds into the room, almost unable to contain her excitement. She turns on every faucet then grabs Ela by her shoulders, leans her forehead against hers and whispers, "Mazhar will be gone for a whole four days! It is for his wife's birthday celebration. He will be taking her and their children to Monte Carlo on his private jet. He hates that kind of thing, but it is her birthday."

Feya starts twirling them around laughing. It's the first time Ela has seen her truly happy. Then Feya abruptly gets very serious. "There will only be three guards left here. One of the ones here will be Yigit, so that means there will be only two guards we need to worry about."

"And why do we not have to worry about Yigit?"

"Well that girlfriend of his broke his heart. When he called her that first morning we were in here, she wasn't alone. I 'comforted' him, of course. Now he is like a puppy dog. He hates Mazhar because Mazhar has always treated him like shit. Mazhar treats just about everyone like shit. Yigit said I didn't deserve to be with that brute. He said he was too afraid to let me know that he cared for me."

"How do you feel about him?"

"Ela, I told you. I have been used for sex, so I will use sex to get what I need. And right now, I need to save our lives." Feya shrugs. "In another world, I could care for Yigit, but in this world, whether willingly or not, he is working for my captor. He is as guilty as Mazhar. I use him, I do not care."

Ela hugs this young woman who has endured hell on earth. She has been hardened by horrible forces, but it has resulted in a suit of armor and sword that she has learned how to wield for her own benefit.

"You are so strong and brave. I admire you. I think it's time to plan." Ela breathes out a sigh of relief. "At least we don't have to try to poison them all. I would hate to weaponize food; I love it too much!"

A few days later, Mazhar addresses Feya, Ela, Yigit, and the other two men who will be left behind to guard Ela and Feya. He speaks in his heavily accented English for Ela's benefit.

"I will expect you two girls to behave. Stick to the schedule. Ela, you will only have one hour a day out of your room. You must spend that hour however Feya wants." He turns to his mistress. "Feya, my dear. These days will be hard for you without me," He chuckles and winks at the other men. "But your big bull will be back to make you happy soon."

All Ela can do is swallow hard to keep from throwing up or saying something cutting. But Feya deserves an Oscar for her performance.

"How will I go four whole days without you?" she pouts. "I will miss you. My bed will be cold and lonely."

Somehow, she is even able to make her eyes misty, which seals the deal for Mazhar. He nods appreciatively and struts past his men, giving them a haughty look.

And with that, the little meeting is adjourned. Yigit hangs back and asks what the women want to do with their hour together.

"I want us to sit in the garden and plan the perfect menu for when Mazhar returns. Ela will advise me and teach me how to prepare the meal."

Feya has taken to cooking like an old pro. She has a natural feel for flavors and textures, and the meals she has prepared for

Mazhar have been so good that he supports the cooking lessons. As predicted, his belief that Feya wants to cook for him feeds his massive ego.

Ela and Feya sit next to the garden's fountain.

"Feya, isn't Yigit going to know you are putting on an act?" Ela says, pulling out a cookbook to look busy. "He knows you don't love Mazhar."

"Yigit believes I must playact so me and him can one day be together."

"He and I. Subjective pronouns. Sorry, force of habit."

"No, I want you to correct me. Then I can live in America one day."

"Let's first figure out how we will get out of here. I don't even know where 'here' is. I can't believe I never asked; where are we?"

"We are near the coast, close to the border with Greece. That is a good thing because we can get a boat to take us to a Greek island then transit to the mainland without papers."

"Maybe we should try to get to Skiathos or Skopelos. They are not so overrun by tourists so they'll have fewer guarded points of entry. But first, we need to get out of here. I don't think that will be an easy task." Ela's eyes search the garden, seeking a way out that she knows isn't there. She sighs. "Sorry, Feya, I don't mean to be a Debbie Downer."

"What is a Debbie Downer?"

"It's just slang for someone who puts a negative spin on things and dampens the mood."

"Oh, I see. No, it's okay. I understand. But it will not be as hard as you think." Feya settles in, clearly eager to reveal her plan.

"I have convinced Yigit that I want to escape and be with him, so he has shared with me the maps of a system of tunnels located under us. The entry point is near Mazhar's office, so this has been the first opportunity to get near it."

Ela frowns. "But Yigit won't let me escape with you. This is his little romantic fantasy and I'm sure I'm not a part of it."

"He cannot leave with me or he will have a target on his back for the rest of his life," Feya says. "His whole family would be tortured and murdered. So, instead, he will help me escape, and stage it so it looks like you killed the other guards, wounded him, then took me along as a hostage."

"Hey, whatever it takes. I don't mind being the fall gal for this one. But is he willing to kill the other two guards and then wound himself?"

"For me, of course."

"Then what does he think is going to happen?"

"He thinks we will rendezvous in six months. That will give him time to heal—he plans on shooting himself in the leg for our escape. And then resign; he will say he failed Mazhar and is shamed and is no longer worthy of his trust, how do you say, yada yada yada."

"But won't he come after you when you don't meet up with him?"

"Leave that to me. Let's just focus on taking what we need. Neither of us have any money, but I will take all my jewelry. Yigit said he can give me enough cash to help me get to Syria. That's where he thinks I am going. We should also take some food and water, just to get us through the first couple of days. Also, dress in layers so we will be prepared for any weather."

"You've thought this through," Ela says, impressed. "I think you've covered everything."

Feya breaks eye contact with Ela, her eyes settling on the middle distance. "I've had three years to think about this. How do you think I survived lying under that animal? I lay there planning my escape many times. Each time differently. But I never knew of the tunnels, so each time my plan was much more dangerous."

Feya's certainty washes away the last of Ela's trepidation. "When do we leave?"

"Tonight."

That evening, Yigit brings Ela her dinner on a tray and gives her shoulder a squeeze before walking out and locking her in again.

Ela is too wound up to eat but forces herself to swallow some food. It will be a long night and who knows when she will get her next meal.

A few hours later, Yigit is there again, this time unlocking the door. Feya comes up behind him and hugs Ela, then hands her a canvas bag filled with provisions and powerful flashlights. They are both dressed in black yoga pants and long-sleeved tops. Feya's blond locks are tucked up into a black beanie accentuating her enormous blue eyes. Even dressed as a cat burglar, Ela can see why Yigit is so taken with Feya.

"Come now, we go to the tunnel." Yigit's nerves are palpable. He has specks of blood on his face and shirt. Earlier, Ela thought she heard two gunshots, which means he killed the other two already.

They enter a small room off Mazhar's office and Yigit uses the keypad next to a door within. When the door opens, Feya takes Yigit in her arms and whispers her goodbyes in Turkish. Then she plunges a large kitchen knife into his heart.

Ela stops herself from screaming. *Is Feya trying to get rid of loose ends? Am I next?*

Feya can clearly read Ela's expression. She laughs. "No, you are safe. You never harmed me or used me." She stoops down to take Yigit's gun and tuck it in her bag. Taking Ela's hand in hers, Feya leads her into the tunnel.

As they travel through the bowels of the tunnel system, Feya keeps her flashlight on the map while Ela lights the way in front of them. When they reach the end of the tunnel, they know there is only one path to take that heads toward the Greek border and freedom.

Chapter Twenty-Four

As the helicopter descends, Emre feels his future slipping away. His heart never felt as full as when he was with Ela. All the fear and stress of the last few years drained away and was replaced with love and hope. Now, with Ela taken, that hope has slipped just out of reach. It is as though he can feel it brush his fingertips but cannot get a hold of it.

He is snapped out of his thoughts when they land with a jarring bounce. That bump is what he needed to know he was still alive, and as long as he is alive, he will be solely focused on finding Ela.

Emre jumps out of the helicopter as soon as it hits the ground. He looks at the others expectantly. "Come on. We don't have any time to lose."

Geoff shakes his head. "We can walk for days, not knowing where they have taken Ela, or we can regroup, gather intelligence from our network, and then develop a strategy. We need to do this intelligently. At this point, we don't even know who has her. All members of the syndicate are being held without bail and all their assets have been frozen, so it could be anyone, anywhere."

Emre realizes that Geoff is right. The emotions surging through him are making him irrational. He needs to allow the others to lead right now. An intelligent man knows his limitations and when to let the experts lead.

He clutches Geoff's shoulders, taking a shaky breath. "I will defer to you all right now. But you have to promise me we will get her back." He turns from Geoff and looks at Iserate and Lizet and doesn't break his gaze until they each affirm what he has said.

After they board the new helicopter, Emre stares out the window over the Italian countryside, his only thoughts on Ela. He can't stop himself from imagining the worst. She was hysterical over the thought of being tortured. He couldn't live with himself if anything happened to her. He makes a promise to himself that when he finds her, he will never be parted from her again and will let her know how much he loves her every single day.

They arrive at a villa on a lake—nothing ostentatious, but comfortable. Another one of Emre's safe houses, set up by Geoff when they began plotting to take down the heroin syndicate. Geoff always said a few safe harbors on every continent can't hurt. Turns out he was right.

They head immediately to the office on the first floor. It is, in truth, a well-appointed operations command center. Geoff, Iserate, and Lizet all get to work immediately. Emre walks around as though he is in a trance, feeling utterly helpless.

"Emre, please go and rest," Geoff says firmly, watching him pace. "We need you in fighting form, old man. I know you will feel more like yourself after a nap and a shower."

He looks at Geoff, turns, and heads to his room. As he leaves the office, he hears Lizet mutter to Geoff, "Did he really just do what you said without an argument?"

About a week and a half after the fiasco in Italy, Emre feels more frustrated than ever. His team is hard at work collecting intel from their networks, yet they are no closer to rescuing Ela. After pacing in his room one morning, Emre joins the others at the conference table. He takes in their grim expressions and before he can even ask, Geoff slides a photo across the table. Emre gasps. It's Ela holding a newspaper dated a few days after she was taken. Next to her, Mazhar sits with his meaty hand on her arm.

"How?" Emre breathes. "He is behind bars. What happened?"

"It appears he had some warning that the raid was about to take place," Geoff says, chagrined. "He has a pretty slick lawyer and has also paid off most of the Turkish law enforcement agencies for decades, so he somehow got out on bail. They are not monitoring or restricting his travel, they have not confiscated his passport. They did freeze his assets, but there is a rumor that he has some mistress tucked away somewhere where he has also stashed significant 'rainy day funds."

For a moment, Emre sits silently. Of all the violent, shady men his uncle worked with, Mazhar is the last one he would ever want in the same room as Ela. Before his heart can break entirely, he snaps himself out of his stupor. "Okay, he's obviously baiting me," he says slowly. "She is just a means to an end." He turns to the team. "I want a plan in place no later than this time tomorrow."

The other three nod and each turn to a screen, getting down to the work they are all trained for. Nothing like a good mission to bring everyone together.

The next day, never doubting that they would deliver, Emre joins them and asks for the plan to exfiltrate Ela.

"There are three things we know," Geoff says, bags under his eyes from the long night. "The first and most important, Mazhar is paranoid, acting irrationally. We must keep this in mind. Second, he wants you to find Ela. It is you he wants, she is just the bait. So he will either plant obvious clues or have someone leak her whereabouts to us. And third, he will have a smaller security detail than usual because most of his assets have been seized."

"Can't we just reach out to him and offer me for her?" Emre says, a bit impatiently.

"Emre, how trustworthy is Mazhar? Do you really think that as soon as he knows where you are that he won't kill Ela? Sorry to be blunt, old man. But you know him better than any of us. Try to think like he does."

"You're right, Geoff. I just got ahead of myself again. Go on."

"From the photo, we can see that she is frightened but wasn't harmed, so any torture didn't start straight away," Geoff continues. "Is that normal for him? You know, to hold off for any reason?"

Emre thinks about everything he knows and all that he has been told about Mazhar. "No, he would usually start right in."

"Well, that is a good sign. There may be something or someone keeping him from harming her. We don't know how long that may continue, but it is good news for now."

"I'm sure more photos will come," Lizet interjects. "I would also bet that we start to receive clues as to Mazhar's whereabouts."

"Why doesn't he just tell me where he has Ela, knowing that would bring me running?" Emre asks.

"Emre, you remember what he is like," Geoff says. "He is making it all so much more difficult than it needs to be because he wants to feel powerful, he wants to outsmart you. He also feels you are a mouse, and he is a cat, and he is playing with you before the kill. He is a buffoon, but a sadistic buffoon."

Just then, Iserate's computer pings. "Merde!" he cries.

They all stop talking at once.

"I just got a notification on a list I am on," Iserate says, not removing his eyes from the screen. "The authorities in South America are searching for a missing person named Jennifer Young."

"Who is looking for her?" Geoff asks, frustrated. "We sent all the messages to her company from Ela's address, saying she was extending her trip and going to a remote area of the Amazon to live with the locals for a few months. Not unusual for an anthropologist to do."

Emre slaps his forehead. "How can I be so stupid!"

The other three all say in unison, "What?"

"Anna! Ela's best friend is having a baby and Ela is to be the godmother. I should have remembered and got word to her. She's expecting Ela to be in contact regarding her visit for the christening." He sighs. "If it wasn't for Anna, I would have never met Ela."

"Where is Anna? Can we get a message to her?" Lizet asks.

"She is in Germany. I can contact—"

Geoff interrupts him. "Sorry, Emre, I can't allow that. You would put us all in danger. You must not contact anyone or even be seen. Clearly Anna doesn't believe the electronic communications we sent—someone needs to talk to her face-to-face. She must be made to understand the danger she is putting Ela in by bringing in law enforcement—Mazhar has paid off police all over the world."

"I should make contact," Lizet speaks up. "I would be the least threatening to Anna. Maybe I'll show up at a mother-to-be prep class. They have those things, don't they? I'm sure it would be the last place that would be on anyone's radar. I'll hack into the registration system to determine which one Anna will be attending."

"Okay, you head out tomorrow and we will keep monitoring for more leaks," Geoff says thoughtfully. "We are just lucky that Mazhar isn't intelligent."

Chapter Twenty-Five

Lizet decides to take a commercial flight to Frankfurt airport, deciding it would draw less attention than a private jet. At the airport, she rents a car under the name Alana Jones, the same as the passport she is traveling under.

After checking into her hotel, she dresses to appear pregnant then makes the forty-minute drive to Freigericht. Lizet heads directly to the community health center and signs into the prenatal class she registered for online. Once everyone is signed in and the class is about to start, she scans the room for Anna. She finally spots a woman who looks exactly like the photo she sourced from Instagram. Well, almost exactly—this Anna is most certainly pregnant.

Lizet takes a deep breath. Despite what Ela said about her Jekyll-and-Hyde act, she's always been more comfortable with the aggressive parts of spycraft than the diplomatic ones. But she thinks of Ela, her new friend who already feels like family, scared and in danger, and approaches Anna.

The woman looks up, face blank at the appearance of a stranger. Lizet puts her hand on Anna's arm and says, "For Jen's sake, please join me at the coffee shop across the street in five minutes." And walks away. The last thing she needs is Anna to cause a scene and draw attention to her.

Eight minutes later, Lizet is sitting alone in the coffee shop, checking her watch every few seconds. She has enough training to be patient. But every time she thinks of Ela's face next to Mazhar in that photograph, she bounces her knee with nerves. Just as Lizet is about to leave, Anna enters with a man.

Lizet stands and shakes his hand. "Hello, you must be Tobias. And Anna, thank you for coming."

"What is going on?" Anna says, not sitting down. "How do I know Jen sent you?"

"I am to tell you she drew an elephant on that neon-pink cast you had on when she came to Germany to help out in the restaurant."

"Okay, that is true, but anyone who was around then would have seen it."

"Yes, and in truth, I am here at the behest of one such person. Do you remember a teen named Emre?"

Anna's eyes widen and she finally sinks into the chair opposite Lizet. "What does he have to do with Jen's disappearance?" She turns to Tobias. "I knew her infatuation with that kid would bring nothing but trouble. Here I am twenty years later being proven correct."

Lizet continues. "Although they hadn't seen each other since that last time at your restaurant, Emre has been looking out for Ela— um, for Jen. He adored her from afar. He grew to be a very successful and powerful man who, along the way, attracted some equally powerful enemies.

"His enemies somehow found out about Jen, who was the only person of significance in his life. Then, a few months ago, in an effort to ensure her safety, Emre took Jen off of the grid and put her in, basically, a form of protective custody. Unfortunately, a few days ago our security was breached. Some very bad people have Jen."

Anna gasps and places a hand over her mouth as Tobias pulls her close to him.

"Please stay calm," Lizet says, forcing a smile. "We must look like friends having a coffee and not draw attention to ourselves. I can't tell you more than I have due to the delicate state of our current mission, which is to extract Jennifer."

"You will bring her back safely, right?" Tobias asks. "Can we help?"

"Our best chance is if we can keep the operation off law enforcement's radar. Emre made sure that Jen's passport officially entered the airport in Rio, but if the police start digging, they will realize that there is no trail after that. At that point, they may get international agencies involved. The people holding her could catch wind of it and start to move her to different locations, which would make our job much more difficult.

"The way you can help is to contact whomever you spoke to down in Brazil, tell them she turned up and it was all a misunderstanding." Lizet gets an idea. "Also, once we find her, we may need to move both Emre and Ela—sorry, Jen—quickly, and Germany may be just the place. Would you be able to keep them near you just for a day, while we arrange to move them out of Europe?"

Anna calms down and looks at Tobias before she speaks. He nods his approval and she says, "I'll call right away and stop the search for Jen or Ela. I remember when the sixteen-year-old Emre gave her that name. Seems like a million years ago." She shakes her head as if to shake herself from her memories. "Anyhow, I will call off the police and, of course, we can hide them both for as long as you need. When you find her, tell her I love her. Oh," Anna says, eyes shining with tears. "And I will wait to christen the baby until she can be here."

Chapter Twenty-Six

In Feres, at a more modest safe house than the others, they are joined by a group of freelance agents—mostly former military who specialized in black ops. After the Sara episode, Emre wasn't sure he wanted to expand the team beyond the four of them, but was persuaded by the others that, with Emre and Geoff waiting in Feres, Lizet and Iserate would not be able to execute the plan on their own.

Once the extraction team is fully briefed, they head out toward the border. It's not much of a problem to stealthily get into Turkey—all the border protections in place are more focused on stopping the flow of refugees heading into Greece.

Hours later, Emre is still pacing and checking the time every few minutes. "I can't stand just sitting here waiting. I feel like I have no control over the single most important operation I have ever been involved in." He runs his hand through his thick hair then looks at Geoff, waiting for some affirmation that everything will be fine. Before Geoff can speak, he hears noises outside.

Geoff shuts off the lights and gestures for Emre to be quiet. He whispers, "It's too soon for them to be returning, and no one else knows we're here."

A piercing whistle tears through the silence—the signal the team established to notify Geoff and Emre that they have returned.

Emre's heart sinks. The team would have just had time to get there and back. They would not have had time to breach the property's external defenses, neutralize the guards inside, and extract Ela.

Geoff stands up, giving a gentle look to Emre. "I'm sorry," he says. Then he unbolts the door.

Ela and another young woman walk through the doorway.

Emre thinks he must be hallucinating. He sees that the women are scratched and dirty but do not have any signs of injury. As Ela looks at Emre he feels an overwhelming sense of relief and love. But in her eyes, her face, her posture, he senses her mixed emotions. It is only a millisecond, then she dons a neutral mask. Her walls are firmly in place. He realizes that no one, not even him, can penetrate those walls. He can only hope that someday soon, when she is rested and restored, they can deal with it all. He wants her to feel safe with him again. He needs her to.

For a moment, Ela and Emre just stare at each other in disbelief. Then Emre can't stop himself from running to her and gathering her up in his arms. Tears slip silently from her eyes, staining his shirt.

"Ela, thank God you are here and you are all right. I will never let anything like that happen to you again. Did Mazhar hurt you?" Before she can answer, he turns to the young woman with Ela. "Who is this?" He eyes her warily.

Ela leaves his embrace and puts her arm around the woman. "This is Feya, and she is the only reason I am unharmed. She has lived through three years of hell, and she planned our escape. She even killed the last guard with her own hands. Emre, you should be forever grateful to her, as I will be." She narrows her eyes at Emre, challenging him to disagree.

Lizet tells them all to calm down. "This has been an emotional time for everyone. Now, take a breath, sit down and let's all hear Ela and Feya's story." She turns to Emre and Geoff. "They were already out of the property and at least a mile into their escape when we found them. I, for one, would love to hear how they did it."

The others sit Feya down, and she tells them the story of the three years of loneliness and captivity she suffered at the hands of Mazhar. "Then, it was like a ray of sunshine when he brought Ela to be my English tutor and companion," she says, smiling at Ela. "She was the only friend I had since my father gave me to that animal. I did not know she had been kidnapped and was being used to lure Emre until a little while ago. But once I did, I began planning how we could get away. I felt it was something that could be done if there were two of us. All alone, I don't think I could have done it."

"But how did you get away from right under Mazhar's nose?" Iserate asks.

"We were very lucky," Ela says. "His wife insisted that he take her and their family to Monte Carlo for her birthday. He was only going to be gone for four days, so we had to move quickly."

Geoff looks from one to the other. "So you are telling me that the house is empty right now? And Mazhar will be returning in three days?"

Feya nods. "He said he would be back on Friday, but it will really be Thursday, two days from now. He always comes back a day earlier so he can act like he returned early just for me. Also, I think, so that he can catch me sleeping with a guard or doing something else he can punish me for. He has never caught me doing anything, but he would never stop trying."

"Well," Geoff says with a grin. "I think we need to repay the little gift of C-4 that he left at the villa. We can get in, plant the explosives, and then detonate them after he enters. That should take care of, at least, the known threat to Emre, Ela, and Feya."

"Although, even if we are successful in eliminating Mazhar, we cannot be certain that all threats against Ela and Emre have been neutralized," Lizet says, glancing at the couple. "Sorry you two, we will still need to keep you off the grid until we can confirm it is safe for you to resume your regular lives."

"What about Feya?" Ela says, placing her hands protectively on Feya's shoulders. "We need to do everything we can to help her. I would have been tortured or murdered if it wasn't for her. I would not have known about the secret tunnel, nor would I have been able to manipulate the guards. I am positive she saved my life.”

“Of course,” Iserate says. “Feya, you will go with Emre and Ela. We will—”

Feya interrupts him. “Thank you. But no thank you. I have been living under lock and key, playing by someone else’s rules for too long. I need to make my own life. Once you confirm Mazhar is dead, I can start living. There is not another soul alive who would be interested in tracking me down. No one even knows I have existed for the past three years. “One thing, though,” she says, fixing her gaze into the distance. “If anyone finds my father, please kill him for me.” Feya brightens. “Now, I would like a shower, something to eat, and then to sleep.”

Geoff looks embarrassed as he says, “Of course, Feya. But first, I must ask one more thing of you. You have already done so much, but we need to know the floorplan of the house and how to find the tunnel entrance. You can eat while we get through the necessary information.”

After Feya provides the information needed , Lizet heads out to meet one of her Greek contacts who will supply the amount of C-4 needed to level Mazhar’s secret hideaway. Geoff and Iserate work with Feya, going over the directions to the tunnel and reviewing the house layout so many times they must feel like they have already been inside of it.

While the others are busy finalizing plans to destroy Mazhar and his hideaway, Emre holds Ela in his lap, stroking her forehead as she falls into an exhausted sleep.

Emre gestures to Feya. "I'm going to put Ela in bed and I think you may want to get some sleep now as well. After your brave escape, you deserve more than a short nap. I think Geoff and Iserate have everything they need."

"Thank you. I am feeling weary."

"If it's okay, you and Ela can share this room. You can be there for each other if you wake during the night."

"Yes, but don't you want to be here with her?"

He gazes down at Ela. "I want to never leave her side again, but this isn't about what I want. It's about what the two of you need most right now."

What he doesn't say is that even if he stayed with her, he wouldn't know how to take care of her after what she experienced. He's back where he started on the *Kayıp Aşk*: willing himself to be patient for the love of his life. He smiles up at Feya. "Rest well, you've earned it."

Chapter Twenty-Seven

Once Lizet returns from Germany, the team spends every waking moment searching for Ela. Mazhar keeps his leaks going, and it isn't long before they are able to determine that she is being held somewhere west of Istanbul, near the border with Greece. Geoff has secured someone from his network of spies to gather more intel on the ground, plying locals for useful gossip.

Relying on his team of experts to bring Ela home means Emre feels helpless. He would happily walk into a trap to save her, but the others insist he must be patient.

One afternoon, Iserate's computer pings. He goes to see what the message says and looks up at the others with a smile and says, "Bingo! We've got the location."

The others crowd around Iserate's screen. "It seems Mazhar has a young mistress he has squirreled away in a large property in Keşan. Some ex-housekeeper got tipsy a week or so ago and was sharing stories of her time there. Word of the conversation finally got back to our man on the ground. An artfully planned leak this time," Iserate admits. He leans back in his chair, folding his hands behind his head as he thinks. "We have to extract Ela while keeping you as far away from Mazhar as possible."

"Iserate, I need to be there," Emre says, brow furrowed.

"No." Iserate says firmly. "If things go well, we don't have to worry. But if we get caught, and you're there, Mazhar kills all of us. If we're there without you, and the team doesn't make it, you're still safe and we can use you as a bargaining chip. We can insist on an exchange—you for Ela. If he wants you badly enough, he will agree. That gives us one more chance to have both of you walk away alive."

Geoff steps in. "One of us will stay with you. If the others are captured, you will need to have someone here to build the next phase of the plan and put together a new team."

At that, they all sit quietly. Iserate finally breaks the silence. "I will go in to get Ela."

Lizet says, "As will I. Geoff, you have been with Emre the longest so you should stay with him. We will go and bring Ela back here to you, Emre."

Emre stands and shakes his head. "I will agree to stay out of the action, but will go with you and wait with Geoff someplace safe. I need to be close. This is non-negotiable."

Iserate, Lizet, and Geoff finally nod in agreement. They know when Emre is immovable.

"What happens after we get her back?" Emre asks.

Lizet clears her throat. "I have part of the answer," she says. "I asked if Anna and Tobias would keep you two hidden in Germany during transit out of Europe. I hope that's okay with you guys. Anna just seemed so desperate to be able to help, I wanted to give her a way to feel part of the rescue of her dear friend. And it will help Ela stabilize from this ordeal. Even a day with her old friends can help ground her."

Iserate agrees. "Good idea, and I actually think transiting them through Germany is smart. The syndicate never had a foothold in that country."

"And after Germany?" Geoff wonders aloud. "We need to stash them somewhere until we determine that they're safe to live normal lives."

Immediately, Emre knows the right place. "Australia. Europe is off-limits because the syndicate's territory extends around it; it's too close just in case there are any stragglers hanging around. The US was the place they planned to kidnap Ela in the first place. Ela lived in Australia and has friends she trusts there. She would feel less displaced there than she would anywhere else." His voice drops down to a whisper. "After this ordeal, she deserves all the peace and security I can give her."

Geoff nods. "But first, let's rescue Ela." He studies a map on his screen. "I think we should set up in Feres, a Greek border town. It's about fifty kilometers from Keşan. Once we have Ela, we can regroup in Feres, then make our way to the Aegean, where we will have a ship waiting." He looks up at Emre with a smirk. "Sorry, Emre, nothing as grand as the *Kayıp Aşk*. But it will get us safely to

Athens where we will be able to move you to Germany then, ultimately, Australia. You will lay low there until we determine that there is no more threat to either of you. At that point, you both can resume your normal lives."

"And you'll be the best man at our wedding."

"Let's hope for that happy ending," Geoff agrees, clapping his friend on the back. "But at this point, I would be satisfied for you both to be alive."

Chapter Twenty-Eight

By the time Feya wakes, the late morning sun is filtering through the curtains, and the bed is empty except for her. She stretches lazily—then at once, the events of the past twenty-four hours come rushing back to her. She looks around as if to assure herself that her memories are real. No drab walls, no eerie silence. It's bright and safe. She hugs her knees to her chest in a moment of pure joy.

Feya skips out to the living room where Emre, Ela, and Lizet are studying some papers laid out on the coffee table. They look up at her with beaming smiles.

Lizet pats the spot on the sofa next to her. "Sit here, we have something to show you." Feya does so, and Lizet fixes her with a soft look. "Ela and Emre want to do something special for you. I have only known you a short time but have never been more impressed with someone's strength and intelligence. I truly admire your spirit and I want you to be open to their offer. You don't have to do everything on your own. There are people who care about you and will be here for you, whatever you need."

Feya sits silently for a moment, eyes locked on the woman. At the compound, Ela had told her about Lizet, that she only takes jobs where she can defend women in need, women who need protecting. Seeing the fierceness in Lizet's eyes, Feya wonders if one day she could do the same thing. Feya nods and returns her attention to Emre.

Emre says, "I could not know how to repay you for your bravery and for saving Ela, who as you know is so precious to me. So I have put together these three proposals and I hope you will accept one as an expression of my undying gratitude to you."

He holds out three pieces of paper. Each detailing a new life for Feya. The first includes the deed to a beach house in Laguna Beach, California, training in any profession of her choice, a personal bodyguard, car, therapy, an annual stipend of $500,000, and a new identity. The second offers a New York City penthouse and the third, a sprawling mountain home in Aspen, Colorado. Each offers the same additional details as the first.

Feya looks wide-eyed at them. "No, I cannot believe this, this is too much. It is too generous." Lizet places her hand on her forearm just for a moment, and Feya remembers what she just told her.

"Feya, actually, it is not enough," Emre says, looking ashamed. "I am embarrassed to say that the only reason Mazhar had the means to live the life he lives is because my uncle made him rich and did nothing to stop him, no matter what he did. I am trying to put an end to that evil so I can look at myself in the mirror and not despise myself and my family. Please, please, let me try to make some small amends for you having your life stolen from you. Please accept. You can think of it as a gift from you to me, as you would be giving me a small sense of reconciliation."

"This was my idea, Feya," Ela adds with a small smile. "At least do it for me—I won't be able to live with myself if I am not sure you're safe."

Feya is speechless but slowly nods her head and begins to weep, first almost silently then in full, heart-wrenching sobs.

Lizet pulls Feya in for a hug then Emre and Ela join in for a group hug. Ela pulls back sobbing and laughing at the same time and says, "I just have one question: beach, city, or mountains?"

"City, of course. I'm a nineteen-year-old European woman, what else would you expect?"

They laugh together, knowing Feya now has a future full of hope.

"Even the dreams I had of freedom didn't come close to this reality," Feya says, pulling back from the hug. "Thank you all so much. Emre, you are so kind, generous, and thoughtful. Now I know why Ela was willing to die to save you."

An awkward silence descends at these words, and Feya sees Ela give an unreadable glance at Emre.

Just then Geoff comes in from the front of the house. "I saw a vehicle approaching. If all went to plan, it should be Iserate and his team."

In all the excitement, Feya had almost forgotten the others had been dispatched to destroy Mazhar's compound.

A few minutes later, the van pulls in through the gates and up the drive. Three people emerge from the vehicle; Feya recognizes one as Iserate. Geoff cautiously walks out, brandishing his weapon. Emre, Feya, and Ela follow.

"What's this? Who do you have with you?" Geoff barks.

Iserate pushes the man forward. His hands are bound behind his back, and he falls on his knees..

"He came back early when none of his guards answered his calls, he knew something was amiss," Iserate says as he yanks hard on the man's hair, pulling his head back to face Emre. It's Mazhar.

Chapter Twenty-Nine

Emre takes one look at Mazhar's defiant face and spits on the ground in front of him. Ela comes close to doing the same. She hoped she would never have to see this man again.

"Why did you bring this disgusting animal here?" Emre snarls.

Iserate says, "He ran out of the house as soon as he realized something was up, so he avoided being killed in the blast, but he was easy to grab on his own. The out-of-shape old bastard couldn't move very fast."

"Why didn't you just kill him?"

"Alive we can extract information from him. We can find out if anyone else is after you. In his death we only gain a moment's pleasure."

Ela watches as Emre's breathing slows. "Okay, that makes sense. But I want him watched every second. I don't trust him for one moment."

As Iserate pushes Mazhar down the hallway towards the cellar door, Feya, who has been silent, approaches him.

"You miserable old piece of shit," she whispers. "I want you to know I despise you. I wanted to kill myself every time you touched me, every time you even looked at me. But I vowed to live just to see you die."

With that, she raises the gun she had tucked away. She aims at Mazhar's chest, then drops her aim down to his crotch and fires the gun. Mazhar seizes up, looks at her with disbelief then slumps to the ground. Ela freezes, shocked into place. This is the second person in as many days that she's watched Feya kill.

Iserate grabs the gun from her and stares at Mazhar's body. "He was our only direct source of information," he says. "It will take months for us to collect what he would have told me in an hour. I would have been happy for you to kill him at that point."

Feya starts shaking. "I have waited three years. I have thought about nothing else. I have pictured this so many times. I had to make sure he could never hurt me or some other young girl again. I didn't think, I just acted."

Lizet steps forward and takes Feya in her arms to soothe her. Ela walks over and rubs Feya's back. To the others she whispers, "I'm sorry, I forgot she was armed."

Geoff and Lizet work on Mazhar to see if he can be saved, at least long enough to get some information out of him, but it is hopeless. If the bullet didn't kill him, it appears his heart gave out with the shock of Feya's verbal attack.

Emre says, "Let's get out of here. Burn the place down. We have a rendezvous on the coastline."

They all get ready in silence. The missed opportunity hangs heavy among them, but Ela can tell that all of them understand why

Feya did what she did. They file out of the house and into the van as Lizet and Iserate torch the place, then join them down the road.

After a few miles, Geoff breaks the depressing silence by singing some silly British singalong. One by one, they each join in. Feya doesn't know the words but hums along all the same. Ela squeezes Emre's arm to thank him.

Morning is breaking as they approach the coast. The beauty of the sunrise's reflection on the sea gives Ela a little hope. But it evaporates as she watches Emre sleeping next to her, and wonders if their relationship can be repaired. She wonders if, at some point, they can get back to the love they shared on the *Kayıp Aşk*. She is so dead inside right now, she doubts she can ever feel that deeply again. She can't imagine feeling pure love for anyone when she's being shuttled from safe house to safe house.

The connection with their transport, a simple ferry well-suited for this crossing, goes smoothly. They sit in the passenger section, much larger than needed for the six of them, each lost in their own thoughts.

A part of Ela wants Emre to sit with her, hold her, and tell her everything is going to be okay, but another part of her wants space to sort out her feelings. She doesn't know where to go from here. From what Lizet was telling her, both she and Emre will be sent to Germany where Anna has arranged somewhere for them to stay while they wait for a plane that will take them to Australia. She was told that Emre decided on the locations because he wanted her to have some familiarity, which would give her a greater sense of security.

She should feel grateful, but she only feels angry. She has relinquished control for far too long now. She let Lizet, Iserate, Geoff and Emre make all the decisions and look where that got her. She still fell into Mazhar's clutches and only escaped thanks to Feya's and her own cunning.

Maybe she will go her own way. She doesn't feel like she can deal with Emre right now, or if she will ever be able to. She can't help but notice his furtive glances. The hope, the desire, the questions in his eyes are suffocating her. She gets up and moves even farther away from the group. She never thought she would long for a boring, predictable life, but here she is.

As they approach the Greek coastline, Lizet lets them all know that there will be an SUV waiting for them a mile from their drop-off area. They will avoid all the authorities by using this route. "After we arrive at the safe house, we will fully brief you on the next segment of the plan."

"Safe house?" Everyone turns, surprised to hear Ela's voice. She hasn't said a word during the whole crossing. "I think that maybe you need to come up with a new name," she says bitterly. "The one in Tuscany turned out to be anything but."

An uncomfortable silence falls. Ela knows she's picking a fight. But before anyone can argue with her, Lizet calls to them that the Zodiac is approaching to take them to shore.

Chapter Thirty

Once they are assembled at the safe house, Lizet begins the briefing. "It's a good sign that our journey here was so uneventful. This may possibly mean that Mazhar was the final threat. I've had reports that everyone else who was arrested is still in custody. Most have accepted deals that will keep them locked up for at least twenty years, a much more lenient sentence than they would have expected. But they did have to provide information on the top layer of syndicate leadership. They will also have to testify against their former bosses. If they even survive prison, once released, they will be on lifelong probation. The authorities will be vigilant in monitoring them. Also, all their assets have been seized, so they no longer have the resources needed to support any force of power. Congratulations, Emre and Geoff, for bringing down this syndicate."

Geoff adds, "And Nigel, who is tucked up in his comfy bed in London. He played a crucial role during the first phase. And kudos to Feya and Ela, first for surviving and second, for escaping, and finally for enabling the elimination of Mazhar."

Everyone shares a brief applause. Emre notices that Ela does not join in.

Iserate laughs and says, "Okay, enough of the kumbaya stuff. Let's get down to business. Lizet, continue."

She turns to Feya. "It will be fairly easy to disappear your current identity. From what I was able to find out, your father—I use that word loosely—and Mazhar bribed authorities and had your birth certificate, school records, and any other documentation basically erased. So half of our task has already been done. Feya and I will just wait here until I am notified that all her new documents are ready. Once I have them, we will fly to New York City on one of Emre's new private jets."

She nods to Emre. "Thanks for replacing your existing jets, helicopters, and yacht. As far as we know, no one knows anything about the ownership of the new vessels, so that adds another layer of security for transporting everyone."

At the mention of the yacht that now no longer belongs to Emre, Ela gasps. Everyone looks at her but quickly turns away, pretending they didn't notice. Emre wants to go to her, hold her, and tell her it will all be fine. He knows it's upsetting, losing the place they both associate with finding each other again and slowly falling in love. But it could not be helped. They were betrayed on the *Kayıp Aşk*, so they had to leave it behind. She doesn't meet his eyes.

Geoff's cough cuts through the silence, then he begins. "Until we can be 100 percent certain that you are totally safe, we feel it's important to get you two out of Europe as soon as possible. But first, we will head to Germany where you can see Anna. She has a place nearby her town where you can stay. We can't have you stay in her home, as there would be a slight possibility it could become a target."

Interrupting Geoff, Ela asks, "Then why are we even going to Germany? The last thing I would do is put someone I love in harm's way!"

Emre feels that last sentence like a punch in the gut. He decides to take the hit. "Blame me. I thought it would be helpful for you to see Anna. Also, she was worried sick when she didn't know where you were. Once she was told what was going on, she wanted to help. She had to do something, so Lizet asked her to do this."

"Never mind. And I do want to see her, so badly I don't even have the words …" Ela says, trailing off.

Geoff continues. "We hope to be in Germany for only two days, then we move on to Australia. We will settle you in Bicton, Western Australia, in a home on Blackwall Reach Parade, on the Swan River. It's a pretty quiet area and the home's layout makes it easy to protect. The plan is for you two to be there for a month, plus or minus a couple of weeks. By that time, we should know if any threats still exist. If there are none, you can each move on with your lives. If there are, we will have to resort to our more long-term plan."

"Excuse me, Geoff."

"Yes, Ela?"

"Why do we have to be held in the same place? What if I just want to stay with Anna?"

Emre's heart sinks. He knew she was hurt, he knew she needed time. But to hear that she may leave him again, just when he got her back, shatters him.

"I guess you don't have to follow our plan," Iserate says slowly, with a glance at Emre. "It is the safest for you. If you want to go off separately, we will just have to revamp our plans and hire another team to protect you as both Iserate and I must guard Emre."

Emre says flatly, "You two can go with Ela. I will take the new team." Then he addresses Ela directly. "You may go wherever you want. Just tell Geoff and he will arrange it." With that, he walks out of the room and out of the house.

When they hear the front door close, Geoff points to it and Iserate bolts out of the room to follow Emre.

Chapter Thirty-One

Ela has never seen Emre so hurt and angry. She's so tired, and she just wants everything back to normal. Although when she thinks about it, she is not sure what "normal" means anymore. Is it her life before that night on the road in DC? Is it the idyllic time they spent on the *Kayıp Aşk*? It certainly isn't her time being held captive by Mazhar, nor this confusing time.

She walks away from Geoff, from the briefing, and from her feelings. She locks herself in her room and sees, on the bedside table, her journal from the *Kayıp Aşk*. She picks it up and holds it to her chest. She thought it was lost. How did it find its way back to her? She picks up the pen that lies next to it, flips open the journal, and finds the next blank page. But before she starts to write, she starts reading from the beginning. The first night on the yacht. Their picnic under the stars. Learning to trust Emre again. Feeling pulled back to him, even when everything told her she should move on. She's been feeling that pull for twenty years.

When she gets to the last entry, she can barely see through the tears. She wipes her eyes, then makes a new entry. All it says is "Try."

After she finally composes herself, she returns to the living room, where everyone is sitting silently. Emre has returned from wherever he went, and is now staring blankly at the coffee table.

Ela takes a deep breath. Although she still feels numb, she is unsure how she will feel in the future. If she walks away now, she will never know. She can always walk away later if she discovers the feelings she read about in her journal are some fantasy. But for now, she will put in the effort to see if they are real, because if they are, it could be exactly what she has spent her life looking for.

She says to no one in particular, "Stick to the original plan. I'm willing to try."

The tension in the room lifts with her words.

"That is good," Geoff says. "It will not delay us and we can more quickly get everyone to safety."

Emre just looks at Ela and nods, still blank.

Geoff asks, "So are we ready to finish the briefing? We only have a couple of things to finalize. Thank you, Ela. We appreciate your willingness to go along with our original plan."

Emre mumbles, "I will not bother you and I will stay clearly out of your way. I am sorry it has come to this."

Ela wants to tell him that no, it hasn't come to anything yet. She wants to give it time and try to see what happens. But she can see that she has hurt him deeply. All she says is, "Geoff, please continue."

The next day, Geoff, Iserate, Ela, and Emre say an emotional farewell to Feya, as well as to Lizet, who will accompany her to the US to begin her new life. Ela feels like she is losing two old friends, which is strange because she has known neither very long. But her heart breaks as she gives each a final hug and promises to see them soon. Then the four of them head to a private airport and take one of Emre's new private jets to a small airfield outside of Frankfurt.

Although they have not spoken to each other, Ela gives Emre's hand a brief squeeze as she heads to her seat.

The sensation of his hand in hers feels good; not electric like it used to, but pleasant. She will take pleasant for now. She is so excited about seeing Anna that she is giddy. She rattles on through most of the flight telling the others stories of when she and Anna were in college and all of the mischief they got into. Well, that Anna got into—Ela was the boring one.

After all she's been through, she needs Anna to right her ship. She hopes Lizet can do the same for Feya—she will need strong friends after the last three years of captivity. Ela takes out her journal and begins her next entry:

Look what Emre is doing for Feya, just because I asked him to. I must remember his kindness. He may have put me in danger, but his intention was to protect me.

A sudden realization hits her; she is amazed that she didn't see it before. She continues the entry.

I was the one who ran away from the safe house. All would have been well if I had just stayed put. And he, nor any of the team, have ever said that to me. They've never thrown it in my face, even when I was making snide remarks about the safe house not being safe. Maybe I need to be accountable for my actions and own up to the part I played in the failure of the original plan.

In light of those sobering thoughts, Ela resolves to be more kind to Emre. To let him know she appreciates his thoughtfulness.

Iserate passes her on his way back from the bathroom as she's scribbling, "Glad to see you using that," he says. "Emre ran back on board the *Kayıp Aşk* to grab it for you. I said it wasn't worth risking his life for, but you know how stubborn he can be when something is important to him." He heads back to his seat without waiting for a response.

Ela is stunned. As life-threatening danger was descending upon them, Emre's thoughts were on what was important to her and what could give her solace. Yes, she is determined to be kind to him and, if possible, mend what has been so cruelly torn from them.

Chapter Thirty-Two

As the jet touches down, Ela cannot contain her excitement at being reunited with Anna. Iserate leads the way out of the plane followed by Emre, Ela, and Geoff. All is quiet on the tarmac and there are two black Mercedes waiting. Anna steps out of the first car and Ela runs right into her arms. After a long hug, she steps back and stares at Anna's enormous baby bump.

"Oh my God! Look at you. That's my niece or nephew?"

"Nephew! And all is well, all the tests came back perfect. Geriatric pregnancy my ass!" Anna is laughing and crying at the same time.

"Of course, I never doubted it for a moment. Just look at you! Pregnancy agrees with you. But I am sorry about the dark circles under your eyes. I'm sure worrying about me has had something to do with those."

"Well, maybe just a bit. But you are safe now so I'll be able to start sleeping again. That is, if your godson will let me. I think he's going to play for the German national team or be a Rockette with all this kicking!"

"That's a good sign, isn't it? When is the little fella going to make an appearance?"

"Any time now. I've been going through minor labor the past two days. I can't believe it's almost time. I'm not sure I'm ready—"

Just then, Iserate steps forward. "We really should get a move on."

Ela looks around for Emre, but he and Geoff are already in the other car, which is about to leave. Ela realizes that, with all the excitement, she didn't get a chance to speak to Emre. To explain what she is thinking and feeling. She was so excited to see Anna, she ran ahead of the others. And now, the time isn't right. She needs to focus on Anna. This whole episode has put Anna through so much during a time when she should have been focused on nothing but herself and her baby boy.

After about forty-five minutes in the car, they arrive at the space Anna has found for them to hole up in. From the outside it looks like an abandoned warehouse on the outskirts of town. Ela is a bit concerned and wonders what the others will say.

Anna unlocks the door and says, "Ta-da!"

The interior is bright, clean, and modern. A large kitchen and living space leads to the hallway. There is an office through a doorway on the right side of the hallway and what appears to be an art studio on the left. Up a flight of floating stairs are four bedrooms placed around a common area that appears to be a conversation, relaxation, or reading space.

After the little tour, Anna looks at them expectantly and they all applaud.

"Well done, Anna. This is excellent. It is a shame we only need it for a day or two," Geoff says.

Anna beams, "It was converted a year ago by a local artist. He plays football with Tobias. It's just a social team, they're really not that good—"

Ela clears her throat pointedly.

"Sorry, I tend to get tangential. Well, anyhow, they have been friends for years and he was telling Tobias that he would be visiting his sister in Paris for a month. Tobias said that my aunt and her family were coming over for the baby's birth and would like to rent it for a few weeks. He said he was happy for us to just use it. He would rather it wasn't empty for a whole month."

Ela hugs her. "Oh Anna, it's perfect! Thank you so much."

"No, thank Lizet. I was going crazy with worry. If it wasn't for her visit and giving me a way I could help, I think it would have destroyed me. Once I had something constructive to focus on, I felt positive and energized. I'm just glad you all like it and that it's appropriate for your needs."

Emre, who has been silent since his SUV pulled up to the house, steps forward then. "Anna, you probably don't remember me, I am Emre," he says, extending his hand. "You were very kind to me when I moved here many years ago. I want to thank you for your kindness then and for your great help now, when we so desperately need it."

Anna just stares at Emre. She takes in what Ela knows is an impressive sight: his stunning looks, his perfect body, his expensive clothes and shoes, the same huge dark brown eyes filled with kindness as when he was just sixteen.

"Wow, I was right when I said you would grow into a gorgeous man."

Everyone just stares at her. Geoff can't hold back a chuckle.

Anna puts her hand up to her mouth. "Oops, did I just say that out loud? Let's just blame it on pregnancy brain. Okay?"

They all laugh. "Yes, you were right," Ela says. "And that outer beauty is only surpassed by his inner beauty." Emre looks up, eyebrows raised in surprise, and meets her eyes for the first time all day.

They all thank Anna and as Emre, Iserate, and Geoff head to the office, Emre gently touches Ela's arm and smiles at her.

Ela and Anna head up to the cozy common area upstairs.

"Are you sure you should come upstairs?" Ela asks.

"Of course, I'm pregnant, not infirmed. Anyhow I was told exercise was good for us."

They settle on the overstuffed sofa and Ela takes Anna's hand in hers. "I want to hear about every moment of your pregnancy. Also, how is Tobias? Will we get to see him? And how does it feel not running the restaurant anymore? Do you feel … um," Ela pauses. "I guess it would help if I gave you a chance to get a word in."

"What, and not be the typical Jen, speaking a million words a minute?" Anna teases. "I will answer all of your questions and fill you in on every kick, backache, mood swing, etcetera. But first I want to hear all about Mr. Dreamy. Jesus, Jen, now that the age difference is meaningless, I vote for you jumping that one."

Oh, how Ela has missed Anna. The easy friendship, the irreverence. That feeling when you just know someone gets you, and your shared history makes you able to say a million things with just a glance or quip. Ela feels all her stress melting away. She starts to feel like herself again.

After she finishes telling Anna everything that has taken place and about the rekindling of feelings between her and Emre, Anna gives her a hug.

"Jen, you know I won't bullshit you," Anna says seriously. "It sounds like this is the real deal. Your feelings, his feelings. Obviously, the situation is crazy, but it sounds like you are at the tail end of it. So, if I'm right, this is the 'L' word. And may I add that it's a bonus that he is drop-dead gorgeous and filthy rich? In my book, the perfect man. Don't tell Tobias I said that. But, damn, girl."

Three hours later, Ela and Anna are still talking when Iserate calls up to them that dinner is ready. "Let's go," Anna says. "This little parasite has left me ravenous."

When they are all seated at the dining table, Anna gets a ping on her phone, "Oh, Tobias is on his way. He should be here in exactly three minutes. We are trying to be exact to help you with this spy stuff."

Geoff laughs and sets serving forks into a large bowl of pasta. "Thank you, it is actually a big help. If we know exactly when someone is expected, we don't have to guess who it is."

"Now, tell me who made this incredible meal?" Anna asks. "Emre, was it you?"

"No, it was Geoff. Just one of his many skills."

"That's good to hear," Anna says, twirling spaghetti on her fork. "If you said you had made it, I would have to call foul on the universe. No one should have the looks and brains you have, *and* be gifted with culinary abilities!" Emre laughs a bit, blushing from Anna's easy praise.

"Okay, Tobias will be knocking in three … two … one!"

Just then there is a tapping on the door. Anna goes to the door and says "Roses are red" and through the door Tobias responds, "You don't even like roses."

Anna turns and smiles. "Yup that's him."

Iserate holds up his hand, gesturing for her to come back to the table. He crosses and answers the door himself.

"Hi," Tobias waves through the doorway.

"Sorry for the extra caution," Iserate says, ushering him in. "But if someone was following behind you and tried to push in, I would rather they run into me than Anna."

"I thank you for that, sir. I am Tobias, Anna's husband and soon-to-be father to that bundle of joy she is carrying."

Ela jumps up and gives Tobias a bear hug. "It is so good to see you. That was Iserate who opened the door, this is Geoff, and this is Emre. Remember him?"

Tobias shakes each man's hand and stops in front of Emre, "Yes of course. You were the industrious young man who would come into the restaurant. You were always the most polite and would pay for your friends all of the time. It is good to see you again."

"Thank you for the kind words. It is very nice to know I was remembered in this way."

Just then, Anna cries out from her seat at the table and the room freezes.

"Oh shit," she gasps. "Those minor contractions I was having aren't so minor anymore."

Tobias springs into action. "Let's get you to the hospital."

Anna shakes her head and between panting breaths says, "No, this is happening now."

Iserate steps up and puts his arm on Anna's shoulder. "I am a fully trained medic. I can deliver your baby, if you want me to."

Tobias says, "Of course."

But Iserate says, "Anna is having this baby, it is her call whether she wants me to do this."

"Yes, would you two stop being so considerate and just get over here and deliver this baby!" Anna shouts.

Emre runs upstairs and brings down sheets, pillows and blankets. Ela runs to the kitchen and puts the kettle on. She's not sure if boiling water is needed, but it's what they always call for in the movies.

Geoff puts on some soothing classical music and dims the lights then helps Iserate gently move Anna to the nest of blankets on the floor in the living space.

Iserate asks Ela to grab a black pouch out of his backpack. She does so, and he unzips it to reveal sterile medical instruments in sealed plastic.

Tobias is sitting behind Anna to provide back support and Ela is holding her hand. As Ela witnesses this incredible endeavor of bringing a new life into this world she is awestruck. She thinks that this is the most physically, mentally, and emotionally taxing process the human body must endure, yet also the most rewarding. Only a few hours after it all began, Iserate checks the baby's vital signs then hands the perfectly swaddled baby boy to Anna.

Ela, Geoff, Emre, and Iserate quietly leave the living room so that the new family can be alone. Upstairs, the four of them sit, stunned by what they just witnessed. Being part of the birth of a child is magical. Ela takes Emre's hand in hers as she sits, thinking of her friends' happiness. They have waited so long for this joy. They deserve to treasure every moment.

All of a sudden, Anna calls from below, "I'm starving. Any chance we can eat dinner now?"

Everyone is rocked out of their introspection and they chuckle. Ela yells down, "Coming! Geez, now that you're a mom you expect to be waited on hand and foot."

Iserate reheats the dinner that was left untouched when little Jonathan decided to make his debut. Ela insists Anna enjoys it on a tray from her makeshift bed with Jonathan sleeping beside her. Tobias can barely tear himself away from his family but Anna insists he joins the others at the table. Emre hears Anna and says, "I have a better idea. We will all just take our plates and join you in the living room. It will be like a big maternity ward picnic."

Ela feels her numbness melt a bit every time he shows his thoughtfulness in these small ways.

After dinner, Geoff insists on cleaning up then suggests everyone gets some sleep. "It's been a big day in more ways than one. Try to get some sleep. Anna, you and Tobias and the baby take the master bedroom, I've got it all ready for you."

When Iserate says he will take the first watch, it shatters the temporary peace they had as just a group of friends who shared in

266

this miracle of life. It suddenly brings back the reality that Ela and Emre are still in hiding.

As Ela lies curled up in bed, she can't stop thinking about the incredible day they had. Traveling to Germany, seeing Anna and Tobias again, feeling the ice that was surrounding her heart very slowly begin to chip away. Sharing in the birth of her godson was like feeling the glow of the sun rapidly melting the remainder of that iceberg. She knows that sleep isn't going to find her anytime soon, so she picks up her journal and begins to write down her feelings. As she looks at the journal, she thinks about Emre risking his life to retrieve it for her. She wants to go to him and tell him that she is sorry she was so cold towards him. That she was traumatized and confused. That she was unjustly blaming him for her own stupid actions. But there will be time enough for that talk. Now, she needs to let him sleep.

As she writes, she comes to the realization that maybe, just maybe, it was all meant to be.

As messed up as the events surrounding my capture by Mazhar were, maybe it was all supposed to happen like that. If I had not been brought to his hideaway, I would not have met Feya. If she was alone there, she may not have tried to escape. Or if she had, where would she be? How would she make it out in a world she had been excluded from since she was sixteen? Would she have found herself at someone else's mercy just to survive? Maybe it was meant to be so that Feya could start a new life, free from burden, free from servitude.

If that is true, I would gladly go through that ordeal. It is also true that Feya has this wonderful opportunity for a new life because of Emre and his boundless kindness and generosity. He didn't even try to make me feel like he was doing it because I asked. He didn't want me to feel obliged at all. He is truly a remarkable man.

Sleep finally overtakes Ela until she hears a tap at her door the next morning. She awakens, fully alert.

"Yes, who is it?"

"It's Tobias."

Her face falls. Part of her was hoping it was Emre.

"Yes, Tobias, come in."

He looks disheveled but ecstatic, as though he is moving through a dream he doesn't ever want to wake from. "Good morning, Jen. I hope you slept well. I spent most of the night staring at my beautiful son. This morning Anna told me that was a mistake. She said we need to sleep as much as we can whenever the baby sleeps because this peaceful time will end soon. I guess babies are pretty chill the first few days, then they own your every moment for the next eighteen years. At least according to Anna. I think she has read too many baby books." He hasn't stopped smiling since he entered.

"Sorry," he continues. "But the reason I woke you is that we are preparing to go home. The doctor will call by later today to check on the baby and Anna and we need to be there when he arrives. Can't have him coming here. Anyhow, Anna would like to say goodbye to you. I guess you may have to move on tonight."

"Oh, I was hoping we would have a few more days."

"Jen, it is fine. This will all be resolved soon and then you can get back to your normal life again. And just think, you got to be here for the birth! That was beyond our wildest dreams. If you were in DC, you would have never made it here in time. So, my dear friend, smile. Let's be thankful for what we have. And remember, everything happens for a reason."

Ela feels like Tobias read her journal from last night. Maybe it's just the universe reminding her, in multiple ways, that she needs to roll with things instead of fighting or running away.

Downstairs, Anna looks surprisingly well and rested. "Oh good, Jen, I was afraid you were going to sleep all day. It's so unlike you!"

"I only fell asleep three hours ago. Give me a break! But seriously, I would have died if you left without me getting one last cuddle of my godson. Hand him over."

As Ela coos and gently strokes the baby's head, she is overwhelmed with love for the little man.

"Wow, I still can't believe you made this human. It's wild. And I already love him so much I feel like I'm going to burst because a body just can't contain that much love. Oh," Ela looks up with a start. "I just realized that we may not be free to travel back in a month for the christening."

Anna and Tobias exchange a glance. "We have already discussed that," Tobias says. "And it's just a silly old superstition to have to christen the baby a month after his birth. We will wait until you are free to come. You and Emre. He has graciously agreed to be the godfather. It's only right seeing that he assisted Iserate with the birth and, according to Anna, is very special to you."

Ela looks across the room to where Emre, Geoff, and Iserate are chatting, and smiles. "Thank you. Thank you for your help, thank you for sharing the birth of your child, thank you for including Emre as godfather, thank you for your love and friendship all of these decades. Now get out of here before I start bawling. I guess I have to give this little guy back to you now." Ela gives Jonathan one last cuddle and hands him back to his waiting mama. "I love you all."

The others join them to say their goodbyes. Emre kisses the baby on his head and speaks softly in his native tongue.

After they leave, Ela asks Emre what he said to the baby.

"It was just a wish for him to have health, happiness, joy, safety, and love all the days of his life. It was something my mother would say over a new baby. Holding Jonathan brought back a wave of memories of my mother that I must have suppressed after she died. I think I was afraid to remember. To love someone so fully and then lose them is unbearable."

Suddenly, he stops speaking. Ela can sense that he's thinking about losing her, first because of Mazhar and then because she returned to him with a heart frozen by trauma. She reaches up and strokes his cheek, staring into his eyes. She holds his gaze, afraid to move away.

She whispers, "Don't ever worry about that again." Then she leans in and gently presses her lips to his.

Geoff calls to them from the kitchen. "Come and have some breakfast, we will have to leave soon."

Ela and Emre can't help but laugh. It seems like the universe is playing with them. The moment they get close, it's time to get on the move.

Ela says, "Let's go eat. We will have plenty of 'us' time in Australia."

Before she walks away, Emre pulls her back to him. "We need to unpack everything that has happened. Your captivity, the escape, all the feelings you have been dealing with. We cannot just sweep everything under the rug. If we do, there is a strong possibility we will trip over it later. I feel like we have been through enough for four lifetimes. I don't want any of it to come back and haunt us."

Ela opens her mouth to interrupt. "Promise me," Emre insists. "Before we move forward, we will deal with all of this. What I want, and hope you want, too, is for 'us' to last forever. I know you, Ela. I don't want you to one day be overwhelmed by all the negative feelings you have experienced during this time because you have suppressed them. You will just pack up and reinvent your life. I don't want that. I want you to be certain, to have purged all your ghosts. Not just you, but both of us. Promise me."

Ela is a bit taken aback. But she realizes that it makes sense. It is the mature way to handle things. And he is right, he seems to understand her patterns. And she agrees, at forty-four it is time to outgrow that childish response.

"I promise."

Chapter Thirty-Three

A few hours after Anna and Tobias leave, the four of them are on their way to an airport outside of Frankfurt. Geoff and Iserate had planned for them to each escort one of the couple to Australia and for them all to meet up in the Blackwall Reach house, but Ela and Emre refused to travel separately and risk what happened when they were taken off the *Kayıp Aşk* happening again.

"Because you are traveling together, we have chartered a private aircraft to ensure your safety," Geoff says from the front seat. "We are headed to a private airfield."

Sitting next to Emre in the opulent aircraft, Ela gently elbows him and says, "show off."

The eighteen-and-a-half-hour flight gives Ela and Emre an opportunity to talk, but sleep keeps overtaking them both. Emre wants to stare at her face for the entire flight, even as his eyes keep drooping shut. They finally stop fighting it and just curl up in each other's arms, sleeping soundly for almost ten hours.

In the limousine from the airport, Iserate and Geoff brief them on their house and their assumed identities. Iserate will be seen as their chauffeur, handyman, and gardener and Geoff will be the valet, butler, and private secretary.

"We can't go over the top with household staff and we don't want to trust vetting anyone new, so we are it."

Ela raises her hand.

Geoff says, "It's not school, doctor, you can just jump in with a question."

"Sorry, I just feel like I'm always interrupting with questions," she says. "When I lived here, I had a housekeeper I would trust with my life. We could trust her to come in and clean. And will I be able to see my friends Ian and Scott?"

"Good news on the housekeeper, I wasn't looking forward to cleaning," Geoff says. "You'll need to give me her name so we can do a full background check on her. It's not that we don't believe you, it's just that it has been a few years and we must do our due diligence. And, yes regarding Ian and Scott. Thanks for giving us their details. We completed our checks on them and they are cleared."

As they pull through the gates and enter the driveway, the modern, three-story home rises up to meet them. Emre can't help but notice the facade is shaped like the front of a ship. Its front walls and windows meet at a point directly in the middle and the upstairs windows are positioned to look like sails. A clever design, as it overlooks a beautiful expanse of the Swan River. This part of Bicton, a suburb of Fremantle, is idyllic.

He steals a glance at Ela to see how she feels about returning to her old stomping grounds. He wonders if he will be able to fit into her life here and with her friends. She seems preoccupied taking in the tour of their new home.

The top floor, which houses two master suites connected by a shared sitting room, is assigned to Ela and Emre. The other two bedrooms and bathrooms are on the middle floor, and the ground floor makes up the common areas: the kitchen, dining room, office, formal living room, family room, powder room, and small library.

Ela runs from room to room then joins the others in the family room. "This is gorgeous! Much more spectacular than the home I had when I lived here."

Emre says, "I would love to see your old home. Maybe we can—"

Iserate interrupts. "Sorry, but we would like Ela to avoid places that were too close to her past life here. With the exception of Ian and Scott, please don't contact your other friends and don't go to the university. It's just for a while. Once we can be assured that any threat against you is cleared, you will have free rein and be able to live normal lives again."

Emre asks, "Really? I was hoping Ela could be able to have a normal life once we got here. It's hard to believe that a dead Mazhar's reach could be this long."

Geoff nods. "We are pretty confident that anyone else who could be a threat to you is either incarcerated and too worried about saving their own skin, or they are dead. But we must be certain, not just pretty sure, before we relax our vigilance."

"I agree, and thank you, Emre, for being concerned for me but I am fine with laying low until we know we are safe," Ela says. "And just think, we get lots of time alone together to have that talk you said we need to have." She smiles at Emre and squeezes his hand.

"Well, when you put it like that," Emre turns back to Geoff and Iserate. "You guys take all the time you need."

Ela asks when she can invite Ian and Scott over for dinner. "I really want to get in that glorious kitchen and cook us all an epic meal. Geoff, you are a great cook, but I miss cooking for friends. It's my love language."

"I'm glad you've enjoyed my cooking but I will be more than happy to have a night off. But let's give it some time. Let's settle in and see if anything seems amiss."

"Okay, that's fair. How should I let them know I'm back and, um, using a different name?"

"If you agree, Geoff will take care of that. He will provide as much information as is safe. Then let them know they are sworn to secrecy and that you will be in touch," Iserate says.

"Any more questions for now?" Geoff asks.

Ela and Emre shake their heads no.

"Okay then, I will prepare something simple for dinner and, if you like, serve it up in your sitting room. I think the two of you need an early night and some peace and quiet."

"That sounds good to me," Ela says.

"Me, too," Emre adds.

Iserate stand up. "Then excuse me, I'm going to check the property line and ensure the gates are secured and all the security cameras are operating. Then, I'll be in the office monitoring the security feeds."

Emre stands and holds out his hand to Ela. She takes his hand, and they head up to their sitting room.

When Emre descends a bit later, he hears Iserate laugh at Geoff. "Could you have made that any more obvious?" he says. "I guess you could have strewn a path of rose petals up to their rooms."

"Hey, the sexual tension between those two is going to get in the way, eventually," Geoff grumbles. "They run more hot and cold than this kitchen tap. Let's hope one of them makes a move so we can all finally exhale. Also, I can't take Emre's moodiness any longer. He was a lot easier to be around when he had his three-date rule. But I have never seen him as happy as he was on the *Kayıp Aşk* as he and Ela grew close. I just want them to find that again."

From the doorway, Emre clears his throat and Geoff and Iserate jump. "I just wanted to get some wine and a couple of glasses," he says, barely suppressing his smile.

Iserate and Geoff look clearly embarrassed. Iserate seems to be studying his cuticles while Geoff selects a wine and hands it to Emre with two glasses. "Sorry you overheard that. I should have just said it to your face."

Emre embraces Geoff. "You know that I consider you a friend beyond everything else. I appreciate your concern for my happiness. I only hope that we can work through everything that has been an emotional burden on Ela. We won't move the relationship forward before that happens. As much as I desire her, I want something permanent. The foundation must be solid before I am willing to build on it. Now that you're finished gossiping, what time will dinner be?"

Emre laughs as heads upstairs.

Chapter Thirty-Four

Ela accepts the glass of wine from Emre's hand. She pats the sofa next to her, but Emre sits in the armchair across from her.

"If I'm that physically close to you, here in our own little world, I will forget all of my resolve to give you the space to work through the trauma you just experienced and the mixed feelings it has created for you."

"Thank you," Ela says. She appreciates the wine's bouquet and takes a sip, savoring what she realizes is her favorite Margaret River cabernet before continuing. "You are truly mature beyond your years."

"It is not years lived that develop maturity, it is what you have survived that builds who you are," he says. "I want us to talk through things, but I also believe it would be helpful for you to see a therapist, if you are open to that."

"I think that would be a good idea. And, it would most likely accelerate the healing process. And you know I'm pretty impatient," Ela winks at Emre.

"Oh God, this is going to be hard."

"That's what I'm hoping for. Nudge nudge, wink wink."

"What am I going to do with you, Dr. Ela?" Emre laughs and throws a decorative pillow at her.

Once their laughter subsides, Ela can tell that it's time to start discussing their feelings.

"Ela, as soon as I first saw you, I was smitten," Emre begins. "You were the most beautiful woman I had ever seen. That long, thick, curly auburn hair, the body of Aphrodite, and those magical hazel eyes. And then you singled me out to talk to, to share ideas with. You made me feel special in front of those horrible boys who were the closest thing I had to friends. How could I not fall head over heels for you?"

"And you were so young," Ela says, lost in the memory. "At first I must admit that I just felt sorry for you. That I didn't like the way those boys were treating you and using you to pay their way. So I purposely approached you and singled you out. But then, as we discussed the books and I got a glimpse of your intellect, your thoughtfulness, and your drive to make something of yourself, all of those things just spoke to me and I started developing feelings for you. But for me, that was uncomfortable. You were sixteen and I was twenty four. I just couldn't allow myself to think of you like that. And, on that last night when I kissed you, and I did it spontaneously just to make those American guys shut up, I felt something I hadn't felt before or since, with anyone except you. It scared me so much that I did what I do best: I ran away."

"I know, Ela. I understood what happened because I felt it, too. And I know you were a decent person and would never cross that line. But I wasn't joking when I asked you to wait for me. That's why I never stopped thinking about you. And why, unfortunately, I kept tabs on you all these years. They say the internet is a blessing and a curse. Between that and your accomplishments, which kept ending up in newspapers, it wasn't difficult to follow your life."

Ela refills her wine glass and offers some to Emre. He puts his hand over his glass. "No thanks. I have acquired a taste for fine wines and champagnes thanks to you, but I only allow myself two glasses, one before and one with dinner. I learned my lesson on that first night of imbibing."

Emre leans forward in his chair. "Now where were we?"

"You were talking about stalking me for years."

"Ha, well, I guess that's correct. But that is where the problems started. I made an effort to keep you well hidden and to also not form attachments with anyone once I was under my uncle's wing. I knew something was shady, but I never guessed drugs. But I knew, even if it was the white-collar misdeeds I thought it was, I didn't want you to get caught up in it. I was waiting for my uncle to die so I could end whatever practices he was involved in. But when I found out how truly despicable it was, and that my uncle's business partners had my parents killed, I decided to stay on so I could destroy them and their drug syndicate rather than just wash my hands of it. Anyhow, I doubt Hasad and Mazhar would have let me walk away once I knew what was going on."

"I'm so proud of you. You put the greater good before yourself. It was a risky move but appears it will all work out in the end."

"But it placed you in harm's way. And that is what we need to really delve into. We need to see if the negative feeling your ordeal gave you can be excised. I will do everything in my power to make you feel safe. To make you understand that I will never put you in danger again. I would give my life for you. I love you. Whatever happens, even if you decide you need to move on and leave me behind, I will always love you."

"I know, I truly believe you. I want to feel safe. I want all this hiding and running to be over. I want what I never thought I would want, a nice normal life. Or as normal as any life could be with you."

Ela and Emre agree to work through the trauma before they make love. They have waited decades, so they figure a bit more time to allow themselves to take things to the next level is no big deal. Ela finds it very reassuring that her emotional well-being is more important to Emre than what they both so obviously want and lust after.

The next day, Geoff joins the others for breakfast on the patio overlooking the pool. He smiles and says, "I have some great news about Lizet and Feya."

"Yes, come on, tell us," Ela says.

"They are officially a couple! Lizet asked if she could be released from her contract and stay in New York with Feya. They want to stay together and see how their love develops."

Ela fist pumps the air. "I'm so happy for them! They get their fairy-tale ending. And I can see that good things do happen to good people. Oh, Emre, maybe all of this has happened for many reasons."

They chat about Lizet and Feya and how they look forward to seeing their future in New York. Then the conversation turns to what their lives will be like while they wait for the all clear.

"Do you think I can be out in public or might I be recognized?" Ela asks. "I did live here for the better part of seven years. I don't mean going to visit old friends or the university, just going to shops and maybe out to restaurants."

"I'm glad you brought that up," Geoff says, taking a sip of coffee. "We still have to make sure no one else is targeting you and Emre. You may want to just make some minor alterations to your appearance. Maybe straighten your hair, modify the color, or wear glasses. What are your thoughts?"

"I'm game! But I will need to get a professional to color and straighten my hair. I'm not willing to risk it myself. Maybe I'll even cut it."

Emre looks horrified. "I love your long hair! Don't change it. Please."

Ela pats his arm. "All of these changes are temporary. I love my hair, too. But a year from now, it will all be back to normal. Too bad Lizet isn't here. She was so good with my hair. But I can't tell you how happy I am that she is with Feya, making a life together." She squeezes Emre's hand, happy that their life together is starting, too.

Ela's days fall into a relaxed rhythm. Other than the fact that she is keeping a low profile and staying around the house until she can alter her looks a bit, she is enjoying having what she would normally feel was a boring routine. Between catching up with her former—and current—housekeeper Diane, reading, cooking, and spending time with Geoff, Iserate, and Emre, the days pass quickly and uneventfully.

A few weeks in, Ela enters a hair salon she has never been to, in a part of town she never frequented. Iserate wanted to bring in the stylist and colorist to the house, but Ela insisted on going to a salon. She wanted a normal experience, her first one in a long time.

Sitting in the chair, Ela closes her eyes and imagines that her life is normal. This is just an everyday trip to the salon. When she gets home, she and Emre will go out to a lovely dinner and walk around the river. Maybe someday.

As Ela leaves the salon, she can't stop looking at her reflection in the shop windows. She would have a hard time recognizing herself. Her hair is dead straight, deep red, and swinging just to the top of her shoulders as she turns her head from side to side. She has decided to go with blunt bangs—or fringe, as they call it here—which frame her face beautifully and make her eyes look enormous. The red color brings out a deeper shade of green in her hazel eyes. Overall, Ela is delighted with her new look.

Iserate is waiting for her a few shops down. He stands there open-mouthed as she approaches. "Wow, I almost didn't recognize you. I have to admit, you knew what you were doing. It is an amazing look on you."

"Well thank you kind sir. Let's go home, I can't wait to see what Emre thinks." She smiles as she links her arm through his. They stroll down the street while trying not to make eye contact with any passersby. She feels safe, but not that safe yet.

"May I speak on a personal level?" Iserate says, once they've reached a quieter street.

"Of course, Iserate. We are like family now. You're the big brother I never had."

"Thank you, I feel the same. I mean, you as a little sister— you know what I mean. I just want to say that Emre loves you. He truly won't care what you come back looking like. Although, I know he will love this look. Who wouldn't?"

"Thanks for saying that. Now may I ask you a serious question?"

Iserate nods.

"Obviously, over the years you have been involved in many scenarios, possibly some like this. Do you think it is possible for a couple such as Emre and me to make it long-term after all that we have been through?"

"That's a good question. To be totally honest with you, it can play out one of two ways. Either the trauma is too much and being with the person you endured it with is a trigger for the PTSD that accompanies it. Or sharing the experience and understanding of it binds the couple closer together."

"What makes the difference?"

"It comes down to being motivated to put in the hard work. You have to be able to get through the trauma and learn how to manage anything you have not resolved. You both do. It is a lot of work, that's why I say you have to be motivated. Motivated and patient. In my opinion, both you and Emre have what it takes."

Ela stops walking and hugs Iserate. "Thank you. I hope we do."

Back at the house, Ela receives applause from Emre and Geoff.

Emre walks around her to take in the full picture. "I wasn't sure about your plan but … wow!"

Ela is beaming. "They did a great job. I love it and I'm barely recognizable. You can finally take me to a restaurant or museum or anywhere!"

"I will take you anywhere you want to go."

Ela stops and gives Emre a very serious look. "Does this mean you like this better than my natural look?"

Emre glances at Geoff and Iserate; they just laugh.

"Well, I feel like this is a trick question, loaded with landmines. What do you Americans say … I'll plead the fifth." Emre winks at Ela.

The next night, Emre is waiting at the bottom of the stairs and Ela makes her way down in a figure-hugging cocktail dress that is such a dark green it almost looks black. He whistles softly as she approaches.

He bows and says, "May I have the pleasure of escorting you to dinner … at a real restaurant?"

"Yes, that would be wonderful. Just like a normal couple that isn't hiding from criminals."

"Almost normal—Geoff will be sitting two tables away. But, my dear Ela, it is the closest we will get to normal at this point."

"I'll take it."

Sitting overlooking the lights of the city playing on the surface of the Swan River, Ela smiles across the table at Emre. It's been so long since she's had a normal night out. She's almost giddy with excitement to be on a real date. She tries to ignore the small part of herself that is still afraid some goon will jump out from behind a bush and snatch her again. That part of her is getting smaller every day, but it still lingers.

"Thank you for tonight," she tells him, taking a sip of her after-dinner port. "It's probably our first real date. I mean, going out on the town. I get to see all the other women stare at you and envy me. I've not had that pleasure before," Ela tries to say this with a straight face but doesn't quite succeed.

"Maybe you didn't see that man over there in the blue sport coat trip over his own feet as he was staring at you," Emre counters. "That dress, you—all so stunning."

Just then, Ela sees Geoff get up and make a beeline to a back door. A minute later, he signals to them that they need to leave.

Ela's heart begins to race and she can't quite catch her breath. She fights to stay composed on the outside, not wanting to draw attention to herself or their situation. She looks at Emre, then at Geoff, grabs her handbag and walks to the door.

"Well at least we got to finish our meal," she says, trying to keep her voice light. "What's going on?"

Emre looks around, just as baffled. Geoff joins them out front as the valet brings the car around.

On the drive back, Geoff lets out a long breath from the driver's seat. "Sorry about that. I noticed a guy lurking around. I thought I saw him the other day when we went shopping for your dress, Ela. Then again at the grocery store when you were shopping for Saturday's dinner. I am just erring on the side of caution. It may be nothing, but I felt it was best to get you both home."

Later that night, Ela taps on Emre's bedroom door.

"May I come in?"

"Yes, what is it?" Emre says, sitting up in bed.

"I guess I got a bit shaken up by Geoff's pronouncement that someone may be following us. Would you mind if I slept in here?"

"Sure, come here." Emre lifts the covers and Ela slides in. She curls up in the baby spoon position and pulls Emre's arms around her.

"Oh Ela. I love you. Now sleep. I'm here and I will make sure nothing bad happens to you." For the first time since she saw Geoff's signal in the restaurant, she feels safe. Ela drifts off within minutes.

In the morning, Ela realizes she slept so soundly she didn't even move. Emre's arms are still firmly around her. She rolls over and kisses him awake.

Emre sleepily opens his eyes then pulls her even closer, returning her kiss with a deep passionate kiss.

"Well, this is making the waiting more difficult. I am only human."

Ela smiles and strokes his back as she arches catlike to press her body fully against his. "That's quite obvious right now. I am only human, too." She brings her lips to his ear and whispers. "Make love to me."

Emre groans. "I would like nothing more, but I want it to be special. I want you to be sure you are mentally and emotionally in the right space. Have one more session with your therapist then, if you feel that it is the right time, we can take the next step."

Chapter Thirty-Five

The next day, Geoff tells Ela that he has met with Ian and explained as much as he could.

"Ian was so excited and will do everything in his power to keep you safe. And he and Scott will come to dinner on Saturday evening. They said they will bring the wine, 'as usual,'" Geoff says.

On Saturday, Emre enters the kitchen to find Ela with what appears to be every pot and pan in use. He watches her checking things off her list as she talks to herself.

"Well, this appears to be a command center and you are the general," he teases.

"You are busy in your office every day, keeping your empire running. With my business in capable hands and me supposed to still be off of the grid, this is now my office. At least for today. Now get out. I have three amazing courses to time perfectly!"

She flicks her tea towel and he holds up his hands in surrender then blows her a kiss before heading off to his office.

What Emre doesn't know is that Ela is cooking a full Turkish dinner so that he can have a taste of home. For the first course she is making a meze platter: spicy bulgur and lentil soup, hummus, baba ghanoush, vine-baked feta, stuffed tomatoes and peppers, roasted chickpeas, nut and yogurt dip, and dolmas. The main course is kababs, both chicken and kofta, with accompaniments of tomatoes, cucumbers, grilled vegetables, parsley, pita, and yogurt sauce. And of course, baklava and Turkish coffee.

The table is beautifully set and everything in the kitchen is in order. Ela is showered and ready to see her old friends. At seven o'clock on the dot, the gate bell rings and after checking the security cameras, Iserate buzzes the gate open for Ian and Scott's car to enter.

Before the car comes to a complete stop, Ela is running out the front door. She holds Ian and Scott at arms length, just staring at them. They both look the same—maybe even better than when she last saw them.

Between her giddy squeals, Ela introduces Ian and Scott to Iserate and Emre. "You already met Geoff. These are my band of merry musclemen. Well, not Emre. He is the man I love."

Ian and Scott shake the men's hands and hug Ela. Ian spins her around taking in her new look. He lets out an exaggerated wolf whistle.

"It's only temporary while we are in hiding, but I'm having fun being a sassy redhead," she says, preening.

"I love it," Ian says. "We were so worried about you when you didn't get in touch with us once your South American adventure was supposed to be over. After speaking with Geoff, we now understand why."

Then he turns to look from Ela to Emre, and back again. "Jen, so this is him? The stunning, sensitive, intelligent boy who stole your heart all those years ago?" He blinks at Emre. "It was all so tragic. You were so young, she was so old. Then she married that emotionally abusive idiot. Then no man ever lived up to her memory of you."

"Okay, Ian, no need to produce a soap opera about it before we even enter the house," Ela says, rolling her eyes. "If you insist on discussing all of my failed relationships and my uncomfortable feelings for a sixteen-year-old, you can eat a vegemite sandwich while the rest of us dine," she teases him but squeezes his arm as she leads him into the house.

The conversation and the wine flows during dinner, it's as though this group of friends has been together forever. In between bites of food and sharing a laugh with her friends, Ela watches Emre as he enjoys his meal.

Emre catches her watching him and rewards her with a smile that warms her heart. It is like they are in their own little world for a moment. Then he laughs too, and she feels like he is reading her mind.

After the dinner, wine and great conversation, Ela feels that she is wrapped in the warm glow of love and friendship. She can't believe how wonderful her life is right at this moment in time.

After dinner, Ian and Ela find themselves alone in the kitchen.

"Is he the one? Is it real?" Ian whispers. "Do you know how difficult it is for a person to live up to a memory that has been viewed through rose-colored glasses for decades?"

"That's the strange thing. He surpasses the memory," Ela says, laying out the cups for coffee. "It's hard to explain, but I know he is my person. I've never felt such a sense of peace just being in someone's presence. And you would think with all we've been through in a relatively short period of time that I would just want to do a runner. The only place I want to run is straight into his arms."

Ian gives her a hug. "It sounds like the real deal to me. I'm very happy for you. Now let's eat this baklava; it looks delicious!"

Later that evening, they sit enjoying a port and catching up on each other's lives. All of a sudden, Iserate and Geoff exchange a look, then both abruptly stand. Geoff puts his finger to his lips and loudly says, "I want to show you all that painting in the office I was talking about." He gives Ela and Emre a pointed look.

By now, Ela is used to this kind of behavior so stands to follow him, but for Ian and Scott, this is all new.

Ian begins to ask, "What paint—"

Ela laughs loudly to cut him off. "Don't play that absentminded professor bit! Come on, you will love it."

And then all, except for Iserate, file into the office. Geoff immediately goes to the screens displaying the live feed from the security cameras.

Emre asks him what's going on.

"Iserate and I have noticed a suspicious person lurking around whenever we escort Ela somewhere. We both heard something outside at exactly the same time. I'm sorry for the bit of acting about the painting—there's always a chance the house has been bugged. We need to make sure you are all secure. If I see anything on the monitors, Iserate will apprehend whomever it is."

"You don't think it's Mazhar's people? Or anyone from the syndicate, do you?" Ela asks. "I was just starting to feel like this is all behind us. I just can't …"

Emre puts his arms around Ela's waist and pulls her close. "I promise that nothing will happen to you. To any of you. I've had enough, too. If I have to call in an army of mercenaries to extinguish every last person who could be a threat to us, I will."

Just then, there is some movement on one of the screens, a shadowy figure creeping behind the pool house. He radios to Iserate, murmuring precise directions to the threat. A moment later, the figure is jumped from behind and taken down to the ground.

Geoff has a muttered conversation with Iserate on the radio, then asks them all to accompany him to a room tucked away off the side of the house. Ela is surprised, as she didn't know that this room existed. When Geoff pushes a hidden button on the wall, she can see why: A bookcase slides out of the way, revealing a hallway.

Geoff leads them into a room where they are on the privacy side of a two-way mirror. "Emre," Geoff says, "I need to know if the person Iserate will be bringing in for us to view is anyone you know from the syndicate. The rest of you are here because I'm not letting anyone out of my sight. We can't be sure this is a lone aggressor."

They are all staring at the empty room on the other side of the mirror when Iserate leads into the room a man who has a dark bag over his head and hands bound behind his back. The man is not acting like some hired bruiser, he is shaking and appears to be pleading with Iserate.

Iserate then removes the bag from the man's head. Just as Emre shakes his head and opens his mouth, Ela, Ian, and Scott start laughing.

"What the hell is so funny?" Geoff asks.

Scott, being the one who composes himself first says, "That's Brayden."

Ela never thought she'd see him again. Brayden looks a bit worse for the wear—as would anyone who got tackled by Iserate. But more than his disheveled appearance, he appears to be crushed under the weight of humiliation.

Emre asks, "Who the hell is Brayden and what is he doing lurking around? He could have gotten himself killed."

"He's Ela's ex-boyfriend," Scott says, wiping away hysterical tears. "He proposed and she turned him down. He is rather pathetic, and we never thought he was good enough for her." Scott says.

Ian adds, "To be fair, she always said he was just a snack, never a meal." He and his husband start laughing all over again.

"Okay, okay, enough you two," Ela scolds with a smirk. "Geoff, you had better let Iserate know that Brayden is no threat, unless you are a gnarly wave he's going to shred," Ela says, sending herself and her old friends into peals of laughter again.

"Well, I for one can't wait to hear all about this 'snack,'" Emre says.

Geoff raps on the mirror and Iserate leaves Brayden and joins them in the room.

"That guy is an ex of Ela's." Geoff tells him, rolling his eyes. "But we still have to make sure he poses no threat. He may not be syndicate, but he is a stalker nonetheless."

Iserate nods. "I guess that's why he is scared shitless. He just keeps crying and saying he only wanted to see Jen." He sighs. "You guys go back to your port and conversation. Geoff and I need to have a little chat with Brayden."

About a half hour later, Iserate and Geoff join the others.

Geoff reports, "Brayden is harmless, or if he ever wasn't, he is now. Iserate laid out would happen to him if he ever got near you again."

"How did he know it was me?" Ela asks from the armchair, now much more relaxed. "It's been ages since I've seen him, and this hair—I mean even Ian said he wouldn't have recognized me if he passed me on the street."

"That was just bad luck," Iserate explains. "He saw you as you were entering the salon. Then he sat across the street at a coffee shop and watched you leave with your new look, then followed us home. He's been stalking you when you went out to dinner or the shops. Once he felt sure it was you, he decided to make his move. And voila—he showed up here."

"Little did he know that you have world-class personal security agents guarding you and a house that we modified with security cameras, a control room, and an interrogation room," Emre adds.

"I think we've had enough excitement for one night," Ian says. "We are an old married couple who watches documentaries for our excitement. We will leave you to it and see you all again soon. Jen, or Ela, I can't tell you how wonderful it is to spend time with you again. And to be able to eat your cooking; there are no words."

After showing them out, Geoff returns to the living room. "Iserate and I have to write up this little incident," he says. "You two should take your port up to your sitting room and relax. Ela—stupendous meal, and yes, I made sure Ian and Scott remembered their doggy bags." He smiles. "Try to get some rest; you worked hard all day. Leave the kitchen, Diane will clean it tomorrow."

Up in their sitting room, as Ela is about to snuggle into Emre's side, he stops her and says, "Come on now, I want the full story on Brayden before you get too relaxed and fall asleep." He suddenly gets serious. "But before that—I can't tell you how special that meal was for me. The fact that you made a perfect Turkish dinner as a surprise. I'm speechless. I couldn't even say anything at dinner because I was so emotional. It was like I was eating my mother's cooking. You are just the most amazing, kind, brilliant woman in the world. Thank you, not just for dinner, but for being you and loving me."

Ela kisses him passionately and he responds, then pulls away and says, "No, you are not going to distract me. Fess up."

Ela quickly tells him all about her relationship with Brayden. "Is that all? Can I get on with trying to seduce you?"

"Actually, there is one more thing I must know," Emre asks. "What the hell is a 'snack?'"

"Oh, that's easy. A snack is someone who is just a fun, temporary distraction."

"Then what does that make me?"

"Emre, my dear, you are a three-star Michelin restaurant at which I will choose to dine for every meal for the remainder of my days."

Chapter Thirty-Six

"I can't wait to hear how you feel after today," Emre says as they are being driven to her final appointment with her therapist. I think twenty years is long enough to wait to make love to you. Don't you?"

"I have to agree. Those first twenty years weren't so bad since we were continents apart," Ela teases. "But I must admit these past few months have been torturous. Every time I see you, hold you, all I want is you."

She smiles. It feels so easy to be honest with him about her feelings.

Emre gives her a serious look. "I want you to know, whatever you say today, I will not give up on us. I will put in whatever work it will take for us to start out on a healthy foundation." He squeezes her hand.

Iserate stops the car and wishes her good luck. "Just text me and we'll meet you right here when you are finished."

Ela sits in her favorite overstuffed chair in her therapist's office. She realizes that she is holding her breath and forces herself to exhale and take a deep cleansing breath. She has her breathing regulated by the time Dr. Madeleine Bay joins her.

When Ela decided she needed professional help to work through this ordeal, she met with a few different therapists. She really clicked with Dr. Bay. She's a no-nonsense psychologist who tells it like it is and doesn't let Ela get away with avoiding what she is feeling. Dr. Bay challenges her when she needs it, always helping her to be the best person she can be.

"Hello, Ela, you are looking well today," Dr. Bay says. "How have you been feeling? Anything upsetting or uplifting happen this week?"

Ela dives in, choosing to explain the whole Brayden fiasco as the upsetting event, and the wonderful reunion with Ian and Scott as the uplifting event.

Dr. Bay asks how the Brayden issue made Ela feel.

Ela thinks for a moment then replies. "I actually felt safe. I was surrounded by people I trust and love. When we realized it was just Brayden, I had to laugh at the absurdity of it. I mean, I now know I am strong enough to withstand what some very bad players can dish out so having this threat turn out to be some man I dumped years ago who wouldn't swat a fly, seemed comical to me. I was prepared for the worst and it turned out to be someone so benign that I almost felt sorry for him. He just wanted to talk to me."

"Did you speak with him?"

"No, I didn't see any point in it. I didn't want to and I didn't owe him anything. I am tired of a society where men feel that whatever they want is what is owed them. Emre is nothing like that. He makes sure that we are equal participants in everything. He always asks what I want; he doesn't make it about him. God knows he had plenty of opportunity to use his power and wealth to coerce me. I mean, he was my sole source of protection, room, board, entertainment. He was basically my world for a couple of months. But he is the most honest and respectful man I have ever met."

"And how do you feel about yourself?"

"I feel like I've grown a lot. I mean, I was a well-educated, successful woman in my own right. Self-made and proud of my accomplishments. But I realize now that I was always working on improving my outward-facing self. These past months were filled with conflicting feelings; first a growing love for Emre mixed with resentment for putting me in danger, and then having to survive without any protections, which resulted in witnessing a lovely young woman build a new life filled with joy. So many mixed emotions. But I forced myself to confront them all and feel them all fully. I mean, really lean into them. This made me grow and mature emotionally. In the past, I would pull up stakes and run away. I didn't have that choice this time. I had to push through and now, I can't see living my life any other way. My old pattern of running away from intense emotions and difficult situations has no value to me now."

As she exits the building, Iserate is waiting with the car door open for her. When she gets in the car, she kisses Emre and looks deeply into his eyes and whispers, "I want you. I'm ready emotionally, mentally, and physically. I want all of you."

"Let's not go home right now," he says, eyes fixed on her mouth. "I think we should go for a drive."

Ela's chin almost hits the floor. "A drive? Now? Really?"

Iserate and Emre try to stifle their laughter, and Ela realizes they're up to something.

A short drive later, they stop at a heliport. Emre walks to Ela's door, opens it, and offers her his hand. They stay linked as they board, and during the short ride to a luxury yacht even bigger than the *Kayıp Aşk*. A smile slowly spreads across her lips as she realizes Emre is giving them back the setting where they rediscovered each other. She squeezes his hand.

Once onboard, a steward appears with a tray holding a bottle of champagne and two flutes. Ela smiles at him and says, "Would you please set that up in the stateroom."

Emre pulls her into his arms just long enough for a passionate kiss before she takes his hand and follows the steward.

Once alone, Emre pours the champagne and clinks his glass to hers. "Here is to us. May our love and happiness grow every day."

"And may we actually be sexually compatible. I would hate to think all of this has been for bad sex."

Emre looks shocked until Ela breaks into a grin and the laughter escapes.

"Sorry, Emre, you are so romantic and I'm such a shit. But humor is better than running away, right?"

"Ela, you do whatever makes you feel comfortable. I'm romantic enough for the both of us."

He then takes the glass from her, places it beside his on the table, and walks her over to the bed. He undresses Ela slowly, caressing every inch of skin as it is uncovered. His mouth follows his hands—her skin feels electric, and she gasps.

She pulls his shirt over his head and runs her hands across his taut, well-formed torso and back. Ela finds his belt buckle and releases it then unbuttons his trousers. She steps back and looks at him in his nakedness. He is more beautiful than she imagined.

After a few moments of feasting with their eyes, they crash together with the passion of all the sexual tension they have endured. They lose themselves in their mutual lust. Their lovemaking traverses the continuum between slow and sensual and fierce and powerful. They spend hours lost in their own world, talking about their future when they manage to rest.

After waking from a short nap, Ela shakes Emre awake.

"Let me rest," he says with a groan. "I may only be in my thirties, but I am human. After I rest, I will be all yours."

"No silly, I'm starving. You wore me out! I need to eat *now*."

Emre laughs, and calls the staff to set up a platter of appetizers in their room.

As Emre is seeing the steward to the door, he says, "I don't have the energy to go to the dining room. I hope this is okay with you." When he doesn't get a response, he turns to see Ela with her mouth stuffed with food. He smiles. "That's my girl. I love a woman who eats with as much enthusiasm as I do. But hey, save some for me."

After Ela has had enough to take the edge off her hunger, she asks Emre if the yacht they are on is his.

"No, I've just hired it for a couple of days. But don't worry. I saw how much you loved the *Kayıp Aşk,* so I will replace her with one very similar to this one. It will be your wedding gift. That reminds me," he rises and reaches for the satchel that Iserate handed him before they boarded the helicopter. "I forgot this."

He returns to Ela at the table, drops to one knee, holds out a small jewelry box. He opens the box, exposing a seven-carat, emerald-cut diamond in a simple platinum setting.

"Ela, I have loved you since the moment I saw you. Since then, we have grown as individuals, and recently, we have grown as a couple. I am positive that you are the person I want to continue to grow with. Please make me the happiest man in the world and say you will marry me."

Ela sits in shock. She knew this would happen eventually, but she did not expect it so soon. As usual, to hide her emotions she says something light. "Boy I must be a good lay. "

Then, when she looks at Emre, so full of love and hope, she feels awful for making a joke. Instead of getting hurt he replies, "Well yes, there is that too, but I thought I would leave it out of the formal proposal. It would make it rather awkward when we tell our friends how I proposed."

They both start laughing.

"You get me. And for that and all the billions of reasons I love you, *yes*, I will marry you."

They spend two days and two nights cocooned away on the yacht reveling in their own special world. A car is waiting when the helicopter lands, but Ian is driving. Ela runs up and hugs him, then asks, "What are you doing here? Where is Iserate?"

"Gee, I thought you would be a bit more excited to see me."

"No, no, I am, I just want to make sure Iserate is okay."

Emre says, "He's fine Ela. He just had to run an errand."

When they return to the house on Blackwall Reach, Geoff and Iserate are on the front porch and when Emre and Ela step out of the car they begin clapping.

"Is this because of this?" Ela asks as she hold up her left hand to show off her engagement ring.

Geoff replies in his most posh English accent, "No, ma'am, sir, it's because you finally got laid. Now you'll finally stop being so grumpy."

With that, they all hug and congratulate Ela and Emre. Scott comes out of the front door and tells them to all get inside. As they enter, Ela is amazed. Every inch of every table is filled with vases of white roses. The dining table is laden with savory treats and the bar is laid with champagne and glasses.

Geoff, Iserate, Ian, and Scott take a small bow. Scott says, "We all wanted to do something special to celebrate the two of you."

Ela looks around overwhelmed with her feelings of love and joy, then says, "What would have happened if I said no?"

Emre says, "I'm a pretty confident guy. And they all knew that I never ask a question I don't already know the answer to. How do you think I became so successful?"

Chapter Thirty-Seven

A week later, Ela and Emre are roused awake by pounding on their door. Emre looks at the clock—five a.m. He jumps out of bed, turns to kiss Ela, then slides into a pair of shorts that had been discarded on the floor during their rush to make love last night. He calls out to see who it is and Geoff replies, so Emre opens the door.

"Good morning, Geoff. Is the house on fire?"

"No, but we have some news that we knew you would want to hear straight away. Can you both join us in the office?"

Emre and Ela enter the office to see Geoff and Iserate standing by the large computer screen, which have Feya's and Lizet's smiling faces projected.

"Iserate and I have very good news for us all," Geoff says. "We have received the final reports from each of our contact points for the syndicate, or should I say ex-syndicate. There is no more threat. Most of the players are dead. Once we released materials that cast suspicion on different members of the syndicate, a raft of execution-style murders took place in various prisons. The ones who are still alive are incarcerated for the rest of their lives and believe the persons responsible for their downfall have been eliminated. We let the lie leak that you, Emre, being so much wealthier than the rest of them put together, were able to bribe your way to freedom. Rumor has it that you are a bit of a cult hero among the survivors because you got one over on the authorities."

Iserate says what they are all thinking. "Now you can all resume your lives unafraid. You can do whatever you want."

The stunned silence only lasts a moment, then it is replaced with whoops of joy. Everyone is talking at once and hugging each other. Onscreen, Feya is crying and holding onto Lizet, who is beaming.

After everyone settles down, they say that they will be in touch with Feya and Lizet soon, then end the video call. Geoff looks from Ela to Emre, then asks, "Where do you go from here?"

Ela looks around the room, then appears panicked. "I don't know. I have been so caught up in the present. I just need some time to think."

Emre squeezes her hand, but she pulls it free. Emre frowns. He can't be losing her now, not after all they've been through together. Nothing in his life will make sense if he can't share it with her. Sensing the emotional shift in the room, Iserate and Geoff excuse themselves.

"Ela, tell me what you are thinking. Whatever it is, I will support you."

She meets his gaze, looking lost. "I'm not exactly sure, but I just feel like the earth has shifted under my feet. I had a life, a business, before all of this started and I need to decide what to do with all of that, how I want to move forward now. And, I need to do that on my own." She says this last part almost to herself, unable to look Emre in the eye.

"Ela, you take all the time you need." He brings her hand to his lips and kisses it. "I must return to London anyway—I have been running my businesses from afar for too long."

"Okay," she says in a whisper he can barely hear.

He takes her face in his hands, kisses her gently then says, "When you feel ready and know what you want to do, let Iserate know. He will stay here with you, or accompany you wherever you want to go. Geoff will travel with me."

Ela holds her hand up to stop him. "I need a deadline. It is not fair to either of us if I just get lost in my thoughts and fears forever. I will have a decision on my personal and professional future made one month from today. I promise. I do love you, I just need to think about the real world and how this will all work. I'm sorry."

"I understand," Emre murmurs. "Well, actually I'm confused as hell right now, but this isn't about me. I promised you I would always protect you." He pauses and brings his fingers to the pendant she still wears. "This was a promise I made to protect you twenty years ago, and that also means that I will give you the space and time you need to be certain about what *you* need. I love you, completely. And to me that means putting your happiness before mine."

He steps back, forcing a smile. This is what Ela needs right now. "Whatever you decide, we both need to be at little Jonathan's christening. So you can let Anna know she can have it one month from today. We will celebrate Jonathan and talk about where our lives are going."

"Do you want the ring back while I decide?"

"No. You keep the ring. You decide whether you want to wear it or not, but it is yours no matter what happens. It is a symbol of my love for you and that is unchanging."

Ela nods.

Chapter Thirty-Eight

That night, they hold each other closely, neither able to sleep. When morning comes, Emre kisses Ela on the forehead and says he will see her in one month. She watches his back disappear through the door, then buries her head in the pillow and cries.

She wishes she wasn't so confused. She wasn't prepared for the news that they were no longer under threat and could live their lives as they choose. One month. She tells herself she can do this. She knows what she needs.

She gets dressed and heads to the kitchen, where she finds Diane wiping down the countertop. Diane has seen her through the tender months after her divorce, and through Brayden. And now she's been here as Ela put her heart back together with Emre. She is one of the people who knows Ela best.

She hugs the housekeeper. "Good to see you. I know I'm a little early for our usual morning cuppa."

Diane gives her a penetrating look. Ela told her yesterday about the big decisions ahead of her. "You know you are like a little sister to me," Diane pauses, waiting for Ela to nod, then continues.

"To be blunt—you know I can't be any other way—you would be a damn fool to let this one get away. I reckon he is the best man you have ever known and will ever know. I think it's him or stay single. You are perfectly happy being single and very capable of taking care of yourself. But, I know you, you are more full of joy when you have someone to share things with. And, may I say, much easier to be around when you are getting laid regularly."

Ela just smiles and hugs Diane again. "You know me so well."

Later that night in her bed, Ela feels the empty space next to her. She can still smell his scent on his pillow and wishes he was here. But she knows that she needs a clear head to decide how to structure her life moving forward. She takes a deep breath then grabs her phone to call Anna. It's a relief to hear her chatter about her new life with the baby, and not about her own problems for a moment.

An hour later she yawns into the phone.

"I'm that boring, really?" Anna teases.

"No, but it's two a.m. here and I'm fading."

"Well, you go to sleep and I will begin planning for the christening. Can't wait to see you and Emre next month. I love you."

"Love you, too. Give Jon a big kiss from his godmother and say hi to Tobias for me."

After she hangs up, Ela wonders if not telling Anna what is going on is the right thing. But she doesn't want to make Jon's christening about her and Emre. She wants Anna to be relaxed.

She finally falls into a restless dream-filled sleep.

The next morning, Ela is on the beach, Ian and Scott walking by her side. Even though she knew she needed to be away from Emre during this decision, she still needed some trusted friends nearby. Ian and Scott agreed to stay as long as she wanted—they even showed up with a full bag, clinking with bottles of her favorite Margaret River wines.

As the three of them walk in the wet sand, she begins. "I know Emre is perfect for me. As a man, he is exactly what I want; it's his lifestyle that I am concerned about. I don't want to be some trophy wife doing nothing all day but shopping and primping."

"If you don't want to marry him and lead that life, I will," Scott says.

"Um, I'm standing right here," Ian says, feigning disbelief. "Remember me? Your not-so-gorgeous, not-so-filthy rich husband?"

"Don't worry, darling, I don't think I'm his type," Scott puts his arm around Ian's back and leans his head on his shoulder.

Their easy banter and affection makes Ela miss Emre even more. But she needs the big picture to be sorted before she heads to Germany. It is too difficult for her to think logically when she is with him. She always gets caught up in the emotional and physical world when they are together. She is concerned that she didn't make that clear to him when she said she needed this time. They decided it would be best not to communicate for this month so Ela could focus and not be emotionally distracted. She looks down at her left hand; she is glad she kept the ring on. It makes her feel like a part of him is still with her.

"Earth to Jen, earth to Jen," Ian says.

"Oof sorry, I was off in the clouds."

"Come on, you need to stay out of your own head. You overthink everything. At times you overthink things to death. Now, talk to us. What is it that you are most concerned about? Let's face it, you know we love you but Emre is six years younger than you. He is gorgeous. You can't be defined as a trophy wife. He would have to be old and ugly, so let's be real," Ian says.

"Well, thanks for the reality check, let me just get my walker and sensible shoes!" She laughs. "But seriously, you know what I mean. I need to feel useful in my own right."

"Have you thought about returning to your pre-abduction life? You still have a business and home in DC, so that's an easy option. Even if you want to marry Emre, he could always move to wherever you are."

Ela screws up her face, "No. I've thought a lot about that and I can't see myself running back to my old life. As they say, *how ya gonna keep her down on the farm once she's seen Paris?* Not that DC or my business is small-town, but the business has boundaries and I can see that I need something bigger, more far-reaching. I've been face-to-face with true evil and have seen how corrupt businesspeople can destroy lives. I want to do more and I want more. Does that sound too grandiose?"

Ian says he understands and that he has an idea. "First you need to bring Marion here. You've always said that she was your right arm and she helped grow your business—I think we need her insight. Then, we need to set up a little brainstorming room. I think I know how we can structure this decision-making for you. "

"I like the sound of this," Ela smiles and laces her arms through Ian's and Scott's.

"Not to ruin this sweet moment, but you are planning on cooking lunch soon, right?"

"That's my husband," Scott adds, rolling his eyes. "His every action is driven by the thought of his next meal!

Chapter Thirty-Nine

Two days later, Marion and Ela are sitting on the third-floor balcony of the Blackwell Reach house, sipping on some champagne and watching the river.

Marion stares at her friend with wide-eyed disbelief. "You have got to be kidding me! I mean, I know you aren't, but things like this don't happen. Well, at least to anyone I know."

"And now, my life is at a turning point and I need you to help me figure things out," Ela says, settling back in her chair after laying out the Emre story to Marion. "I have a few other people close to me who will be working with us and you will meet them soon. I just wanted you to have the whole story first so you all start on the same page."

"It's a lot to digest." Marion admits. "But at least now I know why you've worn that beautiful leaf-shaped pendant every day since I have known you." Marion smiles as she gives Ela a hug.

After dinner, Ian, Scott, Marion, and Iserate lead a blindfolded Ela into the office they spent the afternoon setting up. Ian takes her blindfold off and says "Ta-da! Welcome to the headquarters of 'Getting Jen's life worked the fuck out.'"

A large interactive whiteboard is propped against one wall; the opposite wall has a large map of the world pinned to it. Easels and flip charts are scattered around the room, and markers of every color are laid out on the desk.

Ela is touched that these friends are taking her needs to heart and have set up this room for her. She sees Marion's influence everywhere—her friend really does know her work style.

"We will begin tomorrow," Ian says, hands on his hips. "Tonight, we will relax, play some gin rummy, drink your excellent port, and then have a good night's sleep. We are almost a week into your month of decision-making time, so tomorrow when we are fresh, we will dive in."

"Sounds like a good plan," Ela says. She turns to Iserate. "I know this is the first free time you have had in months, but would you mind working with us on this, Iserate? You know more about Emre's life and businesses than all of us put together. Your knowledge and overall brilliant insights would be a great help."

"I would be honored to help. May I ask just one thing?"

"Oh course, what?" Ela says.

"Would you guys be able to call her Ela, please? Every time you say Jen, I get confused. I have only known Ela as Ela."

Scott and Ian look at Ela for her input.

She thinks. "It's strange, but I only think of myself as Ela. It's like I left Jen on that dark road in DC when Geoff and Iserate's team kidnapped me." She playfully slaps Iserate on the arm, so he knows she's teasing.

"Okay then, from now on you will be Ela, the friend formerly known as Jen," Ian declares.

The next morning, as they gather in the office after breakfast, Ela runs out and comes back dragging Diane behind her.

"I want Diane to take part in this. She knows me well, isn't afraid to speak her mind."

They all agree this is a good idea and welcome Diane.

"Thanks, but who is going to clean this house?" Diane asks.

"Don't worry about that, Diane. We will hire a housekeeper for you. You can just supervise them," Iserate replies.

"Don't that beat all. A housekeeper with a housekeeper!" Diane chuckles.

Ian stands in the front of the room and clears his throat, "I'm going to take the lead today, okay Je—I mean, Ela?"

"You drive," Ela replies. "It's your idea and we have yet to hear it."

"I think the first thing we need to do is to separate the professional issues from the personal issues. Once we determine what is most important in each, then we can bring both models together for you to build your best life," Ian says.

"That sounds great to me. I think that has been what has been causing me so much stress. I'm trying to figure it all out as one big blob. They are two different things and need to be examined separately," Ela agrees.

"The big blob. I think that should be what we label the final step of this," Scott adds. "Phase One will be The Professional Self, Phase Two will be The Personal Self, and Phase Three will be The Big Blob."

They all agree to Scott's silly label. Ela just hopes that it is possible to build a workable blob from what is decided in the other two phases.

"Well, since I'm the only one here who hasn't met Emre and has worked closely with Je—Ela in her business, I will help with Phase One. That will also get me back to DC and the business faster. I will leave the other phases to the rest of you."

They begin work on Phase One. Marion draws a line down the middle of the whiteboard. She writes "Absolute Imperatives" over the right side and "Absolute Exclusions" over the left side.

"I'm basically bastardizing Ben Franklin's Moral Algebra, but we are going to focus on what you absolutely must have in your professional life and what you refuse to have in it," Marion says.

"I must have integrity, compassion, challenge," Ela replies immediately. "Whatever I do must be far-reaching, I would even say global. And it must in some way make people's lives better. I want to help marginalized groups. A lot of what my business is doing now on a much smaller scale. I don't want to have to be driven by profit. I don't want to have anything to do with underhanded dealings. I don't want to get into the weeds anymore. I want to be focused on the bigger picture now."

"This is good, we can work with this," Marion says. "It's time to do some brainstorming, team."

They spend the next few days working through what Ela's professional life could look like: studying business models, examining the market for nonprofit work, talking to some of Ela's former clients. At the end of the week, Iserate asks, "Ela, describe to us, in a perfect world where money is no object, what your professional life would look like, taking into account what you have derived from the past few days."

Ela stands and takes a marker off the table, approaches the whiteboard. She thinks for a few moments, then begins constructing an elaborate business model. She works on this for the rest of the afternoon, telling the others to go and relax for a while. She finds herself possessed with a passion for her professional future that she hasn't felt for a very long time. Working with Marion has reminded her of the satisfaction and fulfillment she got from the work she left behind. That world feels like a lifetime away now.

Iserate stays so he can make hard copies from the digital whiteboard, then clear it to provide more space for Ela to work. They work through the night and as dawn breaks, Iserate downloads the final board of Ela's work.

Ela says that she needs to step away from the work for a day to clear her mind before she reviews what she did. She proposes a day off. The weather is beautiful, so they decide to go to Kings Park for a picnic. Diane declines—she wants to make sure the house is all in order and has a hard time trusting anyone else to work up to her standards.

Ela sprawls on the picnic blanket, letting the sun warm her face. "This next week, we should work on Phase Two, then the following week, I can edit both," she muses. "Once I have the final products, I can work on The Big Blob during the final week. How does that sound?"

Marion nods, taking off her sunglasses to look at Ela. "It has been wonderful getting to know you all and working with you this past week, but it's time I take my leave. Ela, if you need any help or input with the edit stage, we can have a conference call, okay? I would hate to have to make that flight again so soon," Marion laughs and shoulder bumps her friend.

The next day, after Ela waves goodbye to Marion, she feels paralyzed.

"Stop the 'roo in the headlights look!" Scott says. "Come on, woman, this should be the easy bit. You must know what you want for your personal life."

Diane laughs, throwing an arm over Ela's shoulder as they head inside. "Not our girl. She has never taken the time to plan anything to do with her personal life. She waits until some powerful current drags her away from her present situation into the next." Diane narrows her eyes at Ela. "You know I love you, but I have to be honest. You are always running away *from* something, never running *to* something."

This is like a punch to the stomach for Ela. She realizes that what Diane says is so true. She never wanted to be a victim of her life, she wanted to be the captain of it. She vows to herself to make that change today. She will be charting her own life with a purposeful plan from today forward.

"You are right, Diane. Once again, thanks for your brutal honesty. I needed that. I'm ready to get started."

Diane places her hand on Ela's back to soften her words. "Now let's all go in, I'll make us all a cuppa and we can get started. Your decision clock is ticking!"

A week later, Ela is hugging each of her friends and thanking them for their time and hard work. She decided that she needed to work on Phase Three alone. She even sent Diane on vacation. It will be her life, so she should be responsible for the final plan.

Before Scott and Ian leave, she takes them aside for a private conversation. One that could possibly change the trajectory of their careers.

And with that, they all leave and it's only Ela and Iserate left in the big house that now feels so empty.

"I have a lot of work to do to wrap up this property and all operational loose ends before we head to Germany, so I won't be in your way," Iserate says as he makes his way to the front door. "As you requested, I've ensured the kitchen is stocked and you should not be disturbed. It will be as though you are living alone like you did before this all started—or as you put it, before my thugs kidnapped you." Iserate hugs her and adds, "I'll expect to see you in a week. But if you need me, I will always be just a quick call on the intercom system away. Good luck, Ela. I know you will make the right decisions."

Ela sits with her own silence, feeling stronger and more in control of her life than she has ever felt. She makes a cup of tea, grabs a pumpkin scone, and sits at the desk with two documents before her. She is happy with the work they have done and knows that it is better for the input of her friends. They do force her to look at things without any distortion from rosy lenses. But now it's time for her to get down to work on her own. She takes a deep breath, reaches for her professional plan and begins to edit.

Before this month, she might have guessed that this would be the more difficult plan, but it is effortless. It's so clear to her that this is what she wants to do with the rest of her career. After a couple of days, she has tweaked a few areas and now holds in her hands a creative business plan that fulfills her professional desires. She's proud of it—it is so well written and structured that it can be used for funding rounds.

The next day Ela calls Iserate into the office and hands him the Phase One document. "If you would, please share this with Emre. His business acumen is priceless and I value his opinion. He cannot see Phase Two or the Big Blob, but this can be shared. I still need my distance from him as I work on editing Phase Two."

Later that week, Ela finds herself pacing the office holding her personal plan, which is only a few pages long. It is not as extensive a document as the professional plan, which is a rather large tome. But Ela feels its weight not in pounds or kilos, but in its impact on her heart.

Now for the most difficult and most important part: to see if she can make a big blob out of both documents. Will she be able to meld her professional goals with her personal goals? That is the question that has been haunting her since she began this process. It was all well and good to be cocooned in some surreal world with the man she loves, but how will that love endure the harsh realities of the mundane everyday slog? Having your life under threat somehow makes you feel more alive. Having personnel problems just makes you wish your life was under threat.

She realizes she is procrastinating, and scolds herself out loud: "This thing isn't going to finish itself and your self-imposed deadline is swiftly approaching. Get to it!"

When she breaks it down, her personal plan really consists of only three things:

1.   She wants to be her own person and not just an accessory in someone else's life.

2.   She wants to be useful to the greater good.

3.   She wants Emre.

After simplifying her desires and needs to these three points, she realizes that her two plans meld together perfectly.

She can't wait to share The Big Blob with her friends on Friday. She will use tomorrow to shop for a big feast she will cook for her friends after the unveiling.

On Friday evening, Ian, Scott, Diane, and Iserate are seated in the formal living room, Marion is on the big screen conferencing equipment. Champagne and hors d'oeuvres are on the table to the side of the room. She even made sure to order Marion a delivery feast from their favorite Korean restaurant in DC.

"Thank you all for everything. Please fill a glass and a plate but save room for the main meal which will follow. Marion, I see you received the delivery from Anju! You all can see that I made very few modifications to the work we did together. I took my personal plan and categorized everything and was able to reduce it to three guiding principles. Once I did that, it all fell into place.

"The main focus of my business will stay the same: We will help indigenous communities protect their land and cultural heritage. It will become a nonprofit, serving communities that do not have the resources to access these services otherwise. We will expand to have offices on the ground in South America, Africa, Europe, and Australia, in addition to the Washington, DC, office. The team that was temporarily running things in DC have agreed to be the permanent team, and Ian will head up the Australian office that will cover the Australasia region. Scott will be the vice president of human resources, and responsible for hiring everyone else we need. Once personnel are in place, Scott and his team will keep us in compliance and make sure everyone is fairly compensated. We don't want to become part of the problem of corporate greed. We want to help make people's lives better, and that includes our own employees. I will no longer be the lead anthropologist in the DC office. I will focus on the overall enterprise—its vision, strategy and, most importantly, its fundraising and financial viability.

When you look at the three guiding principles of my personal plan, which are, to be my own person and not just an accessory in someone else's life, to be useful to the greater good, and to be with Emre, you can see how the business plan and my life plan complement each other perfectly. The business reflects who I am in my own right with my own expertise, it will keep me active and mentally stimulated, it is focused on the greater good and, in my new role, I will be able to base myself out of London and only travel when it is necessary for the health of the business, which will enable me to be with Emre and live our life together, yet not be stuck in each other's pockets."

Ela takes a bow to the applause of the friends.

The next day, on the flight to Germany, Ela says to Iserate, "Well, are you going to tell me?"

"What?"

"Don't play coy. Tell me what Emre said about my business plan!"

"Oh that." He reaches into his computer bag and withdraws two bound documents. "He sent these. He said you can do whatever you like with them. You can accept them as is, make any changes you deem necessary, or shred them and use them as confetti at your wedding."

"So he's pretty confident that we will be married?"

"I would say so. He honestly doesn't believe that anything can come between two people who love each other as you two do. Maybe he's naive, but I am sure not going to be the one who tells him that."

"Not to worry, my friend. I'm pretty sure that he is right, as usual."

"Although he projects confidence, I don't believe he will be truly at peace until he is your husband," Iserate adds.

Ela runs her hand through her hair as she thinks about the documents in her lap.

"I don't want to read these."

"What? Why? He doesn't mean to upset you."

"No, no, Iserate. I just want Emre to tell me his thoughts and ideas himself. I want to make sure I don't misinterpret any of his feedback. As we know, he is a business mastermind. I would hate my ego getting caught up on some constructive criticism because I misinterpreted what was written."Ela hands the two documents to Iserate.

"That's a good idea," Iserate says with a nod. "It's best to do this in person."

"So you really think he is not at peace?"

"Not fully. He is one who believes in not counting his chickens before they hatch."

Ela gets a mischievous glimmer in her eyes and says, "I have an idea. Will you help me hatch it?"

Chapter Forty

Upon arrival in Germany, Ela is delighted to see Anna and the baby waiting for her. After hugs, kisses, and snuggles with baby Jonathan, Anna grabs Ela's hand and whistles when she sees the ring.

"He didn't come to the airport," Anna says, before Ela can ask. "He wanted you to have time to settle in before he saw you. He mentioned something about not wanting to overwhelm you. To be honest, I think he would just rather your reunion be more private than this. Just in case it doesn't go the way he hopes, he doesn't want an audience."

She smiles conspiratorially at Ela. "He arrived two days ago and we've had some lovely talks. He is very special. If you don't marry him, I will. Well, if I wasn't already married with a babe in my arms I would."

"You are the second of my dear friends who has said that." Ela feigns concern. "Maybe I had better watch out." The old friends laugh together.

"Well, I am so happy to see you and little Jonjon. I'm still trying out nicknames. As his godmother, I get to assign the nickname you know. I think that's written, maybe in the Ten Commandments, Queensbury Rules, or some such place. But it is true."

"Yes, godmother. Whatever you say. Sure."

Di Toma

When they are sitting in the kitchen sipping Earl Gray tea back at Anna and Tobias's house, Ela fills her in on what's been going on over the past month, then tells her the idea she had on the flight over.

"I love it! What can I do to help?"

"You are busy enough with the christening. Iserate will rope in Geoff to take care of it all. I bet when they were government spies, they never dreamed they would be doing what this crazy American woman has asked them to do."

She nibbles on a scone as Anna details the plan for the weekend.

"We have loads of family from distant parts of Germany and the US staying with us, so I'm sorry you won't be staying here. But I was able to get the place you stayed before. Our friend is in Paris again. I think he has a lover stashed over there. Anyhow, we will have a run through of the christening at five-thirty this evening. That will just be Tobias, me, you, and Emre, then I thought we could come back here for dinner. Our families are going out to some touristy dinner at a castle, which we were able to get out of because we are so busy with the christening plan. We really aren't that busy but wanted to have some time just the four of us—well five if you count Jonathan. We made a bunch of the food we used to serve at the restaurant. Kinda nostalgic for us all."

Anna volunteers Tobias to drive Ela to the house. She opens the familiar door, and makes her way to the living room. There she finds Geoff and Emre. Geoff jumps up and embraces her.

"It's been a minute, my dear. So wonderful to see you. I was just heading off. I told Iserate I would help him with some grocery shopping." He gives Ela a wink before he turns to Emre and says, "Is that all for now?"

"Yes, Ela and I will be tied up the rest of the day with the christening runthrough, then dinner with Tobias and Anna. Go and enjoy yourself. We will see you tomorrow when we all head to the church."

"Thank you, see you both tomorrow."

After they hear the front door close, Emre walks up to Ela and holds out his arms. After an eternal moment, she falls into them and they hold each other. Just standing there in each other's arms. Not speaking, not moving, not wanting to feel anything except their bodies melding together.

Emre is first to break the silence. "I've missed you. I hope the time and space apart gave you what you needed."

"I've missed you, too. And yes, thank you for understanding. It did."

"I didn't understand. But I don't have to understand how you feel for your feelings to be valid. I just need to be supportive of them."

"You are a smart man, in so many ways."

"Thank you. By the way, Iserate said that you did not want to read my response to your business plan."

"Yes, I want you to talk me through it. I want to make sure we are on the same page. I don't want any silly miscommunications because of some rogue inference I may make."

"Shall we do that now?"

"No, today and tomorrow are all about the christening. We will review your documents the following day, on Monday."

"Okay, that's fine. Are you going to rest now?"

Ela smiles and shakes her head no. "I'm going to shower, then crawl into bed."

"Oh, okay. I'll leave you to it."

"You didn't let me finish. I am going to shower and crawl into bed, and I expect you to be there waiting for me."

With that, she walks out of the room slowly and sensuously.

An hour and a half later, Ela wakes and looks at the clock, "Shit, shit, shit, we are going to be late. I can't believe we fell asleep!"

"Calm down, Ela. We have plenty of time. We are only fifteen minutes from the church. And I *can* believe we fell asleep. Our love making is always rather athletic, to say the least. And after a month without each other … well, need I say more?"

Ela laughs and shows her agreement with a deep kiss. Then she hops out of bed to get ready.

Emre unsuccessfully grabs for her. "What, no round three?"

Ela selects a simple knee-length denim skirt and black silk sweater and Emre has on black jeans and a blue chambray button-down shirt. They stand side-by-side in the full-length mirror admiring themselves.

"We make a lovely couple, don't we?" Ela asks.

"I agree. Now that we are no longer in hiding, I think we need to get some photos taken. Can you believe that we don't have one photo together?"

"That's true, I hadn't thought about that. I'm sure we will have some taken at the christening tomorrow."

He looks at her hand. "I noticed that you are still wearing your engagement ring. So maybe in a few days, we can have some official engagement photos taken."

"Yes, I'm wearing it because we are still engaged, aren't we? Or have you changed your mind and wanted to get one last roll in the hay before you walked out on me?" Ela stands with arms akimbo, displaying exaggerated indignation.

Emre starts laughing. "Please keep your day job, I don't think there's an Oscar in your future anytime soon!"

On the drive to the church, they are both quiet. That comfortable quiet between two people who are in sync. Emre is concentrating on the unfamiliar roads and Ela is at peace thinking about how natural it is to be with Emre again. Their silly banter, their passionate love making, their mutual respect—it is all still there. No awkwardness, no hesitation. They truly must have been together in a past life. This type of harmonious relationship usually takes years to build. Not the years apart that they have had, but years of the day-in, day-out sharing of lives. She mentally scolds herself, *No more overthinking. Just be grateful and enjoy your good fortune.*

The rehearsal goes well, and dinner afterwards is fabulous. As they take their first bites, Ela and Emre look at each other and start laughing.

Anna looks up smiling "Are you going to let us in on the joke?"

"It's just that the food is so nostalgic for us," Ela says. "This all began when I was cooking in your old restaurant and Emre would come in with his group of horrid friends. Just think, if they were nice to Emre, none of this may have happened. It just feels like we have come full circle, twenty years later," Ela smiles as Emre nods in agreement.

Emre entertains them with stories of what he really felt about his group of horrid friends.

"I should have never wasted my time with those terrible German teens—except of course it wasn't a waste of time because it brought me my Ela," Emre says thoughtfully, chewing on a bite of enchilada. "But at the time I was investing in my future, so to speak. I wonder what all those boys from those important families are doing now."

"Not much, from what I hear from the old neighborhood," Tobias says. "And over the years, their families have lost much of their clout. So your old pals have been working rather boring jobs with little to no career path. I guess they should have paid more attention to their education rather than thinking they could ride their families' coattails."

"That they should have, but I wish them well. We were all doing what we thought was the best thing for ourselves at the time. I think I was always just more future-focused than they were. I like planning and developing strategies for myself and my businesses. Some people are just wired like that." He turns to Ela. "Speaking of plans and strategies, Ela is a natural at it. We need to follow up on some planning she did recently."

"Not tonight, my dear. We agreed to wait until Monday to discuss work," Ela replies, eyes sparkling. There's something important they have to do first.

Chapter Forty-One

The christening day is bright and sunny. A large group of friends, family, and some of the church's extended congregation gathers to celebrate little Jonathan. The party afterwards is a festive affair filled with loved ones of all ages enjoying food, conversation, and laughter together.

The next morning, Emre wakes and reaches over to Ela, only to find her side of the bed empty. At first, he assumes she has just gotten up to grab a cup of coffee or tea and will be back soon. After thirty minutes, Emre begins to worry. But as he heads to the door, he sees an envelope on the bedside table with his name on it.

His stomach drops. Has Ela done a runner? Somehow, she went from the loving passionate woman who shared his bed last night, to a scared woman who runs away from emotionally charged situations. But he can't figure out what he did or didn't do, or if someone said something that spooked her.

He slowly approaches the envelope, touching it tentatively with one finger as though it may shock him. He then takes a deep breath and opens it, then reads the short note.

Happy Monday. Sorry to leave so early. I didn't want to wake you, so I quietly snuck out. I will be busy all day. Be ready at three p.m., Geoff will drive you to meet me." Have a good day.

Ela x

He realizes he has been holding his breath and exhales, then takes a long, deep breath. He feels his heartbeat start to slow down. He loves her for all the mystery, but is glad he is healthy and not prone to heart failure. He thinks that maybe she is just putting off discussing his response to her plan. Oh well, nothing to do about it now. He has no idea where she is.

Thirty minutes after Geoff picks up Emre, he is pulling the car into a grove of hazel trees. This time of year, the trees are bare and the woods are quiet.

Emre looks at Geoff as though he has lost his mind. "What in the hell are we doing here? I'm in a wool suit with business documents to present and you stop to look at trees?"

Geoff replies, "Just get out of the car and follow me. Leave the documents. I want to show you something."

Emre, mumbling about the absurdity of stopping to look at a grove of trees on their way to a business meeting, begrudgingly follows Geoff. They walk up a narrow path and as they enter a clearing in the center of the grove, Emre sees Iserate, Lizet and Feya, Tobias, Jonathan and Anna, Marion, Ian and Scott, and even Diane! There are also a few people he doesn't know but recognizes from Ela's business website. They are all beaming at him.

As they slowly part, he sees her. Ela, in a flowing sage green dress covered by an ivory-colored floor-length cape lined in faux fur, her hair dyed back to its original beautiful auburn color, full and curly. It's not as long as before, but still so Ela. She is holding a bouquet of ivory roses, standing before another person who is wearing a white caftan. And it hits him. This is their wedding.

He starts to walk toward her and she says, "Is this okay?" He runs the rest of the way up the aisle and picks her up, and says, "Yes, a thousand times yes!" And just as they kiss, a light dusting of snow begins to fall. The first snowfall of the season.

Epilogue

The large conference room at The Twenty Two, with its commanding views of London, is the site for the fifth annual business planning meeting of International Cultural Communities, part of The Eden Foundation.

Ela, looking like the world-class business leader that she is, stands at the head of the conference table sporting a Brunello Cucinelli business suit she picked up on their last romantic weekend away in Italy.

Before she begins, she shares a small smile with Emre, seated next to her at the table. She tucks away a foil-embossed envelope that had just come in the mail into her portfolio, sliding it over to him. It's an invitation to Lizet and Feya's wedding.

So many wonderful things have happened over the past six years. Ian and Scott have a son and daughter, Diane has started her own cleaning business employing two dozen cleaners, Emre and Ela got married, and Ela started this amazing enterprise.

Ela opens her arms wide and welcomes everyone.

"Thank you all for being here. It is good to see that all our head offices are represented; we have the teams from South America, Africa, Australasia, the US, and Europe all here. We have a lot to celebrate before we begin our planning sessions.

First, a brief history of how your parent organization, The Eden Foundation, came to be. As you know, I am an anthropologist who once ran a small consulting business out of Washington, DC. I had developed a business plan that would convert it to a non-profit with additional offices across the globe. For those of you who haven't met them already, I'd like to introduce you to our senior vice president of operations, Marion Carder; our senior VP of human resources, Scott Archer; and Australasia region senior vice president Ian Archer, all of whom have played vital roles in the development of my dream, not to mention the nurturing of my soul.

My dream was to be able to help as many indigenous communities as possible; removing the barriers to funding they need to ensure their liberty. I knew that it would take me out of the field, so to speak, and I would be taking on the overall leadership, developing the vision and obtaining the funding to make it all possible. That brings us to our silent partner, as I like to call him. He has no choice but to be silent, as I rarely let him get a word in edgewise. But that's the challenge of being my husband.

"Six years ago, he read my plan and loved the idea. He also had a large sum of money, an inheritance from an uncle who earned his money in illicit ways. So he took those ill-gotten funds and set up an endowment to enable International Cultural Communities, ICC, to be formed and to run in perpetuity. But there is no free lunch, as they say. The funding was so large that Emre, our silent partner, wanted me to establish an umbrella foundation, of which ICC would be a part. The Eden Foundation encompasses nonprofits that focus on social justice, climate change, healthcare, and education. These funds are being used to improve the world we live in, trying to give a voice to those who struggle to be heard and those who just need a helping hand.

"The funny part of this story is that Emre was concerned I would not like his addition to my plan. He thought I may think he was usurping my space. But that couldn't be further from the truth. All I saw was that he truly believed in my vision. I actually would not even hear his suggestions until after we were married. I'm glad I waited, or people may have thought I married him because of his support for my business plan.

"Just one more bit of history before we get started: People always ask about the foundation's name. They wonder if there is some biblical reference, and I have to laugh. It's from a book title—*Martin Eden* by Jack London. It's the book my husband was reading the first time I saw him, and the first thing we ever talked to each other about.

"Okay, enough of my reminiscing," she says, toying with the pendant necklace that hasn't left her neck in decades. "Let's get to work on another highly successful year!"

Acknowledgements

You know your life is rich when you have wonderful people surrounding you and cheering you on. I have a rich life. I was fortunate enough to have some fantastic initial readers who got to meet Ela and Emre in their raw form. I appreciate the suggestions and encouragement of those readers. The first to read *Ela* was my wonderful husband, Mike Snipes, followed by dear friends: Rachel Bano, Brenda Kamph, Patty Murgolo, Irene Payne, and Mercedita Quiros. Thanks to all of you for reading *Ela*, and for providing ideas, encouragement, and perceptive feedback.

In addition to the wonderful insights from friends and family, I hit the jackpot by having the world's best editor, Lori McCue. Her enthusiasm for this novel, along with her superb editing skills, combined with her ability to (gently) get me to see where I needed to make changes to provide the best possible experience for the reader, culminated in a much better novel than it would have ever been without her. Thank you—thank you—thank you!

My daughter, Madeleine, provided excellent feedback and tough love along the way. It was she who talked me into self-publishing. I was telling her that I loved writing and editing but loathed the query process—her response was simple. "Don't do it, self-publish instead. Do what brings you joy!" She also made the introduction to my brilliant editor.

Di Toma

Thanks also go out to a truly creative photographer, Marco Ciurnelli, for my author photo. And, very importantly, thanks to my cover designer extraordinaire, Julian Legendre, who somehow captured the essence of *Ela* in visual perfection.

Reading Group Discussion Prompts

1. Did Ela and Emre's age difference bother you? If so, why and if not, why not?

2. How did you feel about Ela and Emre's chemistry and compatibility? Did you root for them or not? Did your opinion change over the course of the story?

3. How did the side characters contribute to the story and the romance? Did you have a favorite and least favorite side character? If so, who and why?

4. At any point in the story, did you want to yell at the characters to do something differently? If so, when and what would you have told them to do?

5. What part of Emre's youth do you feel made him into such an emotionally evolved man in adulthood?

6. What main aspects of emotional growth did you see in Ela over the years?

7. Which location in the novel would you most like to visit?

8. If the book was turned into a movie, who would you cast as the lead characters?

9. Which character would you most like to spend a day with?

10. If you could ask Ela one question, what would it be?

11. What was the most memorable and shocking moment or plot twist in the book?

12. What was your favorite quote or scene in the book?

13. What do you think Emre and Ela are up to 10 years after the events of the novel? What about Lizet and Feya? Anna, Tobias, and Jonathan?

14. Which characters would you most like to read a sequel about?

15. Both main characters have closer relationships with their found families than their blood relations. How are Ela's relationships with her loved ones (Anna, Ian, Marion, Diane) different from Emre's (with Geoff, Iserate, etc)?

16. Do you think Ela and Emre could have found happiness if they hadn't found each other again in adulthood? How might the story have been different if they had reconnected a decade earlier than they do in the novel?